HOME FRONT

HOME FRONT

a novel by

PATTI DAVIS

with

Maureen Strange Foster

CROWN PUBLISHERS, INC.
NEW YORK

Published by Crown Publishers, Inc.
225 Park Avenue South,
New York, New York 10003
CROWN is a trademark of Crown Publishers, Inc.
Manufactured in the United States of America

Library of Congress Cataloging-in-Publication Data

Davis, Patti.
  Home front.

  I. Foster, Maureen Strange.   II. Title.
PS3554.A93762H65   1986   813'.54   85-30859
ISBN 0-517-55952-8

10   9   8   7   6   5
First Edition

to my husband,
for his love and support . . .
and to all Vietnam vets

special thanks to
Shad Meshad and Dennis LeBlanc
for their help and insight

HOME FRONT

★ Prologue ★

W E WERE HUSTLED INTO THE SHINIEST LIMOUSINE OF an endless motorcade. I peered through the window at the madness that grips the capital on Inauguration Day, not easily distinguished from a fifties movie in which flying saucers descend on the metropolis. The crowd seethed, streets were blocked off, helicopters whirred overhead, and the sound of sirens bounced off buildings and came ringing back to my ears. Time fast-forwarded. Moments later, under a steel-gray sky, my father was sworn in as President of the United States.

At the White House we were led upstairs, where servants were waiting to introduce themselves and other officious people bustled in and out of the rooms. My father quickly gravitated to the living room, sat on the couch and looked around, as if trying to absorb the fact that this was now his home.

"Can I get you anything, Mr. President?"

"Sir, the motorcade is scheduled to depart at eight o'clock."

"Some papers have been delivered for you, sir."

Brian wandered into the living room, rotating his head from the high ceilings to the amber paintings to the plush carpet.

"So this is the company housing they gave you, huh, Dad?" He pushed on a section of the wall as if it would open onto a secret passageway. "Kinda old. Hope it doesn't have termites."

"Brian," said my mother with a distressed look, "have you

1

been wearing those cowboy boots all day with your good suit?''

He looked down. ''So that's why that photographer was shooting my feet.''

My father was examining a stack of papers, licking his finger to turn the pages. ''You know, Harriet, I don't think we should have used that old family Bible for the swearing in today. The binding was crumbling off. I thought the whole thing was about to fall apart and blow away.''

''Well, it didn't, dear. Everything was perfect. Elizabeth, did you tell the switchboard you were expecting a call from Greg so they'd be sure to put it through?''

''Twice, Mom.''

''When is he due to arrive?''

''Sometime tonight.''

My mother was carrying on conversations as she ducked in and out of rooms, inspecting furniture, drapes, walls.

''There's just so much history here! Imagine all the people who have been within these walls. But, good grief, I just can't wait to redecorate.''

I tried to imagine, to be awed, to be anything but what I was —numb. It seemed like a scene I'd wandered into by mistake. I looked out the window and saw people gathered outside the distant gates, pressing against the metal, staring through the bars. They'd be surprised to learn that I felt like the outsider, that as they stood beyond those gates they were more a part of this historic event than I. Though I felt awkward and unreal, the inauguration was not a surprise to me; it was something I'd started preparing myself for, though not successfully, when I was still playing with dolls.

★ 1 ★

WHILE I SAT WAITING FOR THE PHONE TO RING, ALL the years leading up to this day flickered through my mind. . . . I remembered a night before our house had gradually filled up with a plethora of elephants—glass, porcelain, carved wood—and pillows bearing a crocheted replica of the White House and the bright red words GO ALL THE WAY. Remembering, I felt a coldness that started in my knees and traveled up to my stomach where it stayed—for years, it seemed.

That night in late 1965 we were gathered in my parents' bedroom in our home in California, the room where all family conferences took place. My mother and father sat in the two ice-blue damask chairs that framed the fireplace, and I perched on the end of their bed, completing the semicircle appropriate for such occasions. Brian was sprawled on the floor in eleven-year-old indifference to whatever made his presence here more important than what he'd been watching on TV. It was a summer evening; I listened to the crickets sing outside the French doors that opened on the garden. A warm wind found its way down the chimney, stirring up the scent of last winter's fires.

"The reason I wanted us to sit down here together," said my father, "is that I've made an important decision."

I felt my stomach tighten and my eyes search for an escape.

3

Above the mantel I saw the portrait of my mother and me, painted when I was about two years old. How far back can we remember? A girl at school who stabled her horse next to mine once told me she could remember what it felt like to be inside the womb. She remembered being born. Some people say they can recall things that happened even before this—in lives past. I wonder most about the things I can remember feeling, and yet can't recall.

In the portrait, conspicuous amid all the light, watery colors, are my eyes—dark and wide and wondering—staring, it seemed, at nothing in particular, but filled with questions. Every time I walked by I was drawn to my own, younger eyes, but I could never fully remember how that painting came to be. I recalled the wrought-iron stairway, where dampness clung to the walls and our footsteps made hollow, echoing sounds as we walked up to the artist's studio. But as many times as I'd tried, I could never take my memory past those stairs.

"Elizabeth, are you listening to your father?"

"Yes, Mom."

"No, you're not. You're staring into space again."

I looked back at my father, who was waiting.

"I'll be announcing this decision soon," he continued, "but I thought it only fair to tell you kids first."

"Mom knows already?" Brian asked idly, taking aim with an imaginary rifle at a crystal vase perched on a side table.

"Of course she does," I told him.

She does and so do I. It was easy to see it coming over the last few months—the speeches, the headlines, the strangers coming and going—and yet hadn't I known long before then? I'd sensed it as a child, fearing it without knowing what it was, already feeling the force that was destined to sweep us all away.

"I've given this a lot of thought," he went on, "and I've decided to run for governor."

Brian turned to face them, propping himself up on his elbows. "Will I have to change schools?" he asked, not bothering to hide his distaste. "Do we have to live in Sacramento?"

"We'll cross that bridge when we come to it," said my mother.

Unlike my parents, I preferred to scout as many bridges—real or imaginary—as I could, then map my course accordingly. I sat staring at the curlicues in the Oriental rug, losing myself in their endless puzzle.

"Is there anything you'd like to ask?" said my mother. "Something you'd like to say?"

I looked up at my father. "What made you decide this, Dad?"

"Well, Beth," he said, turning to face me, "you're a smart girl. You've seen what's happened here over the last few years. A lot of folks have been counting on me—important people, good people. You wouldn't want me to let them down, would you?"

"Yes! Why are they so important? Why are they more important than we are? Why can't—"

"Elizabeth!" My mother's voice sliced through my complaints. "This is a major decision in your father's life. It's a big chance for him and you should be very proud. There are even people who think he could be president someday."

"President!" Brian bolted up. "Where would I go to school then, in the White House or something? There probably aren't even any kids in Washington!"

"Come on, Brian," I said, "that's not the point."

"Well, what is the point you're trying to make, Beth?" my father asked patiently.

I didn't know. Was I trying to tell him that I didn't want him to be governor, that I wanted him to have nothing to do with a life that he and my mother had been striving toward for so long? I thought about the closet in Brian's room where we used to hide when we were younger. The light clicked on when the door was opened and went off when it was shut. It was the darkest place I'd ever been and I wanted to be there now, but sixteen was too old to be hiding in closets.

"Well, I've finished my speech," said my father. "Sure hope I haven't ruined everybody's day."

Brian went back to the television and I went out by the swimming pool and looked down at the city lights, twinkling like diamonds on black velvet. I was home for vacation from Devon, a boarding school in northern Arizona, where no lights could be seen at night, only miles of dark desert where sheets of wind blew the earth smooth and sent balls of tumbleweed skipping and bouncing past fork-shaped cactus.

I wondered if my life there would change, if people would act differently toward me once my father became governor. I didn't wonder whether or not he would win the election—I already knew the answer to that.

★ 2 ★

I WAS EIGHT WHEN I BEGAN TO NOTICE THAT THE CONVER-
sation at our dinner table invariably turned to politics. At
that time my father, Robert Canfield, worked in radio and TV as
a spokesman for National Motors. I think I would have liked it
better if the talk had been about cars—at least that was something tangible, something an eight-year-old could understand.
Instead, our dinners were suffused with opinion and philosophy
and interpretation and words like "mandate" and "liberals"
and talk of Ike and Nixon and Castro and Khrushchev. There
were musings about campaigns and supporters and the electorate
and Democrats and Republicans. I didn't care one way or the
other and I wished the whole business would just vanish from
the face of the earth. To me politics was more than just the names
of people I didn't know and words I couldn't understand. There
were distant rumblings—warnings that the earth I stood on
could shift at any moment. It became a dangerous presence in
our house, growing larger and more threatening until it lived
with us and slept in our beds. It crouched under the dining room
table, waiting its chance to swallow up all that I counted on in
my world.

"There's nothing on TV," I'd wail when political events mo-
nopolized the stations for days at a time, depriving me of all my
favorite shows. Whatever was going on couldn't possibly be as

important as "Tombstone Territory." One day, my father said to us, "If the air raid sirens ever go off, I want everyone to run to the dressing room because there are no windows in there." Their dressing room was large and every wall was mirrored. Anyone walking in immediately multiplied. I didn't absorb the full impact of his warning, but I dreaded the idea of spending hours in a small room surrounded by reflections of myself. Years later, it occurred to me that the only advantage of using their dressing room as a bomb shelter was that the shattering mirrors would probably kill us before the radiation did.

Although I couldn't identify my nemesis clearly enough to attack it, I wasn't going to stand passively by, and I had no intention of giving in. When it came to politics I didn't want to listen and I certainly didn't want to talk. When the conversation turned in that direction, I became suddenly, deliberately, and extremely intent on whatever happened to be on my plate. Creamed turnips mesmerized me for minutes at a time; a dab of mint jelly clinging to the edge of my lamb chop put me in a trance. I fixated on the puddle of chocolate milk at the bottom of my glass like a gypsy reading tea leaves; I counted my peas, and then I counted pearl onions. All the while, talk of the Russians and senators from the East Coast buzzed over my head. From time to time they would pause and ask me what I thought, and I couldn't be accused of lying when I replied, "Me? Oh, sorry. I wasn't listening."

Sometimes I got away with it. The conversation went on without me. At other times I wasn't so lucky. My father would fill me in on the salient points of whatever was under discussion and then ask my opinion again. Since I'd already exhausted every possibility for diversion on my plate, I tried approaching it from a different angle. I would say, "I don't know." This, unfortunately, didn't work very well. I wondered if I might be cursed with the look of someone bound to have an opinion. Some people just don't look like the "I don't know" type. A last resort was simply to agree with whatever seemed to be the more popular view—which wasn't hard to ascertain since my parents generally presented a unified front. This didn't always work, either. Maybe I didn't look like the type of person who would be likely to agree with their point of view. I made a mental note to watch more old westerns, study the guy with the poker face—and cultivate it.

Finally, and with a certain amount of desperation, I deployed a new strategy. At dinner, I started falling off my chair. This did succeed in creating a diversion, but only temporarily; after I returned to my chair, the conversation returned to politics. My solution: keep falling. I worked my way up to falling six, maybe seven times at a meal. Aside from the fact that I was constantly hungry—having spent most of my time in transit from the chair to the floor—my parents were beginning to suspect that there was something seriously wrong with me. I noticed that they began eying me suspiciously at various times of the day, apparently trying to figure out if I fell off of every chair, or just the one at the dinner table. Little Brian sat in his own chair staring at me with wide eyes and smiling, as if he knew exactly what was going on.

A new chair was moved to the dining table for me, a heavier one, with arms. It was more difficult—I couldn't be quite as subtle—but I succeeded in falling off that one, too. Then began their conversations, conducted in hushed tones, that I managed to overhear.

"I'm terribly concerned about Elizabeth," my mother said to my father one night, after I'd excused myself from the table to watch "Laramie." I peeked through the opening between the double doors and saw her lean toward him, conspiratorially. "She seems to have trouble staying in her chair. I've never heard of anything like this before. Maybe we should call Dr. Harrison."

Teachers at school began studying me as if I were one of the classroom gerbils. I assumed that my mother had called the school and asked if her daughter had displayed any unusual behavior, such as, for example, falling off her chair.

I was taken to Dr. Harrison for a checkup. After tousling my hair and pinching my cheeks, he began searching my chest with his icy stethoscope. When he shoved the thermometer into my mouth I began to fear that I had gone too far. What if they decided that I was suffering from some rare illness, and started treating me for something I didn't have? Injections . . . foul-tasting medicines . . . maybe even surgery! Amputation! I remembered my grandfather once telling me about a man in his hometown of Winnetka who had a disease called dropsy. I wondered if that could have anything to do with dropping off things —like chairs. I didn't know what the treatment for dropsy was, and I didn't want to find out.

I decided to end the whole business. I sat at the table for the duration of the meals with a nonchalance that seemed to deny anything strange had gone on before. Soon the chair with the arms was removed, and the original one returned.

My father's hardy good looks and persuasive voice sold an awful lot of cars for National Motors, for which he was highly paid. In the late fifties, National was embroiled in a well-publicized and somewhat embarrassing scandal, involving a failed nuclear tractor-trailer in which they'd invested millions. When the story broke we watched him on the local news, pursued by reporters as he was leaving a restaurant.

"Will National really take a beating on this one, Mr. Canfield?"

"I guess they're just a little ahead of their time," said my father with a wink.

"It's rumored the trailer had a problem with radiation leakage!" shouted another as my father stepped into his car, leaving them with a wave. "Any truth to the rumor that it went off course and they tracked it down with a Geiger counter?"

When we all went out together people recognized his voice—on the street strangers recognized his face—and in time men in important positions saw that my father's homespun likability could sell a great deal more than the latest model station wagon. Not long after this, he began making speeches, and politics, as I had long feared without knowing why, took over our lives. My father began having meetings in the den with groups of men who looked like bankers. Then the entertaining began.

One day my father said to my mother, "Where did you get the idea to invite *them* for dinner? I wouldn't have thought of it." And she said, "Bob, this is what you have to do if you want to get anywhere." Week after week the people came, smoking cigars and cigarettes and pipes and drinking Scotch and talking, talking, talking. Some were senators; some were introduced only as "mister." I was taught to shake their hands and say "How do you do?" I didn't know exactly what they did, other than talk about politics. Their wives wore furs and jewels and when I asked a tall blond lady if her rings were real she looked down and said, "Of course, darling," just as my mother whisked me into the other room.

"Why do these people always have to come over here?"

''They're important, Elizabeth. They can help your father a great deal.''

''Help him do what?''

''Never mind, dear. Why don't you go upstairs and play with Brian?''

My father, educated and articulate, moved easily among the social elite that plugged into the world of politics. He fitted in so well that in time he became a highly paid speaker for the Republican Party. He had always been an eloquent man. Once during his years with National, he addressed an assembly at my school, saying how proud we all should be that our country's auto industry provided the nation with such fine, modern, safe transportation. I remember being proud of him and at the same time frightened; whatever it was that made him so special was the reason I'd never be able to keep him all to myself.

My father spoke to others, his father-in-law Samuel spoke to him, and I was frequently reprimanded for not listening to either of them. Grandpa Samuel said I should behave as my mother did when she was my age. ''When Harriet was a little girl, she never talked back and she never fidgeted in church.''

Grandpa Samuel was acutely aware of who was fidgeting and who was listening. He was the preacher at the First Presbyterian Church. Every Sunday I was buttoned into a starched organdy dress and led into the pew between my parents. As Grandpa Samuel's voice boomed over us I watched the sun move across the panes of stained glass . . . and I fidgeted.

After the service, we'd go back to his house for lunch. My grandmother died before I was born, but she stared at us from pictures on walls and bookshelves, in high-necked lace blouses and black velvet to her chin, which made me wonder if her death had been caused by choking. There were dishes of candy around, and they were always filled. While Grandpa Samuel told my father how to ''hold an audience in the palm of your hand— you've got to know how to grab them,'' I'd discreetly puncture chocolates with my fingernail to see if I liked what was inside.

One day when there were no chocolates, only hard candies that hurt my teeth and took too long to dissolve, I sat on the couch and tried to look interested as Grandpa Samuel gave my father a lesson in public speaking.

''You see, Robert, there are what we call buzz words—words that grab people's attention. Words like freedom, morality, responsibility, family. And you've got to know how to use your voice to accentuate these words—increase the volume, raise the pitch—and of course it never hurts to quote the Scriptures, son, to back up your message. Take advantage of all the tools the good Lord gave you.''

Years later I sat in an auditorium where my father was making a speech for one of the presidential candidates. In a rich, firm voice he talked about freedom, the responsibility of making a moral choice, the strength of the family unit ... and I remembered that day at Grandpa's. The validity of his lesson was evident all around me as people wiped their eyes and rose to their feet in thunderous applause.

When the party's presidential candidate was in desperate need of help, my father was often called on to give speeches to rally the public to the Republican cause. His efforts didn't perform any miracles at the voting booths, but crowds responded to him and his message with fervor—and the men who came to visit him in our den groomed him to be the next candidate for governor.

⋆ 3 ⋆

STANDING BY THE PHONE AT BOARDING SCHOOL ONE November night, I looked out the window to the line where the glow from the lights ended and the darkness began. I watched the leaves scrape across the ground, pushed by an errant wind, and heard an owl call out from somewhere in the blackness. I knew my life would never be the same again. I knew I would have to confront this change, or run from it—and I didn't want to do either.

"Elizabeth, dear, this is something your father has wanted for a long time. You know that. I think you should at least congratulate him."

"Mom, can I ask you a question?"

"Of course, dear."

"Why can't you call me Beth like everyone else?"

My mother is too tactful a person to sigh, but I could hear her patient look screaming at me over the wires.

"I don't think this is the proper time for jokes, dear. You know how important this is."

Not having inherited my mother's tact, I sighed freely. I never wanted him to run in the first place. How could I pretend I was happy that he won?

There was a brief silence. "Your father is in the next room talking to some people. I'm going to get him and put him on the phone now."

"Mom, wait—" Her presence vanished from the other end. In a few seconds I heard the double doors snap closed, and my parents talking in whispers.

"Beth?"

"Hi, Dad."

"How's everything at school, honey?" He sounded robust and filled with enthusiasm. His dream, or one of them, had just come true. I sensed that he was entirely comfortable with his new power. There was no reason for me to think that he was any different from the man I had known all my life—the man who helped me bury my goldfish after it had floated motionless in the aquarium for two days while I insisted it was only sleeping.

"Beth," he finally said, folding me into the crook of his arm and lifting me onto his lap, "your fish isn't sleeping, honey, he's dead."

"Does that mean he won't wake up, ever?"

"Yes, but he's someplace better, in a beautiful lake where he can swim as far in any direction as he wants."

"Is that where we'll go when we die?"

He looked at the floor for a long time, his brow furrowed. "Something like that," he said.

We buried my goldfish in the yard and marked his grave with a cross that my father made from sticks and twine. As I watched his hands fumble with the tiny sticks, I felt I could ask him anything.

Now, on a night years past those days, I feared we'd crossed a threshold into an unfriendly world . . . and he'd become a stranger to me.

"School's okay, I guess." The rustling leaves, the hoot of an owl, the black night outside the window beckoned to me, a fantasy world in which I could lose myself.

"Is it snowing on you tonight?" He was trying to make it easy on me.

"Dad, I . . . I know this is a very big occasion for you."

"Yes, there's quite a bit of excitement here tonight." I heard the door open in the background, the rumble of voices.

"It sounds like they're waiting for you, Dad. I don't want to keep you."

"That's all right, Beth. They can—"

"I just wanted to tell you, Dad . . . I just wanted to say . . ." I'd sworn that if she put him on I wouldn't do this, I wouldn't cry. I watched the tears fall from my chin to the mouthpiece on the phone receiver.

"Yes?"

"I know how much this means to you and I'm . . . I'm really not feeling well tonight, Dad. I think it's the flu. Tell Mom I'll call her next Sunday. . . ."

My roommate came in that evening and found me on the bed in a crop of Kleenex.

"Sweetie pie, what are you doin' sittin' here all by your lonesome in the dark?"

Delia was Devon's femme fatale. I'm sure there was some truth to the rumor that in her home town of Phoenix she caused a small riot by stepping out to the ice cream store in a halter and shorts.

Delia flipped up the switch for the overhead light, and I turned to face the wall.

"Turn it off, Deel. It's past lights out."

"I thought you were crying . . . you *are* crying!" She turned off the light and came over to the bed, and sat beside me. "Now what could possibly be the matter with you? I've never seen you cry like this before."

"I'm all right," I said, patting my eyes with a tissue and trying to collect myself. "Really, I'm fine."

"The hell you are," she said, pushing my bangs off my forehead. Then she leaned forward and whispered, "What is it, honey? You can tell me. It's a man, isn't it? Now come on, you didn't go falling in love without lettin' your old roommate in on it, did you?"

I shook my head, blew my nose, and started collecting the wadded up tissues that surrounded me.

"Then what is it, sugar?"

I put the tissues in the wastebasket. "You wouldn't understand, Delia. Really, you wouldn't.

"A cow's balls, I wouldn't. You just try me. Come on, tell me what's got you so upset."

I'd calmed down by this time, and sat down on the bed beside her. "My father won the election."

"Why, honey, that's just marvelous! You mean these are tears of joy?"

"Not exactly."

"Well, honey, you must be excited about it. Your family's

famous now. Hell's bells, sugar, you're royalty is what you are! You're sittin' on top of the world.''

''I don't expect you to understand, Deel. It's just that . . . ever since I was a little girl I was afraid of something happening, but I didn't know what. I sensed something. . . . I was afraid that some tidal wave was going to come along someday and sweep us all up.''

''Bethie, you should be happy! Don't be afraid. Jesus, ain't a girl on this hall wouldn't give up everything to change places with you.''

We sat talking in whispers, barely able to see each other in the moonless dark. Suddenly there was a tapping on the window— her boyfriend Greg. ''Hi, it's me!'' Along with a blast of freezing air, he slipped through the window.

''Hey, guys.'' He put his arms around Delia and she shut the window behind him. I curled up in the corner of my bed and buried my head in a book, but he made it his business to notice me. He stuck his face at me and said, ''Hey, Betsy, what's the big deal? Whatchoo cryin' for?''

''You're here,'' I told him. ''Isn't that reason enough?'' I slammed the book closed and went to the closet for my coat.

''What's with her?'' he asked Delia.

I shot her a look to keep her quiet, but it was too late.

''Her father was just elected Governor of California.''

''No shit,'' he said, turning to me with that cretinous grin of his. I grabbed a pillow and blanket from my bed and headed for the door.

''Congratulations, little governor's daughter!'' he said.

''Beth, where are you going?'' asked Delia. ''It's after curfew!''

I spent the night in the laundry room, trying to decipher the future.

Greg was seeing a lot of Delia, and I was hearing a lot of both of them, in the way of moans and groans and occasional shrieks coming from Delia's bed at around one in the morning. Sometimes on the nights of their lurid assignations she left the window open for him so he wouldn't have to tap and wake up the world, though if there was a single girl in our dorm still unaware of Greg and Delia's affair she must have been in a freezer awaiting the twenty-first century. Burying my face in the mattress and clutching two pillows over my head helped keep the noise out but presented another small problem, suffocation. While Delia sighed and Greg puffed and the bedsprings creaked I lay there wondering how long it could possibly last and worrying about whether, if they were found out, I could be held as an accessory to illicit lovemaking. At a place like Devon, sex on the grounds was probably reason for expulsion, although I could see the school officials accepting a nice fat check from parents as a peace offering. I lay there cursing Greg for being able to slip in at night so easily, and so often. I'd heard stories about some of the kids sneaking up to the hayloft in the barn to have sex, and wondered why these two insisted upon the privacy of my bedroom. From time to time when I lifted my pillow to get some air, the array of sounds coming from their bed piqued my curiosity, a foreign language I tried to interpret. Since they were keeping me awake anyway, maybe I could learn something.

Devon was in the middle of the desert, about seventy-five miles north of Phoenix. It functioned as a cattle ranch as well as a school, one of its unique selling points being that the entire student body participated in the biannual roundups. The first fourteen years of my life had been spent not on the open range but on the suburban lawns of Woodland Hills and Bel Air, and the only cowboys I knew were on television. But when a brochure for Devon arrived in the mail, the idea of going to a school that was also a ranch intrigued me. I took the color brochure into the garden and sat under the orange trees studying it for hours until I almost had it memorized. My parents finally gave in to my pleas; they even told me that I could have a horse of my own and keep it stabled at school. I took my first riding lesson the day after I arrived, and in my four years at Devon I spent more hours on horseback than in any other activity except sleep. As for the roundups, those of us who weren't creative enough to come up with excuses were doomed to four days on horseback chasing cattle, who have an uncanny ability to decide en masse to go in exactly the wrong direction.

The brochure represented Devon as a "strict, elite environment" that offered a "good education as well as a healthy exposure to the land." As for the elite environment, you couldn't argue with that. At Devon everybody's parents were somebody. I've never felt that being born to somebody who had achieved something important made you elite—it's more of an accident than anything—but I don't think too many kids at Devon shared my view. Most of them had a kind of thoroughbred mentality, as if accomplishment could be inherited, like nearsightedness. In an attempt to thwart temptation, Boys' Camp and Girls' Camp had been placed so far apart you could have dropped a small asteroid between them, but it was almost impossible to control a hundred and eighty teenagers in the middle of the desert. You have to wonder how serious a school is about strictness when a girls' dorm, consisting of single-story motellike buildings, has little supervision, inviting easy entry by predatory characters at one in the morning.

Delia and Greg could jump from hatred to uncontrollable passion in a matter of hours, exhausting everyone except, apparently, the two of them. It was impossible to keep track—not that I cared—though I couldn't help noticing when they hated each other; I finally got some sleep. Apart from the fact that he was invading my privacy I found it easy to dislike Greg because he was obviously of the opinion that his blond hair and conventional good looks gave him license to voice his opinion even when it wasn't wanted, which as far as I was concerned was always. I could never figure out what Delia saw in him, though I had no trouble figuring out what he saw in Delia.

After my rendezvous with the laundry room I resolved never to speak to Greg again. *Never* came on the afternoon he approached me on campus and said, "I just want to say goodbye." Although I hated giving him the satisfaction that I even remotely cared where he was going or why, he caught me off guard.

"What do you mean, goodbye? Where do you suppose you're escaping to, three weeks before finals?"

"U.S.M.C.," he said, and in his typical haughty manner off he went. Too bad there wasn't a sunset for him to walk into. I was irked by his calculated air of mystery, but curiosity pushed me to the fore.

"I hear Wonder Stud's enlisted," I said to Delia, taking care not to raise my eyes from the book I was reading.

"He's perfect marine material," she told me. "Can't you just see that lover boy in uniform, out there kickin' ass to kingdom come?"

"I thought you had to be eighteen to join," I added nonchalantly.

"No doubt," she said. "Probably lied about his age."

"Lied to you, you mean. Wouldn't surprise me if he was twenty-one."

The next two weeks I slept so soundly I missed three morning classes. I hoarded sleep, perhaps fearing that Greg would unexpectedly return and I'd have to start drawing on reserves. But he didn't come back; he was gone for good. One day when I was studying in the room, Delia came back from class wearing a look of terror.

"You won't believe it," she said.

"How many guesses do I get?"

"I think I'm pregnant."

⋆ 4 ⋆

DELIA LOOKED AT ME EXPECTANTLY, AS IF SHE'D JUST
asked me a life-or-death question to which she was
positive I had the answer. She clutched her books tensely to her
chest, a shield against enemy weapons. I sat there ogling her as
if I'd forgotten the English language.

"Well?" she demanded. She threw the books onto her bed.

"What did you just say?" This was the best I could so—stall
for time until I figured out what she could possibly expect of me.

"This is no joke, honey." She plopped her purse down on my
desk and began fumbling for a cigarette. I'd never seen Delia the
least bit nervous before. Again, she looked at me. "Well?"

I put down my pencil. "Okay, Delia. First, we have to find out
if you're *really* pregnant." The response in her eyes wasn't
promising. I explained reasonably, "Maybe you're just late."

"Late? Honeybun, I haven't seen the sight of blood in two
months. That sound like late to you?"

Questions raced through my mind, the foremost being . . . why
me? Why ask me these questions? What did I know? My sexual
knowledge had been expanded minimally by what I'd managed
to overhear coming from Delia's bed when Greg was around, but
I was still embarrassingly uneducated. Delia knew this, yet she
was looking at me as if I were the only person in the world who
could help her.

"Maybe there's some other explanation."

"Sure there is, sugar. Menopause."

"Delia, all I'm saying is you should be absolutely positive before you start getting hysterical about this."

"No sweat, honey," she told me. "You're calm enough for both of us." She looked down and studied her cigarette. She'd had a cold the last few days and I mentioned to her that maybe she ought to do something about it—meaning cut out smoking for a while. She assured me it was okay—she'd switched to menthol.

"Come with me to the john," she said.

We walked down the hall and into the bathroom. Somone was blow-drying her hair, and a couple of freshmen were standing at the sinks putting false eyelashes on each other. We went into a shower stall, ran the hot water, and Delia lit up, so the steam could conceal the smoke from her cigarette.

"Delia, wait for me back in the room."

"Where are you going?" she called out after me.

"Just wait there!"

It was only a couple of hundred yards to the main campus building, where the nurse had her office. I held my collar up to the wind, and began to run. I was panting when I got there.

"Yes? Can I help you?"

"I ... uh ..." What was I going to say? "I think I'm pregnant and I need to know the symptoms"? I figured that after she got through placing an emergency call to my parents, she'd start sewing a scarlet *A* on my sweater.

"It's my head."

"A headache?"

"Right ... a terrible headache." I collapsed into a chair, massaging my distressed forehead. "It's killing me right here ... and here ... I can't study ... I'm seeing double. I barely made it over here. ..."

"I'll be right back. I'm just going to get a thermometer." When she disappeared into the back room, the phone rang. While she talked I scanned a row of books on her desk, grabbed one that looked like it might be helpful, and bolted out of there. I ran back to the dorm, my guilty eyes darting around for witnesses. If I were caught, the emergency call to my parents would definitely be placed. I ran faster. I could always say I was just borrowing the book as a favor to a sick friend. As I raced back to the dorm I cursed Greg and every memory I had of him.

"Where've you been?" cried Delia. I went to my desk holding up the book so she could see the title. "*Women and Their Ailments?* Where the hell'd you get that thing? Not the school library, I bet."

"Not with these pictures." I flipped the pages. "Let's see . . . pregnancy . . . pregnancy . . ."

"I told you, Bethie, you're wasting your time. Lordie, girl, didn't you ever watch 'As the World Turns'?"

"Here! Okay." I looked at Delia and announced, "Bloating." She put her hand on her stomach, and nodded.

"Really?" She nodded again. "Okay. Nausea?"

"For the past five days."

"Okay, wait. How about this one? Breast and nipple tenderness."

"Gee, I don't know. Nobody's touched 'em since—"

"Quit screwing around and just tell me how they feel!"

"They're sore."

She lifted her hands and cupped them around her breasts. She pushed her thumbs against her nipples. She didn't look happy. I closed the book and put it down, and stared out the window. I could see someone studying in one of the classrooms across the way. At that moment I would much rather have been reading Chaucer or boning up on the latest archeological finds.

Delia's eyes pleaded with me. "You know what I've gotta do."

I was afraid this was coming. I looked back at the window.

"The only doctor I know is my family doctor, and he'd tell my parents in two shakes. They can't find out about this. You met my parents, Beth, you know what my daddy's like. He thinks I'm Betsy Ross and the Virgin Mary and that lady from *Sound of Music* all rolled into one. Why, if he got wind of what's been goin' on around here, he'd shit shingles."

I rested my head in my hands and then stood up. "Where are you going?" she asked.

"Just over to the corrals to take a walk. Will you be okay for a little while?"

I pulled my jacket around me and pushed my way into the wind. I watched my feet make little explosions of dust as they landed on the road. The sun was halfway gone and the remaining light painted the desert a deep rust, like Mexican pottery. Sometime before the last bit of sunlight surrendered, I remembered something. Not long before, I'd been in the dentist's office in Phoenix having a cavity filled. While I sat captive in the chair with cotton wads and strange gurgling instruments stuffed in my mouth, I amused myself by eavesdropping on as many conversations as I could. What I heard was the nurse and the receptionist talking about a friend of theirs who'd had an abortion. I was sure they mentioned the name of a Dr. Mead.

I went back to the room and suggested to Delia that we check out of school to visit her parents in Phoenix for the weekend. Then we could invent an excuse to remove ourselves from the house for most of the day. I gave her the money I'd been saving to buy a new bridle for my horse, and between us we had a little over a hundred dollars.

On Friday Delia had a clothes sale at school, which brought in another ninety. The only thing I had of any value, besides my horse, Harmony—and that was where I drew the line—was an antique gold ring that belonged to my great-grandmother. I pawned it in Phoenix, and altogether we had a little more than the five hundred dollars she needed.

The address Dr. Mead had given us was on the outskirts of the city, an old clapboard house set back from the road. It looked as though hovering trees and the neglected jungle of a front yard were there to deliberately discourage outsiders. A pair of eyes peered at us from around the door; it was held at an uninviting angle by a chain that wasn't released until we'd given our names, both of which were borrowed from characters in books. Once we were inside, my eyes went directly to the tiny bloodstain on the apron worn by the woman who let us in. Shades were drawn on every window; the only relief from darkness in the middle of the day was the light from the lamp in the corner. The room smelled of Lysol. The woman with the bloodstain had vanished. Delia looked around solemnly. She may have been smiling a few minutes before, but she didn't look happy now.

"You okay?"

"I'm okay."

The woman returned. "Which one's Hester?"

Delia was staring off into space; I gave her a nudge with my elbow. "I am," she said, finally.

"Come with me."

They disappeared through a door that looked as though it led to a kitchen. I tried to imagine a kitchen that had been turned into an operating room. I could hear voices, but I couldn't understand what was being said. I found a chair and wondered what the house had looked like when people had lived there, when it was still a home. I saw sunlight streaming through red-checked curtains, spilling across a polished wood floor and hook rugs. I thought of a family having breakfast at a large, round table, of children running through the rooms.

Months before, Delia had come into our room laughing. "Take a look at this, honey!" she cried, climbing up on a chair. "I'm gonna blow it up like a balloon and hang it from the ceilin'." In her open palm was something shaped like a ring sealed in a clear plastic. I knew that whatever the thing was I was supposed to know, and be laughing along with her—not saying, "What *is* it?"

Delia was a cowgirl with the body of a Las Vegas showgirl. Since the age of six, her dream had been someday to ride on the rodeo circuit. Once she tried teaching me the finer points of chewing tobacco, but I must not have been paying attention when she advised against swallowing the juice. The sickly brown stuff found its way down my throat to my stomach, which promptly rebelled. Delia spent the rest of the night laughing about it.

"It's a rubber, babycakes!" she howled. At least I knew what a rubber was, but it seemed Delia, of all the girls I knew, could find a better use for it than hanging it from the ceiling. She stood on the chair with her hand on her waist, grinning at me. "Well, I'll be a heifer in heat," she said. "You're a virgin, aren't you?"

"Delia," I told her, "just because I don't go around advertising my sex life like some people doesn't necessarily mean I don't have one."

"Don't be embarrassed, sugar! You just haven't met Mr. Right Stud yet, that's all."

"Oh, sure. Somebody like Greg Howell, I suppose." At any point in time I could have broadened my sexual horizons, at least on a theoretical level, by listening in on Delia's detailed lectures to our dorm mates about sex and the budding debutante. At Devon, Delia had become a guru of the erotic, and girls clustered around her in awe of her expertise: the glories of the male organ ("you mean you actually *touched* it?"); the bliss of the "climax"; the ecstasy of being "all filled up." All right, I admit to having heard a few words here and there, though it was hard to believe that what she was describing could possibly be enjoyable. The mechanics of it all made it sound as though you'd need a box of equipment and at least three assistants to make it work. Could my own parents possibly have done any of that stuff? Worse, could I have been conceived that way? When I was in the third grade, a freckled girl with no front teeth whispered in my ear that babies are made when a man puts his "thing" into a woman. When I got home from school I marched right into my father's library and said, "You didn't put your *thing* into Mom to make me, did you?" He looked like he'd seen a rattlesnake. "Harriet!" he called, "Harriet, would you please come in here and get your daughter? I think she has some questions for you."

I wasn't wearing a watch, and had no conception of how much time had passed since Delia was swallowed up in that room. I walked over to the window and peeked around the edge of the shade. The shadows had hardly moved from where they were when we walked up the driveway.

Out on the road a boy was riding a bicycle. I thought of how many hours I used to spend riding my bike past the manicured yards of our neighborhood, pretending I was on a country road and the lawns were open fields. It seemed like a long time ago. I wished I could trade places with that boy for just a few minutes. He was riding toward a car parked farther down the road. It was probably his parents in the car waiting for him; maybe he was just learning to ride. But he didn't stop, and they never moved. Soon he was out of sight, and the car was still there, facing the house. Suddenly I was acutely aware of the danger in what we were doing. What if whoever was in the car was watching the house? What if they knew what was going on behind these dark windows? I moved abruptly back, out of sight.

When I was five, my mother went into the hospital for a few days. With my father spending most of his time with her, and only the maid left to discipline me, I got to have pizza for dinner, watch television whenever I wanted, and play in my mother's makeup drawer. But her homecoming was more exciting than all of that. She brought with her a little brother, who I was sure was the result of my nightly prayers for "someone to play with, God —and you can make it a girl or a boy, I'll let you decide."

He was little and splotchy and my mother said, "Now don't keep coming into the nursery and waking him up, Elizabeth. He's not very strong yet and he needs his sleep." I kept coming in, but I whispered so I wouldn't wake him up.

"Brian," I'd say, leaning over his crib as far as I could, "as soon as you're big enough you can sneak out with me at night and look for leprechauns. They come out and dance when there's a ring around the moon."

When he was barely a year old, I crept into his room one night when a smoke-ringed moon shone through my window and unleashed visions of dancing leprechauns in my willing imagination. I lifted him up, soft and sleepy in his rabbit-print pajamas, and held him tightly as I slid open the glass door that led into the garden. It was a warm summer night and Brian curled up on the grass and went back to sleep, not at all interested in leprechauns who might at that very moment be dancing in pools of moonlight. Our collie Heidi came over and stood by him protectively, whining faintly at this untimely intrusion on her domain.

"Elizabeth, what on earth are you doing?" My mother was standing in the doorway, and her voice filled the garden. "My heavens . . . is that Brian you've got there on the ground?"

"Um, well . . . we were looking for something."

"I see, and do you mind telling me what you were looking for in the garden at this hour of the night?" The moon was shining through her nightgown, showing the outlines of her body in silhouette. "Well, Elizabeth?" She scooped Brian up in her arms. "What were you doing out here?"

"Looking for leprechauns."

"Leprechauns?" There was a long pause. "Get back to bed. You can look for them in the morning."

I could have told her that they don't come out in the morning, that they don't even come out every night, but she had already gone from the moonlight back into the shadows of Brian's room.

The woman with the stains appeared at the kitchen door.

"You can come in and see your friend. She'll be fine, she's just a little weak." There was more blood on her apron than before.

She pulled me past the kitchen, down a hallway and into a tiny room. Delia was lying on a cot with a blanket over her. A sliver of light found its way past the shade and landed on her cheek. She looked awful. Her skin was blanched.

"She can rest here for a while. Here's some Kotex to take with you, but you better get some more." She was gone.

"Delia, how do you feel?"

"Okay, I guess. I just need to lie here for a while." Her eyes were half closed.

I took her hand in mine. My only thought was of how much I wanted to strangle that bastard Greg, but it seemed like a good time to keep it to myself.

Delia's skin was so pale that the afternoon sun seemed to shine right through it. I looked at the veins in her face, like some delicate embroidery.

When we got back to her house I told her parents that something she ate at the movies upset her stomach, and she was going to bed early. The next day, when her color had come back, I suggested that we return to school early on Sunday, to keep her parents from noticing anything about her that might seem different. While she rested in the dorm, I spent Sunday afternoon exercising both her horse and mine, and cleaning out both corrals. I welcomed the pain in my arms and back; somehow it seemed fitting that I be in pain, too.

Early Monday morning I woke to find Delia out of bed and already dressed in her riding gear. I rubbed my eyes.

"Delia, what are you doing?"

"Gettin' these lazy bones back in motion, sugar. What's it look like?"

I rubbed my eyes. "Are you sure you're up to it?"

"Maybe I am, maybe I'm not, but two days under the weather is my limit. See you at breakfast!"

I was a little worried about her, but mostly I felt relieved that she seemed completely back to normal. I put my head back on the pillow for one more hour of sleep, and woke up feeling better than I'd felt in days.

One morning later that week I walked to my mailbox, not a thrilling trip because I rarely found anything there of interest. It was late November. The sky was full and gray, and the winds were turning wintry. I buttoned my jacket against the chill and unlocked my box. The envelope I took out was in handwriting I didn't recognize, and I couldn't make out the peculiar return address. But the name at the bottom of the letter gave me a jolt.

★　★　★

Dear Beth,

I know we never got along too well, but I just felt like writing to someone. Actually that's not true—I felt like writing to you. I guess we got into a rut of giving each other a hard time, but I want to tell you now that I always kinda dug you. I remember one day when Doug's horse took off with him and you went after them like the Lone Ranger and stopped the horse. Pretty spunky—and brave, I guess. I wouldn't have done it. Anyway, I was thinking about that today, and about you, so I'm writing. Hope it's not a shock.

I'm in Boot Camp now. Lots of fun. Since I quit Devon life has been a series of disillusionments. Admittedly, I was naive to quit school—it's a big bad world out here. And no, there is no Santa Claus. I've met a lot of one-way people. I'm not getting taken, though, cuz I can hack it. One way or another, I'll make out.

I've never been one to run from a fight. I got in a fight with this dude here. I expected to slug it out but the first thing he did was kick me in a tender spot and, while I was down, he stomped on my face. When I did get up he had a rock in his hand. I finally won, but now I know how the game is played.

When you leave the sheltered society of Devon, watch out for yourself. There are all kinds of people waiting to gobble you up.

I haven't lost faith in my fellow man, I'm just wary. Thanks for listening.

Greg

★ ★ ★

I was tempted to throw the letter away and not tell Delia, but something made me tell her. In the news there was more and more about the war in Vietnam; I wondered if someday Greg would end up there.

"Write him back, Bethie. You can see how lonely he is."

"Write *back?* You'd better get back in bed, Delia. I don't think you're fully recovered. Where's that thermometer—"

"Listen to me, honey." She sounded serious. "I think it always rubbed him wrong that you two didn't hit it off. He sorta... admired you, and... well, what I'm trying to tell you is, I think he secretly liked you better."

"I'm deeply moved," I said. This was getting worse by the minute. "Do you actually think that I could write to him after what he did to you? Don't tell me you've forgiven him already."

"There was no need forgivin' him, sugar."

"Are you serious? You mean you're not even mad at him?"

"No reason for it, Bethie."

"I don't believe I'm hearing this."

"I probably should have told you before—"

"What?"

"It wasn't him, honey."

I just stared at her.

"It was Dunstreet."

"Dunstreet! This can't be real! Our history teacher was the *father?*"

She nodded and sat down on the bed.

"Wait a minute. If you were sleeping with—and Greg was—what makes you so sure Dunstreet was the father?"

Delia looked down at her knees, then back up at me. "Promise me you won't tell the other gals, okay?"

"Sure I promise. But—"

"Those times Greg was in here, we never really did it, Bethie. We were just—well, you ever hear the expression 'dry humpin'?"

This was too much. What about the glories of intercourse? The fabulous male organ?

"Honey, he never even took off his underwear."

I couldn't help myself. I started to laugh—but Delia laughed the loudest. When she finally calmed down, she told me that the night she slept with Grover Dunstreet, eight weeks before, was the first and only time she'd ever gone all the way. She reminded me to keep it to myself.

⋆ 5 ⋆

AFTER THE ELECTION, MY PARENTS' TIME WAS DIVIDED between Sacramento and Bel Air. Christmas, I was relieved to learn, would be spent in Bel Air. Once home, I decided to write to Greg. I sat in my bedroom, which seemed smaller with each visit. When we moved to that house from Woodland Hills, it had seemed enormous to me, with built-in shelves up to the ceiling. I had to stand on my tiptoes to see the top one.

There was a porcelain doll in my bedroom then that was always kept on a shelf just beyond my reach. It had been a gift from my father's mother, who died when I was very young. I have vague, unfocused memories of a small, birdlike woman with large blue eyes and gray-black hair, but the rest of the picture is fuzzy.

Each year the doll was moved a shelf or two higher to ensure that I wouldn't play with it. "It's irreplaceable," my mother said, "an antique," as if that explained the strangeness of having a doll I couldn't play with. There she sat, white porcelain face and painted black hair, looking pristinely down at me in her Victorian dress, flanked by the *Encyclopedia Britannica* and a Baccarat elephant. Once she reached the top shelf, she stayed there for a full year and then, when I shot up another two inches, she disappeared. I asked where she was and my mother said, "I sold it. We needed to make room."

"She didn't take up that much room," I told her, but my

mother was already in the garden, clipping roses to fill the crystal vase in the dining room.

Things had a way of disappearing in our house, with no warning and little explanation. There was a painting in the living room of children marching in a line carrying signs that read "Chocolate!" Up close, none of the children had faces, just oval shapes without features. But if I stood back against the opposite wall I could see faces on each one. Eyes, noses, smiles, frowns suddenly were visible to me.

One day the painting was gone. In its place was a gaunt Oriental man whose eyes seemed to be focused on his shoes. I asked where the other painting was and my mother said they had sold it. I asked what would happen if I grew anymore—I was already the tallest in my class—would they sell me to make room?

"Elizabeth, I don't know where you come up with these ideas. I think we should cut down on your television time."

I sat staring at the paper on which no more than "Dear Greg" had been written. Whatever animosity I felt toward him seemed trivial in a setting of blinking lights on the tree, the singing of carols, and the smell of pine. I suspected that his holidays were devoid of many of the things that we grew up expecting this time of year. My Christmas glow mellowed me, and besides, I couldn't help being curious about his life in the military. At the same time I couldn't bring myself to pretend that we'd had some kind of rapport we never had. As I wrote, I even mentioned his arrogance as one of the reasons.

On Christmas Eve, I received this:

★ ★ ★

Well, Betsy,

Offhand I'd say you were pretty much correct in your evaluation of me. If I'm guilty of being hostile maybe it's because I've never found anyone I could completely trust. And it may be that same hostility that sent me into the Corps, where I'll spend the next four years of my life. I'll be in Vietnam soon and they play for keeps over there. No pussy-footing around there—so I'll hang onto my shell—it might be the thing that keeps me alive.

I've got so many disjointed concepts of human relationships drifting through my mind. With this uncertainty swirling around in me, it's hard to find a set of values or an "ideology" to stand on, and that's disconcerting to someone like me—someone who's always liked to have things cut and dried. That may be why I joined the service. But recently I've become aware of a strain in my character that enjoys dealing in the abstract. I guess that sort of puts me in limbo, huh? Marine material? Who knows? I guess I'll find out soon enough.

Greg

★ ★ ★

I didn't tell my parents about Greg. The dinner table conversation was peppered with comments about the war. A part of me wanted to be eight years old again, so that I could make it all go away, at least temporarily, by simply falling off my chair. As a child I was frightened by political talk but without knowing why; it was a child's fear of the unknown, of great, dark movements out of your control or comprehension. Now, what little I knew or felt about the things they mentioned made me equally fearful. The war was discussed in terms of maneuvers and philosophy and ideology—all very abstract. As they had done when I was a child, my parents still attempted to include me in their political discussions by asking my opinion. They talked about the importance of making Vietnam safe for democracy, and asked me what I thought. Episodes related in my high school textbooks echoed in my ear, and I said the first thing that came to me: "Isn't that like making the prairie safe from the Indians, or Hawaii safe from the heathens?" My parents gave each other a look. Then my mother said, "Elizabeth, where did you hear *that?*"

When I got back to Devon after the holidays, there was another letting waiting.

★ ★ ★

Dear Betsy,

Well, here I am at Camp Pendleton. They're teaching us some great stuff. It's almost laughable that a nation supposedly thriving on peace can teach us how to be such efficient killers. Things weren't bad enough in '44 and '45—

now with an M-79 (a grenade launcher—we call it the thumper) and an M-16 (looks like a toy) I have the same firepower as 150 men in World War II. Outa sight, huh?

The M-16 takes a bullet that is .001 larger than a .22. If that little bitch hits you in the wrist from a quarter-mile away, she'll rip your arm off at the shoulder. It takes a magazine of twenty rounds. On full automatic, it can fire all twenty shots before the first empty casing hits the ground. If one round can do all that damage, just picture what one marine can do with a rifle on automatic.

Also, God help the VC that gets into hand-to-hand combat with any one of us. I've learned a dozen ways to kill with my bare hands. It's a fine world, isn't it? Do I sound bitter? Hell no! I enjoy blowing another man's head off! Oh, I'm gonna fight like hell to stay alive, but, dammit, that can't be what we're meant to do on earth. I still believe that mankind can be more constructive than this.

Take Care,

Greg

★ ★ ★

I wondered if my occasional letters did any good. I hardly knew him—maybe not enough to be of any help at all. I told Delia about his last letter, and tried to get her to write to him, too.

"Sugar, it's all over with us—life goes on, you know? Look, I think it's peachy that you two are writin' to each other. I always knew he was sweet on you."

I began to feel responsible for Greg. It was a burden I wasn't sure I was ready to bear, and yet I liked it. I wanted him to confide in me. Nobody I knew at Devon seemed at all concerned about this faraway war that was snatching young men to fight for some obscured cause. Little by little I felt closer to Greg. In my next letter I asked him how he thought he'd feel if he had to kill a woman, or a boy. Maybe a boy just like him, confused about what he was doing, but compelled by some sense of duty or patriotism. How could he reconcile this in his mind?

★ ★ ★

Dear Betsy,

Your question is one that we all ask ourselves here, but not for long. My answer is that I know that I can do it. I've lost two buddies in Nam so far. I've got a score to settle. I don't really feature getting my tail blown away, but neither did they.

I think I have a pretty fair idea of your general attitude on the war. But let me give you a suggestion—don't get too theoretical or idealistic in your viewpoint, because when that happens you can't be objective.

All the guys who are finishing their training got orders for Nam—which likely means a big push on the NVA anytime now. A lot of gooks are going to wish to hell they'd never been born.

As Always,

Greg

★ ★ ★

Gooks? The evening news, which I managed to watch by dropping in at a faculty member's house at the appropriate time, was becoming an eerie reality; the day after I got Greg's letter, the battle of Khe Sanh began. It would come to be known as one of the worst slaughters of the war, and one of the longest. Although I'd been watching the events of the war on the news for months, it had never seemed as real to me as this. Khe Sanh was more than just news on television—it was something I'd been warned about, and I watched in horror as the warning unfolded into a grisly reality.

February was usually a grim month. Devon was so far north that the snow came early and stayed late. What had once been white crystalline snow was a slushy mixture of mud and ice that stubbornly refused to melt. There was nothing to do but wait for it to end. That first week I received an elated message from Greg.

★ ★ ★

Dear Betsy,

I'm a Marine! I finished Boot Camp at 11:00 yesterday, had a day base liberty, and right now I'm on my way back to Camp Lejeune, North Carolina, where I take my Infantry training. Right now they're placing me in Intelligence —I think it's a pretty good Specialty. I'm going to be here until March 3rd, then I go out to San Diego for my Specialty school. I'll be in Vietnam by May. Maybe it hasn't hit me, or maybe I'm just pushing it out of my mind, but I'm not worried about it . . . yet! The worst part is that I'll be there for a whole year.

I'll write more later—

Greg

★   ★   ★

Inside the letter was a photo of Greg in uniform, scrupulously neat, his thick blond hair cropped short and his smile radiant. On the back of the picture he had written: "If supporting Vietnam is right, and opposing it is wrong, I'm somewhere in between. I'm not for or against, I'm just learning. Think of me that way always."

During those grim winter weeks I'd been spending my indoor afternoons curled up with a notebook, sifting through my troubled thoughts and putting them into poetry. In response to Greg's letter, I wrote him:

> *Once upon a time a deer fell,*
> *a child grew up,*
> *a man went to war . . .*
> *and all became puddles on the earth.*

Spring slowly warmed the desert, and the cacti that were covered with menacing thorns blossomed with delicate flowers. I became absorbed in our exchange of letters, and with the week-to-week events of the war. I read and reread books like *The Red Badge of Courage* and *Lord of the Flies,* anything having to do with man's relationship to hostility and war. Greg's letters were coming less often. He said he had little time to write. In one letter he told me:

I happen to know that forty hours after the USS *Pueblo* was stolen, two BLT's (about 1200 infantrymen) were on their way. I also know that the task force that went over there was nuclear-powered. This sort of thing scares me because it means that guys who are at Devon now will be fighting one way or another—if not in Nam, then in Korea or some other two-bit country.

And then, in late April:

★　★　★

Dear Betsy,

My departure date will come between May 5th and May 10th. We fly out from El Toro Marine Air Station to Hawaii, have a stopover, then fly to Okinawa. We spend a couple of days there and draw jungle boots, jungle combat clothes, rifle, bayonet, packs, cartridge belts, etc. Then on to Da Nang. That's probably where I'll be stationed, 'cause I've been assigned to the 1st Marine Air Wing. I don't much feature the idea of spending a year in the combat zone. There is one way of coming home early, but when I hit the States I plan on walking off that plane.

Signed by destruction machine
#2,498,683

★　★　★

After the assassinations of Martin Luther King and Robert Kennedy, I was tormented by thoughts that we were a country gone crazy. During the summer, while I was home in Sacramento, watching TV coverage of the war became my evening ritual. My parents studied my morose fascination with the news much the same way they studied me when I used to fall off my chair—just another phase I was going through.

My father was a tall man with steel gray hair and eyes that seemed to mirror whatever shade of blue the sky was on any given day. I used to touch the corners of his eyes where the skin had gone crinkly from years of laughter, and ask how I could get my eyes to do that.

There was a hill in back of our house in Woodland Hills where we used to walk on Sunday afternoons. It was "our hill"—the best kite-flying hill in the whole city, I thought. My father taught me about the wind; how to make the kite spin and dive on the different currents. One time I stood on my tiptoes, stretched my arms as high as they would go and asked him how high I would have to reach to touch God. My father knelt down so that he was my height; his eyes were like little pieces of the sky. He said, "You don't need to reach up at all, Beth. God is everywhere."

I held onto his hand, wondering if my fingers would ever get that long, and told him that when I grew up I was going to be a sailor. I'd live in a lighthouse and work the foghorn, and once a year I would get on a ship and sail around the world. He played with my ear and told me I'd probably get bored after a while just working a foghorn, and that it was dangerous, dirty work to sail around the world, not to mention the low pay. He managed to convince me that I'd be better off setting my sights elsewhere.

I took his advice, and decided instead to train myself for a career as a veterinarian. I opened a bird hospital, with space available for butterflies should any be in need of medical attention. Brian was four, old enough, I decided, to be appointed veterinarian-in-training. Our house had several massive plate-glass windows which frequently caused birds in flight to meet with disaster. Brian would come around the corner with a limp bird in his hand and holler, "I found another one!" Then, armed with Popsicle sticks and masking tape, we'd bind up whatever we decided was broken—and we'd add another bird to the ward, a row of old shoe boxes lined with Kleenex. Brian was an eager assistant. I came out one day to find him trying to get a thermometer in a bird's beak; he thought it looked feverish. The gardener, on the other hand, was no help at all, muttering in Japanese about how he couldn't water with all those boxes in the way, and filling up the holes I'd dug for worms—bird nutrition was another aspect of our medical program. The appropriate diet for butterflies presented a different challenge, although trial and error taught me they didn't respond well to grapes or Cheerios.

One day I found a butterfly that I diagnosed as having fainted. I put it in a jar and went to search my parents' medicine cabinet for something to revive it. I had every confidence that I would find some treatment for fainting since their medicine cabinet took up half a wall and contained remedies for everything: common ailments such as coughs, constipation, and headaches; childhood diseases that had already come and gone but the medicines were still there just in case ; and remedies for other diseases that one would probably have to travel to Africa to contract. I remember hearing my mother on the phone when I had the flu, asking the doctor which medicine she should give me, taking at least fifteen minutes to list the ones she already had. But usually a new one would arrive and space would be made for it, too.

Finally I found an ammonia inhaler. The label said to break it open under the patient's nose to revive him. I didn't know where a butterfly's nose was or if it even had a nose, but I figured if I just put the broken inhaler in the jar the fumes would eventually reach its nose, wherever it was. About half an hour later I heard Brian screaming for me to come quick. I got there and found that my orange butterfly had turned cobalt blue. We gave it a solemn burial, along with its many predecessors, under the jacaranda tree.

An end to my veterinary career came shortly after that, when our gardener refused to enter the yard until it had been vacated of the animal ward that was becoming an animal morgue and not smelling at all the way a nice suburban backyard should smell. Soon after, my father gently suggested to me that there might be some other career I'd like to pursue when I grow up—a librarian, perhaps.

Now my mother watched as I spent hours in front of the TV news and one evening she finally asked, ''Contemplating a career in broadcasting, dear ?''

Just before school started, Delia called and told me she wasn't going back to Devon. She was vague about the reason ; something to do with her parents having found a better school for her. I wondered if the transfer could have had anything to do with what happened the year before, but it looked as though I wasn't going to find out on the phone. She promised she would keep in touch. My new roommates, Chris and Marin, spent most of their time giggling—about what, I never did figure out.

★ ★ ★

Dear Betsy,

In basic they taught us all about survival in the jungle and how to use M-16's, but nobody told me what a beautiful country Vietnam is. There are greens here you never saw in your box of Crayolas. I have a new friend over here named Trenton. He tells me I'm too serious and every time

he catches me waxing philosophical he comes up with some
joke to get my mind off everything. His girlfriend sent
him a letter with song lyrics by Phil Ochs, and he told me
they were too ''deep'' for him but I might like them. The
song goes like this:

Soldiers disillusioned come home from the war
Sarcastic students tell them not to fight no more
And they argue through the night,
Black is black and white is white
Walk away knowing they are right
Still nobody's buying flowers from the flower lady

Keep the faith,

Greg

★　★　★

When I knew Greg at Devon, I sensed that he was a time bomb.
After a football game in which Devon was narrowly defeated,
Greg jumped on one of his own teammates, accusing him of losing the game. Both of them sat out the next few games: Greg as
punishment, and his teammate as the victim of a broken nose.
The anger I saw in his letters frightened me, and I wrote him
about it. He wrote back:

★　★　★

You're right. If I was angry enough I'd take on the world.
I just can't see sacrificing an ideal for fear. Fear is all
relative, and although it is ever-present, it can be controlled. The only thing I really fear from day to day is
being captured. That'll never happen to me, though, cuz
I'll never give up. They'll either kill me or get tired of
chasing me. Stark as that may sound, that's the way it is
for me. I'd rather be a KIA than a POW.

★　★　★

The news had become a nightly chronicle of horror; men carrying bodies, or whatever was left of bodies, men who were visible

one minute, gone the next. I tried to imagine how I'd feel if I saw Greg in one of those gruesome reports. Sometimes I thought I did see him. My heart would stop until I was sure it wasn't him. But the faces, like his, were all so young. A year before, I'd had little idea of where or what Vietnam was. Now I was hearing about areas of that jungle country with strange-sounding names: Khe Sanh, Da Nang, Hue. With the news coverage and letters from Greg, Vietnam seemed not very far away at all.

★ ★ ★

Dear Betsy,

Scuttlebutt has it that we may move to Quang Tri or Dong Ha in the not-too-distant future. I'm now in Phu Bai, about 15 miles southwest of Hue. It's a dusty old place, about 110 degrees between eleven and three in the afternoon. The past three nights the VC have hit our perimeters, and boy were we sweating it out. But I'm still here.

As Always,

Greg

★ ★ ★

November brought crisp winds that snatched leaves from the trees and sent them scurrying across the ground in orange whirlpools. When I first went to Devon I thought it strange to see autumn in the desert, but in time I looked forward to the smell of leaves and fall's palette of colors. Sometimes if I stood still I could almost smell the approach of winter on the edge of autumn's wind. That month I spent hours riding my horse through shiny afternoons, loving the feel of the wind. One day on the way back from the corrals I stopped at my mailbox and found a letter from my mother, a postcard from Brian showing a cat standing backward on top of a donkey, and a letter from Greg.

★ ★ ★

Dear Betsy,

My mother passed away. They're giving me two weeks' emergency leave. After the funeral, I'll be spending time with my father and family. But I'm going to come to Devon for a few days, probably around the 18th. I look forward to seeing you. Don't worry about me—my mother was sick a long time. In some ways, this is best.

Since I've managed to write to you all this time without mentioning Delia, I should probably say something about it now, since I'll most likely be seeing her when I'm there. The jive is I just don't expect Delia to scope out the changes in me since we last saw each other. I suppose I should have written to her from the beginning, but I just didn't know what to talk about. We never did that much talking. In those days my main concern with any woman was getting her into the nearest bedroom. Hey, I'm not knocking sex—four days and nights with a beautiful Chinese woman when I was on R&R made lovemaking that much more enticing to me. But getting to know a couple of nurses over here who are without a doubt some of the finest women I've ever met has taught me that there can be more to a relationship with a woman than getting it on. And I consider you to be a woman.

Being here changes a guy in more ways than one.

Until then,

Greg

★　★　★

I closed my eyes and tried to picture Greg's face, to remember the sound of his voice. Because the familiarity we now shared never existed when he was at school, I had to search my memory for visual images of him. I spent a lot of time staring at his picture.

I couldn't tell what Greg expected to happen when he saw Delia, but I had a feeling that when he learned she had left school he might be relieved. I had no intention of telling him about the abortion.

The message I got from his letter was so mixed it made me dizzy. On the one hand he was saying he wanted his relationships with women to be "productive," but the comment about the Chinese woman made me nervous. What exactly did he expect of me? But, more important, what did I expect? I was torn between feeling flattered that he considered me not a girl but a woman, and knowing that *woman* was a word I would never have used to describe myself. Even though Delia turned out to be bluffing about her sexual expertise, I was embarrassed about my virginity. I was terrified of the possibility that he, in his not so oblique way, was leading up to having sex with a woman who happened to be named Beth—but at the same time the idea filled me with excitement.

The truth is that I was less threatened by the idea of having sex for the first time than the fear that my utter lack of experience would embarrass me. Would he stop in the middle and laugh at me for being so inept? It would have been bad enough if I'd simply never had intercourse with a boy—or, should I say, man, since Greg considered me a woman—but I'd never even been touched, at least nowhere that mattered. When I was twelve my mother told me that there are three places a boy may put his hand: in your hand, around your shoulders, and around your waist. Once, in the tenth grade, I was dancing with a boy who had his arm around my waist. It kept creeping downward and I kept pushing it back where it belonged. That was the extent of my steamy history.

When I was nine my mother gave me a book that told how salmon do it, how four-legged animals do it, and finally how primates do it. What I had yet to figure out was exactly what a man *did* inside you. Did he move, did he just stay there, how long did he stay there? On a few sleepless nights my curiosity led me to explore the crevices of my body, but I was still ignorant. What I needed was a step-by-step description from someone who had firsthand experience, but I certainly wasn't about to ask for it.

What made it all so laughable was that I had a reputation at Devon for being an "easy lay." Later I realized that I was to blame for giving a false impression of myself by looking the way I did. In my eagerness to break away from my parents' dictates of fashion I did myself over in a look I considered rebel chic—but which translated to the boys at Devon as hot to trot. Preparing for my debut before I even left home, I stayed up nights huddled under the bedcovers with a flashlight, straightening my skirts while my parents thought I was asleep. Upon arriving at school I broke out the heavy artillery—white lipstick, black pencil for raccoon eyes, and thick layers of mascara. One eye remained hidden at all times by a Veronica Lake sweep of hair. I was hobbling around in skirts that fitted like masking tape and I had a problem with depth perception because of my hairdo, but I thought I looked terrific. One day I walked past some boys in the rec room and heard them whispering about what a slut I was.

I remained calm until I got back to the dorm, and then went crying to Delia.

"Well, honey, what do you expect? Look at the way you're dolled up. You look willing so they say you're willing and then make up stories to back it up. You know how fellas lie to each other."

Actually I didn't know how fellas did anything. "Well, what do I do about it?" I pleaded through my tears.

"To start with, sugar, put a washcloth to that sweet face and start wearing some clothes you can breathe in." Now that she mentioned it, my sweaters were a little tight. The hooks of my bra were clearly visible.

I launched a campaign to change my image and salvage my tainted reputation. It was eventually successful, but I suspected that most people thought I'd simply pulled myself out of the depth of promiscuity and renounced my lustful ways. Greg may have been one of them, and that was what worried me. If he had sexual thoughts about me now he probably assumed I would know what to do about it. I was curious and excited and thoroughly terrified.

"Hey, Beth, what're you doin'? I got a letter from Greg today, first one in a long time. Said he got an emergency leave 'cause of his mom dying."

I squinted into the afternoon sun to see where the voice had come from. Doug Purcell had been Greg's buddy when he was at Devon. He was tall, with freckles that looked like splattered paint, and as I looked at him standing against the sun, his hair reminded me of a copper teakettle. He was the star of Devon's mediocre football team, which gave us little grounds for communication, but Greg had written him sporadically, and we'd talked about that.

"I know, I was just reading his letter. I guess he'll be here in about a week. Mail takes a long time from over there, doesn' it?"

"Uh-huh. Well, he'll probably be one wild son of a bitch once he gets a few miles away from the war. You better watch out. He's most likely pretty horny by now." He winked at me and walked away. I could tell by the movement of his shoulders that he was laughing.

* 6 *

EVERY SUNDAY MY PARENTS ATTENDED THE ELEVEN o'clock services at Brentwood Presbyterian Church, then returned home for an early dinner. Sometimes friends were invited, or relatives, or some of my father's political associates and their families. Sunday dinner was always my favorite meal of the week. Sunlight poured through the French doors in the dining room and sparkled on the silver borders of the special china my mother used to set the table. The plates gleamed like the insides of seashells, and there was a single red rose painted in the center of each one. The enormous serving platter had a bouquet of roses, and the smaller pieces, like the creamer and the sugar bowl, had little rosebuds. Everyone seemed to smile and laugh more than usual, and when the subject of politics happened to come up, one of the wives would say, "No shop talk on the Sabbath," or, "Enough of that; Betty wants to tell us about the wild party she went to in Washington last week," a suggestion that would invariably turn my mother's smile into a disapproving frown.

No one paid much attention to Brian and me, enabling us to be very creative with the food on our plates—hiding vegetables under potatoes, arranging meat in wide patterns that gave the illusion we'd eaten more than we had. The meat patterns were Brian's downfall. Since he'd only reduced the quantity by one

43

bite, it was hard to make it look as though he'd eaten more than that. Somewhere around the time that his second set of teeth made its appearance, he'd developed an intense aversion to meat; he thought it was too hard to chew and was convinced he'd choke on it. My parents tried everything, including telling him that his teeth would fall out if he didn't exercise them vigorously by chewing meat. The ever-skeptical Brian looked at them and said, "Good. Then I'll get false teeth and you'll stop bugging me to eat this stuff. Who cares about eating dead animals anyway?"

At Devon, I made my weekly call home about five o'clock on Sundays, when I knew they'd be finished with dinner and the guests would be gone. They expected my call and were always there to receive it.

"Hi, Mom."

"Elizabeth, how are you, dear?"

"Elizabeth quit school to join the Carmelite nuns, but Beth is fine, thanks."

"Oh, hush. Is it snowing there today?"

"Not yet, but we expect it to. It's freezing outside."

"And how are things in school?"

"Fine. In English we're reading *1984*. It's the one where—"

"Yes, yes, dear, I'm familiar with it. Dear, your father and I heard that you have a friend serving in Vietnam."

"You know, Mom, I've never been able to figure out exactly how parents 'hear' things. Is it clairvoyance—or is there an FBI agent in my laundry hamper?"

"Elizabeth, what an absurd thing to say."

"I'm serious, Mom. I've been wanting to ask you about this ever since the first grade. Remember the day I came home from school and you told me you 'heard' I lost my hair ribbons? How about the time you 'heard' I pushed Charlotte Olsen into the water fountain?"

"Elizabeth, you have the memory of an elephant. But I'm not giving away any of my secrets. Someday you'll be a mother and all these mysteries will come clear to you."

"Thanks. In the meantime I think I'll search my room for bugs."

"Honestly, I've always said you and your brother watch way too much television. What is that silly show . . . the 'Missing Impossibles'?"

"Right, Mom. Is Dad there?"

"He's just inside, I'll put him on."

"Hi, Dad."

"How's everything?"

"Just fine, Dad. Did you have any company today?"

"Jeb Henley and his wife were here."

"I don't think I've met them."

"He's one of the party men, honey. They're asking me to help campaign for some of the congressmen in the next election."

"They never leave you alone, do they?"

"Thank heaven for that. Now, Beth, your mother and I hear you're corresponding with a boy in Vietnam."

"Yes..."

"Well, when you come home we'll look forward to hearing all about him."

On the way to the corrals, I considered other ways that information could leak out. Maybe my mail was steamed open, read, and then resealed. I'd seen that in a movie once. At the moment, though, I had more important things to think about. Greg would be at Devon sometime on Friday, and I'd conjured up several scenarios for his arrival. In one, I pictured myself riding Harmony along the main road that snaked its way through the desert and led travelers to Devon's wooden gate. As a car approached I would recognize Greg and I'd gallop up to the car, faster and faster until finally I rode neck and neck with him, and then... in another scene, I saw myself walking out of class, and Greg would be waiting outside the door, and then... this was as far as I got. When it came to the point of speaking to him, my imagination sputtered and died.

Friday's dawn struggled to be seen through a dark sky bloated with clouds. By noon the rain was relentless. The ground was thick and slippery with mud, and trying to keep dry was an exercise in futility. The rain found its way under umbrellas and through hoods and the sky gave no promise of reprieve.

I tried to occupy myself with reading, straightening my drawers, and occasional halfhearted attempts at homework. I wandered into the other rooms, plopped down on a bed and shared in whatever conversation was going on, but I was prepared at any moment to hear myself paged, either for a phone call or for a visitor. It occurred to me that the road might be impassable and that Greg would call and say he wasn't coming. By dinner time he'd neither arrived nor called.

My mother once told me the story of the time she waited and

waited for a man, the man she planned to marry. She was a senior in college when they became engaged, and she waited one night in the Chicago station for the train he promised he would be on. Outside it was below zero; the snow was thick on the ground and still falling. As warm as it was inside the waiting room she was too anxious to sit in there, and stood shivering on the platform waiting to see the lights of the train in the distance through the snowy night. Finally a voice over the loudspeaker announced that anyone waiting for the train from Boston should report inside. There she was told that the train had been derailed just outside Chicago, and the injured passengers had been taken to a nearby hospital. When she got to the hospital she learned that her fiancé was not among the survivors. She was devastated. She told me she thought she would never love another man, but later, when she met my father, she knew right away that they would always be together. She said he probably didn't think of it that way—and she certainly would never let on. You have to be smart with these things, Elizabeth, she told me. Don't show your whole hand.

They were sitting in a posh restaurant when my father, by candlelight, proposed to her. She told me that despite the elegant surroundings she was a little disappointed because, since childhood, her fantasy was that her husband-to-be would propose to her in a canoe out on a lake, strumming a ukulele while down on one knee. I can imagine my father's dismay when she told him this; in a restaurant he might have dug up a ukulele somehow, but the canoe would be more difficult. When he took her back to her apartment, though, he repeated the proposal on his knee.

I made my way through the barnyard in the dark through sheets of rain. The lights that usually illuminated the ground had exploded from the impact of the downpour, and rivulets of churning water crisscrossed the ground. Despite a lot of concentration and a hopscotch technique, I reached the door of the dining room with my boots and jeans splattered with mud. I was through the door before I saw him. He was sitting at a table surrounded by kids, and from the animation of his gestures and the reactions of the audience I could see he was regaling them with war stories.

I felt like a drowned rat and knew I looked worse, and considered sneaking out—but it was too late. He came toward me and grabbed my shoulders and hugged me almost too tightly. I was aware of the hardness of his muscles and the smell of Old Spice around his face and neck.

"I wasn't sure you were coming . . . with the storm and everything."

"Yeah, the road's pretty bad, but hey, compared to Nam it's a piece of cake. Hey, Betsy, you look great."

"Oh, you bet." He was still standing close, and I could see flecks of brown in his blue eyes. His front tooth had a small chip; I wondered if it had always been like that.

I was relieved of my awkwardness at our first meeting by a faculty member who was kind enough to point out that dinner had started. We sat at the same table where Greg had left an enraptured group waiting for more tales. As he took a seat he opened with, "You know, I saw your movie *The Green Berets* last night. It was good for a few laughs." I wondered if that explained his new John Wayne—style swagger, or if everyone in Vietnam walked like that.

"For instance, take the scene where the helicopter crashes. I fly in that kind of bird, and what happened in that flick is impossible. You remember when the bird took a few hits and a fire started in the nose?" Some of the kids shook their heads vigorously, while one or two retained a certain skeptical detachment.

"Well, a Huey will never catch fire anywhere but just to the rear of the door, and when it does, the crew has six to seven seconds to get the bird down before it explodes. I've had too much experience with crippled birds to believe that crash at all. A Huey will drop straight down and impact in a horizontal position, bounce about ten feet in the air, and hit upside down. Falling from the altitude it did in the flick, everybody would have died."

The skeptics may have wanted to speak up, but they didn't. I didn't blame them. Greg spoke with such authority I wouldn't have wanted to be the one to contradict him. I did wonder what he would do, though, if John Wayne suddenly appeared in the dining hall, walked slowly toward him in his commanding way, put his hand on Greg's shoulder and said, "How's that, son? You mean you'd like to tell me how it's *really* done?"

Most of the boys at the table were so captivated they couldn't eat and listen at the same time. I wondered how many of them would end up in the war. The meal seemed unusually long, and when we passed our plates to the end of the table, some of them still full of food, I realized there was an entire evening ahead with nothing planned. On some Friday nights they ran a movie, but not on this one. I felt as though Greg was my date and I was under pressure to find some entertainment for him. Fortunately Doug Purcell came up and said, "We were just going to shoot some pool for a while—wanna come?"

The rec room across from the dining hall had two pool tables, a soda machine, and four couches. The couches were frequently moved around to conceal whatever couple was occupying them from whoever might walk through the door. During several games of pool Greg continued to relate stories and field questions about what was going on in Nam. "Beautiful country, man—green, lush—too bad I gotta see it this way."

Greg challenged me to a game of pool, and when it was over told me I was better than he expected, probably because he didn't beat me as badly as he'd beaten everyone else. I told him I was tired and was going back to my room.

"I'd better walk with you," he said, laying his pool cue across the table. "You never can tell, there might be some wild coyotes out there tonight."

The other boys in the room started hooting, and Greg was smiling as he walked out. Doug hollered, "My man, don't do anything I wouldn't do!"

The rain had stopped and the moon danced in puddles as we walked to my dorm. In the quiet moments that fell over us I stared at my feet as I navigated around the mud. Then suddenly we both spoke at the same moment.

"Go ahead," he said. "I did enough talking for one night."

"I was just going to say that. I mean, that you did a lot of talking tonight. Not that I mind or anything. I was just going to point that out."

"Well, you know how it is. No, wait a minute—I guess you don't. My first civilian audience, that's all. I guess I got a little carried away."

"I never thought of myself as a civilian before. You really do feel like you're different from everyone here, don't you?"

"I am different."

"You are in a way, but that's only until your time as a marine is up. When you come back you'll be one of us again. A civilian."

"Maybe," he said. We stood at the front steps of my dorm. Raindrops fell from the eaves onto the tops of our heads.

"I guess I'll be turning in, too. I've been driving all day. See you tomorrow, okay?" He was looking right into my eyes, and his hand was on the small of my back—one of Harriet Canfield's off-limit zones.

"Okay . . . good night." I opened the door quickly and went inside. I was so tired of thinking, of the nervousness in my stomach, of wondering what would happen, that I was asleep in minutes.

The next morning was sunny and clear. The only reminders of the storm were puddles, the smell of wet earth, and the way everything looked as though it had been scrubbed clean. Greg wasn't at breakfast. I decided to occupy myself at the horse corrals. I shoveled manure and mud out of the stalls, bathed Harmony, trimmed his mane, and scrubbed out his water trough. At some point I heard the lunch bell ring, but nothing was mandatory on Saturday.

I was bent over cleaning my horse's hooves when I saw a pair of boots on the other side of his belly.

"I thought I'd find you here," said Greg. "I came to see if you wanted to go riding with me. I got permission to use one of the school horses."

"Sure, that sounds great. Why don't you go get saddled and meet me back here?"

The afternoon was clear and windy, and time was forgotten as we found new paths across the desert. We laughed about Greg's obvious inexperience with horses, and I tried to show him how to hold the reins, but my instructions were smothered in laughter. We followed the creek bed to a spot where trees arched across, blocking the sun and leaving it damp and cool underneath. We got off the horses and let them wade in the water.

"Greg, I'm awfully sorry about your mother. What was wrong?"

"Cancer," he said. He reached over and put his arm around my shoulder, looking straight into my eyes. "Don't be sad, Betsy. She's been sick ever since I can remember. We all knew it was only a matter of time. It was hard knowin' all along that she was gonna go, but thinking back on it, I'm glad I knew. If I hadn't I might've been your typical jerk teenager and treated her lousy. We didn't have a lot of years, but they were good ones."

For a moment, we were silent.

"I guess you probably know that Delia isn't here anymore."

"Yeah, Doug told me last night. Hey, Betsy, look." He pointed
to the creek, where our horses were nuzzling each other. "Looks
like they've got the hots for each other. What's the matter,
Betsy? You're blushing."

For the first time since I'd gotten Greg's letter about coming
back, I was relaxed. I felt that I was with someone I knew, who
knew me just as well. By the time we got back to the school,
evening had claimed half the sky and the sun clung to the horizon. We stopped at the barn where I helped Greg unsaddle his
horse, and rode beside him as he walked uphill to where the
school horses were kept. Then we went down the other side of the
hill to the private corrals. When he tried to help me with my
horse, we ended up laughing all over again. "One day I guess
I'll have to get myself some riding instruction," he said.

"When you come back to the States, my services are available." I was afraid I'd said the wrong thing, but he nodded and
smiled.

When we were finished, all that was left of the sun was a ribbon
of orange smoke between the sky and the desert. We sat on the
railing of the corral listening to the sounds of night as it settled
on the desert, watching a three-quarter moon grow whiter as the
sky grew darker. My horse rested his head on my shoulder.

"You know, in Nam the nights are so dark sometimes I swear
the moon is farther away from that country than anyplace else
on earth. And the stars always look dim. They never twinkle."

We sat there for a while longer before he took my hand and
said, "Let's walk up there."

He was pointing to the hay barn. Perched on top of the hill,
the barn was open on two sides with bales of hay stacked under a
sheet metal roof. I'd heard of couples going up there, so I knew
exactly what going to the hay barn meant. The moment I felt
would come eventually came so suddenly that I didn't have a
chance to be afraid. We walked up the hill and scrambled up the
bales of hay to the highest one. Greg lay down, smiling up at me.
I could see the moonlight making patterns out of the shadows,
and I was about to say how beautiful it looked, but I didn't want
to disturb the lovely silence.

His arms reached out for me, and when I knelt down beside
him, he took my shoulders in his hands and pulled me gently
down. His mouth felt warm and protective as it traveled across
my face and down to my shoulders. He moved my body across

his and to the other side of him, and as he opened my blouse, he followed the movements of his fingers with kisses. I felt the wind across my breasts, and then the heat of his chest against mine. I began to drift as in a dream, and it became harder and harder to think, to form words. . . .

"Greg?"

"Please, don't tell me to stop."

"I don't want you to stop. I just want to tell you that I've never made love before."

He looked into my eyes. "You're kidding."

"Of course not. You're not . . . well, disappointed or anything, are you?"

"Disappointed? Hell no, girl. What gave you that idea?" He lay next to me on his side, his hand gently cupped on my breast, as if he were holding it for safekeeping.

"I just want to be good for you, that's all, But I don't really know—you know."

"Oh, Betsy, you are good for me. You're the sweetest girl I've ever known." He leaned over and kissed my chin. I laughed.

"What's so funny?"

"There was a time when the last thing you'd have called me was 'sweet.'"

"Maybe, maybe not. But anyway, that was a long time ago."

He moved his body onto mine, kissed my cheek, and whispered in my ear, "Just think of this as a first time for both of us."

"What do you mean?"

"I've never made love to a virgin before."

I saw the reflection of moonlight in his eyes. "You know, you'd think I'd feel cold in this place," I told him, "but I feel warm all over." He hugged me tightly, and with all the strength I could discover in my arms and legs, I hugged him back.

Afterward I felt somehow glad that it had been Greg and no one else. I trusted him, and wondered if it would be possible ever to feel this safe with anyone else. I looked at his face and his body where shadows and moonlight seemed to be competing for attention. I wanted to remember every detail. As I lay there in his arms I thought about not being the same as I was before; I'd seen a man's body for the first time and touched him, and had him inside me. I was changed forever. The feeling was elusive, a little frightening, and wonderful.

During my week of worrying about lovemaking I had wondered if my years of horseback riding, as I'd heard the girls say, had broken my hymen. Judging from the sliver of pain I felt when Greg was inside me and the blood on the hay, I decided my horse was innocent of all charges. We pulled out the red-stained pieces of hay and scattered them to the night winds.

On the walk back to the barnyard, I was grateful that I felt no obligation to talk. I sensed our bodies fall into rhythm as we moved together, and noticed that Greg was no longer walking like John Wayne. We said good night with a quick kiss and a long look. I went into my room and was happy to find it empty. I went to bed without showering, sinking deep into the covers, loving the darkness and the new smells that came from my body. I imagined Greg sleeping alongside me, and I pushed myself against the wall to make room for him—just for practice. I wondered what it would feel like to roll away from making love and fall asleep together, our legs entwined.

I used to go into my parents' bedroom when the maid was making up their bed. After the sheets were pulled back and the pillows were in a pile in the center, I'd try to figure out which pillow had belonged to my mother and which to my father. My mother's smelled of Jungle Gardenia, and my father's was wrinkled—he had a habit of pounding it into the shape of a watermelon and wedging it between his arm and cheek. The creases in the pillowcase left creases on one side of his face; sometimes I could still see them hours later. I fell asleep picturing Greg in his bed, embracing his pillow, slipping into dreams.

⋆ 7 ⋆

WHEN DAWN WAS STILL A FAINT LIGHT EDGING ITS way across the sky, I woke up. There was a sore place inside me where Greg had been, and as I stretched and yawned I smiled with my memories of the night before. I rolled over toward the window, nestled my chin into my pillow, and watched as the sun pushed its way above the horizon. When I finally got out of bed, I walked over to the mirror and stood before it, trying to detect any subtle changes in my body. I went closer to the mirror, studying my figure from each side, then from the back.

"I bid two hundred," said Marin.

I jumped. She was leaning on her elbow, smirking.

"Sorry, queenie, didn't mean to startle you."

"What are you doing?" I whispered, grabbing my bathrobe from the closet door.

"What am I doing? That's a funny question coming from somebody parading in front of—"

"Shhh," I told her, tying my robe with great modesty. "You'll wake Chris."

"Chris is already awake, thanks" came the voice from the upper bunk. "Could you two continue this discussion in the closet?"

Marin laughed, rustled around in her covers, and nuzzled back into her cocoon. I turned back to my new self in the mirror, this

time scrutinizing my face. My skin looked pasty, my eyes pleaded
for one more hour of sleep, and my hair darted off the left side
of my head in an absurd cowlick: Take me to your leader. I
wondered how couples could possibly stand to look at each other
in the morning. In the movies, women woke up looking as though
on the way back from the bathroom they had made a fast detour
through Elizabeth Arden's. I'd always found it hard to pay attention to the dialogue because I was too busy wondering why, if
her lipstick was fresh and bright, it wasn't also smeared all over
the pillowcase. Mascara raised another question. After a couple
of torrid hours in bed, did these women slip off to the bathroom
in the dark to remove their eye makeup? If not, why didn't they
wake up the next morning with black circles under their eyes?
These were problems I'd have to solve before I could think about
getting married. I could always creep out of bed in the morning
before my husband awakened, wash my face, put on some
makeup, creep back into bed and pretend to be fast asleep—but
there had to be a better way.

The wake-up bell on Sundays rang at eight-thirty, a reprieve
from the usual six-thirty clamor that jolted everyone from sleep
during the week. When the bell sounded, I was already stepping
out of the shower with freshly washed hair. I proceeded to blow-
dry my lanky brown locks into some form of style. When I was
satisfied, trying to ignore the fact that my thin hair held a style
for only thirty minutes, I went back to the room and asked Marin
if I could borrow one of her sweaters.

"Beth, is this some holiday I don't know about?"

"What do you mean?"

"Hey, come on. You usually spend Sundays at the corrals,
which you're not going to do in one of my sweaters. And by the
way, I've never seen you blow-dry your hair for your horse before."

"I promise not to go there with your sweater. I just want to
wear it to breakfast. I'll let you borrow my suede vest..."

"Throw in the matching skirt and you've got a deal."

I sat in the dining room in Marin's pink angora sweater, picking at my food and trying not to stare at the doors where I
expected Greg to appear at any moment. Two cups of cold coffee
sat in front of me, and I went over to the buffet line for a third.
You had to be at least a junior to drink coffee; I never liked the
taste but it seemed a shame not to take full advantage of my

seniority. When I got back to my table and sat down I sneaked another look at the doors, and there was Greg, standing with his entourage. He caught my eye and waved his arm in the air. It felt as though half the dining room turned to see whom he was waving to, and I avoided their looks by concentrating very hard on stirring cream and sugar into the coffee I was too nervous to drink.

My mother once recounted her first date with my father, when she'd had the poor judgment to order soup, only to find that her hands were shaking so badly she couldn't hold the spoon steady. "Never order soup on a first date," she told me, and I wondered if this was the warning all mothers gave their daughters about first dates with men. I picked up the coffee cup to test the steadiness of my hand and, seeing the coffee come dangerously close to the rim, decided it was too risky.

When I glanced up a few seconds later he was making his way across the room, in my direction. I imagined that the entire room fell quiet and two hundred pairs of eyes were on the two of us. My hands quivered, and my stomach mocked me with rumbles and flutters. I was positive that everyone in the room knew what had happened the night before, in detail. When he finally got to my table, he knelt down on one knee next to my chair—all the other seats were taken. Then he took my hand from the table, and brought it to his lips.

He said something to me after the kiss, but I couldn't hear his words because the room had filled with applause and cheers. I was beyond blushing; disintegrating might be a better word. My embarrassment paralyzed me so that it took a few moments to realize that this was the happiest I could remember ever feeling. Suddenly my entire body felt warm inside, the way it had in the hay barn.

"What did ..." I cleared my throat. "What did you say?"

The fellow next to me had gotten up and given Greg his seat.

"I said 'Good morning, beautiful.'"

"Good morning to *you*."

"How ya doing? Did you sleep okay?"

I nodded. "How about you?"

He shook his head, smiling. "It's amazing how well you can sleep when you're not worried about getting shot at." He picked up my coffee cup and took a sip. "What would you like to do today?"

His assumption that we would spend the day together took me by surprise, but I liked it. I liked the fact that he asked me how I had slept; a question I'd been asked a thousand times in my life, yet coming from Greg at this moment it seemed terribly forward, and fraught with suggestion.

"We could go riding," he said, "but you might not feel like getting on a horse."

I felt myself flush, but I laughed as if men said things like that to me all the time. "No, I guess I don't." He was laughing, too, and for that moment there was nothing else in the world. I loved his smile, I loved mornings, I loved that tan dining hall that smelled exactly like every dining hall in every school everywhere. I loved the fact that we'd both washed our hair—even that seemed sexy.

"Doug wants to throw the football around for a while this afternoon. Why don't you come, too?"

"Yeah, okay. Maybe I will." A tidal wave in the desert couldn't have stopped me.

"Hey, Betsy," he said, before returning to his pals, "you look real pretty today. Nice sweater."

I returned to the room and carefully replaced Marin's prized possession before going to the corrals. I let Harmony loose in the ring so he could roll in the dirt and run around. Watching him buck and run, I called out, certain he understood me, "I wish I could give you the whole desert!"

When I walked down to the football field, the grass was slashed with afternoon sun. I sat in the bleachers and enjoyed Greg and Doug's carefree duet, running free across the quiet, empty field and sending the ball spinning in long arcs between them. When Greg waved at me, I noticed how the sunlight seemed to lick the muscles of his arm. His skin was shiny with sweat, and I remembered how his body felt against mine. I sank into the warm bath of my thoughts, watching Greg and Doug run between sun and shade, as clouds drifted across the sky in stuffed animal shapes. When they finished they came over, and Greg, panting, said, "Boy, that felt great. It's been a long time." The three of us sprawled out on the grass, content to let time pass with only occasional attempts at conversation. When the sky began to look like evening, we walked back to the barnyard.

I don't know what your plans are tonight, Greg," said Doug, "but the rest of us poor students have to go to chapel. Some things never change."

"Yeah, well, I planned to go, too," said Greg.

"Who're you kidding? You don't have to go, you're a visitor! No rules for you, soldier."

"Well, I'd like to go."

I tried to figure out what was going on behind his words—he seemed so distant.

The chapel was an A-frame with the wall behind the pulpit made entirely of glass. Greg guided me to a pew which, after the previous night, struck me as being a little close to the front. Against the night sky, the Reverend Thorpe delivered his sermon on "The Sanctity of the Family." He was employed by Devon to conduct the weekly service and to serve as adviser or, if need be, disciplinarian, to any student whose moral fiber was fraying. He was tall and thin, except for a round belly that gave away his weakness for sweets and his habit of drinking whatever wine was left over from the communion services. He had a way of squinting when he talked to you that made you think he was trying to ferret out any signs that the devil had taken up residence in your person.

The reverend covered several aspects of his chosen topic, including the importance of love and fidelity between marriage partners. Desires of the flesh, he stressed, are God's way of encouraging us to procreate, not to sin. Greg pinched my arm, so I kicked him in the foot. The reverend moved on to the obligation of children to be obedient members of the family unit, which reminded me that I'd forgotten to make my weekly call home. On the way out, I told Greg, and asked him to walk over to the phones with me.

"Hi, Dad, it's Beth."

"Beth! We were thinking of calling you. How are you?"

"Terrific. Just a little busy with"—I looked over at Greg, who was grinning—"studying, you know. How are you and Mom?"

"Fine, fine. Hectic, as usual. You know how it is up here."

He was referring to the governor's mansion in Sacramento. I made every effort to schedule my visits home to coincide with their trips to our house in Bel Air, because the mansion gave me the jitters. It was impossible to have any privacy there, and the guards always looked at me as though they were positive I was hiding contraband in my underwear. To reverse the admonition of the day: No one trusted anyone under thirty. On one of my visits up there I accidentally pressed a button hidden behind a curtain, and within seconds sirens were blaring and a fleet of helicopters descended on the roof.

I asked him to put my mother on the extension, and made my apologies to both of them for cutting the call short. I said I had to rush back to continue studying for an exam on Monday morning. Greg was entertained by the whole thing, and a little bemused. As we walked away, he asked, "Are your conversations always that brief?"

"Usually."

"What's it like, anyway," he asked, "having a governor for a father?"

I shrugged. "It's like having anyone for a father, only more so." He laughed. "What's your father do?"

"My old man? Oh, I don't know. Since he left the military, this and that. Owns a couple of stores. Ran for councilman once. Spends a lot of time at the Legion."

"The Legion?"

"Yeah, you know. American Legion. Clubhouse."

"Oh."

He put his arm around me as we walked. Somewhere between noticing how the afternoon sun had tanned him and taking his hand, I realized where we were going.

The hay barn was streaked with moonlight. Without words, we climbed to the same spot. As we took off our clothes, I thought I saw a scarlet stain still on the hay, and smiled. Greg pulled me to him. His body was already becoming familiar to me—the curves of his muscles, the texture of his skin.

"Greg," I said, "I'm still a little sore."

"I'm sorry, Betsy," he said, holding me close. He kissed my cheek. "Then we won't—"

"But I want to," I told him.

"Then we will," he said, smiling. "But it's okay, you'll see. I don't have to be inside you."

He touched me in places that made my whole body shudder, like waves cresting and breaking one after another. My breathing had strange sounds mingled with it—sounds that seemed to come from a place in my body I'd never been aware of before.

Moonlight spilled over us. I knew it was getting late. From somewhere far away, I heard the footsteps before I heard the voice.

"Okay, you kids. I'm going to count to ten before I come the rest of the way. Give you a chance to get decent.'' It was the night watchman. We bolted upright with the shock of cold water on a sweet sleep.

''Jesus, Greg,'' I whispered, ''what are we going to do?''

''Take it easy,'' he said, handing me my blouse. ''Here, put this on. And stay behind, I don't want him to see you.''

Herb Stoller had been Devon's night watchman for sixteen years. He was widowed, well past retirement age, and content to sleep through the days to surface at night, flashlight in hand, ignoring the protest of arthritic joints. ''I love these kids,'' he'd always say. ''They keep me young.'' It was clear that he hated turning anyone in for anything, which was part of the reason he avoided the hay barn. He seemed to make an obligatory check about one night a month.

Greg brushed the straw from his jeans, and stood up. He was buttoning his shirt when the beam of Herb's flashlight pierced the darkness, exploring the side of the barn where Greg climbed slowly down toward the outside. I kept myself hidden, peering over bales of hay to glimpse Herb's face above the flashlight beam. He looked kind and grandfatherly, better suited to rocking children on a porch swing than thwarting the amorous adventures of teenagers. Undoubtedly, the latter was more entertaining. Suddenly the light caught Greg's face and I heard Herb say, ''Now listen, son, I . . . hey, I know you! Greg, right? Greg Howell? You been off in Vietnam, ain't you?'' He sounded as though he were seeing Bogart's ghost.

''Yes, sir. I'm just here at Devon for a visit.''

''Son of a gun! You're here for a nice friendly visit and mean old Stoller catches you in the hay barn with your lady friend. Young soldiers never change, eh, son?''

''No, sir. I guess they don't.'' Greg pulled a piece of straw from his hair, and let it slip to the ground. I felt so sorry for him standing there in that ridiculous beam of light, trying to be a gentleman. And succeeding. He put one hand behind his back and waved to me.

''What branch of the armed forces you in, son?''

''Marines, sir.''

''Tell me, son, what's it like over there in that Vietnam?''

''Well, it's like . . . war, sir.''

''Yes, I reckon it is. Not like the Korean War, though, they're sayin', and not like W.W. II, neither. I was in that war, just a kid, like you. Had a girl back home, too, like you. Thought I'd go crazy till I saw her again. Terrible thing about war, the way it—'' He looked at Greg. ''Yeah, I know how it is.'' Greg cleared his throat.

''Well, son,'' Stoller continued, ''ordinarily I'm supposed to turn kids in, if I find 'em messin' around up here in the barn. That's what they pay me for. Not you, of course, you're well past this now, but as for your lady friend . . . well, my eyes ain't too good these days. For all I know you was up here all alone, just settin' and enjoyin' the way the moon looks from the good old U.S. of A.''

''I sure do appreciate that, sir. Thank you, sir. My girl-friend, well, she appreciates it, too.'' Greg reached out to shake Herb's hand, and the old man obliged. Then old Herb put his fingers to his head and gave Greg a salute. Greg did the same.

''Good luck over there, son. I'd like to give you the same advice my old man gave me, rest his soul in peace.''

''What's that?''

Herb looked into Greg's eyes. ''Make damn sure you come back alive, so you can beat the shit out of the bastards who sent you there in the first place.''

''Yes, sir!'' I saw the flashlight beam move across the ground, and Herb was gone. Greg came back into the darkness, and sat down beside me. He took a piece of straw from the ground and played with it in his fingers. I got up on my knees, and turned to face him.

''What a charmer.''

''Yeah, sweet old guy, isn't he?''

''No, I meant *you*,'' I told him.

''Aw, he was just an old pussy cat.''

''He liked you. You were the son he never had.''

''What makes you so sure he never had a son?''

''Nothing at all, but he was crazy about you, and—''

''Oh, yeah? And what?''

And so am I, I thought.

Greg looked off in the direction that Herb had gone moments before.

''What's on your mind, fella?''

He turned to me. ''Betsy, I'm leaving tomorrow.''

''Is that what's bothering you?''

I thought of how far he was from me, and how close death was to him—a breath away. It left me with a hollow, churning feeling, a mixture of fear and helplessness, and sadness that boys like Greg were dying for someone else's war.

I had arranged for my horse to be taken into Phoenix a week before the holidays, but I wondered if that would be soon enough. Winter was tightening its grip. Somewhere in the wind was the smell of snow. I didn't know at the time that one of the worst snowstorms in history was lumbering toward us, and would leave half the Western states under six-foot drifts.

One night as I went to sleep I had the uneasy feeling that everything was too quiet. In the morning I looked out and the world had turned white. It was a magical world, clean and glistening, an enchanted land that should belong to wizards and unicorns. Unfortunately, it also belonged to my horse who, never having seen snow, was not at all enchanted. Crunching across the ground, my breath leaving white trails in the frozen air, I got to the corrals and found Harmony wild-eyed and frantic. The temperature was well below thirty degrees and the sky seemed to creak with the weight of further snow.

Within a week it became treacherous for vehicles forced to travel the long road from Devon to the highway. There were reports of cattle freezing to death, and Indians on reservations farther north running out of food. One evening in the middle of dinner the electricity went out, and we were without lights and heat. Where before it was a warm, welcoming cluster in the dark desert, Devon now melted into the bleak landscape, white as far as the eye could see. Amazingly, the phone lines still stood, and I called the company that was to transport my horse. When the trailer arrived, I jumped in the cab of the truck to guide the driver to the corrals. The heater was the first warmth I'd felt in a week. Harmony was still frightened by this strange white stuff, and apparently decided that his corral was the last bastion of safety. When I started to lead him out to put him in the trailer, he threw his head up and reared in panic. He finally relented, but only after his hooves had narrowly missed my head several times.

Classes were canceled; the only priority was to keep warm. Food was rationed in an effort to conserve what was left on the premises. None of us were equipped to handle this hardship, but my roommate Chris complained the loudest.

"Can you believe it? The pipes are frozen! How am I going to wash my face—stick it in the snow or something?"

"Don't you know anything about roughing it?" said Marin. "Use cold cream, for Christ's sake."

"Very funny," said Chris. "And how about the toilet? It won't flush!"

I told Chris to fill up a bowl of snow to wash her face, and pee outside if she had to.

"Pee in the *snow*, like an animal?"

"Okay, Scarlett, use the damn toilet. But don't come crying to me when it gets so full it spills out on the floor." That picture must have made an impression, because she finally went outside, cursing all the way.

The school arranged for buses to shuttle us to Phoenix, where we could fly home. The drive, which normally took ninety minutes, took close to three hours. I was scheduled to leave at 4:00 A.M. A little past eleven I crept into bed wearing as many layers of clothing as I could manage, and attempted to get some sleep before boarding the bus. Chris and Marin had left on earlier buses, so I was left with a roomful of frozen air all to myself. A snowdrift peaked outside my window and powder continued to fall, and I lay there thinking that I might fall asleep and awaken hours later entombed in snow. In my mind was a picture postcard of a Western landscape blanketed in snow, a pure shimmering paradise, but inside the pioneers' covered wagons only pneumonia, suffering, and death. Although I knew he was on his way to safety, I had the awful feeling Harmony was freezing, like the cattle on that ranch nearby; a slow, burning paralysis, then permanent sleep. I was weighted down with layers of blankets, but I couldn't get warm; after days of icy air I was chilled from within. I had gloves on, and two pairs of socks, and a muffler. The glowing dial on my watch said one-thirty, and I hadn't slept a moment.

I thought of Greg, in a place so far away from here that it never snowed. The images in his letter ran again and again through my head, the sadness, the pain, the nightmares. Snow, war, Valley Forge. In two centuries, nothing had changed. Words formed themselves in my shivers. I lit a candle and, huddling in blankets, wrote a poem:

> *War, man's dark mistress,*
> *who lingers in the shadows of calm days*

when killing for victory
is like the smoke of distant memory.
But her long finger waits to beckon.
On warm, slow nights
echoes of past heroes and wars of valor
curl around the shoulders of young men
destined for yet another battlefield.

At five minutes to three I began going through the closet in the darkness, looking for something I could wear to the airport. I had no illusions about keeping warm, and days before I'd given up trying to look presentable. At this point, it was just a matter of covering up, hiding beneath layers of wool that had long since lost their dry-cleaned sweetness. As I crouched on the floor pulling a sweater over my head, I felt something wet against my leg. Oh, no, not now. Not tonight ... Warm blood made its way through my layers of clothing. There was nowhere to wash, and the thought of having to strip down in this refrigerated room ...

Six hours later I was pushed by a crowd of passengers into the terminal at Los Angeles Airport. After an hour on a heated plane I could still feel ice in my bones. I didn't need a mirror to know that my unwashed hair was matted around my head, and my clothes were hopelessly wrinkled. I heard my mother call, ''Elizabeth! Elizabeth dear, over here.'' We made our way toward each other through the crowd. She was impeccably dressed in a tweed suit, and greeted me with a smile of fresh lipstick. When I found myself embracing her, I saw no need to hold back my tears.

⋆ 8 ⋆

WE RODE HOME IN THE LIMOUSINE THAT HAD BECOME a constant in my parents' lives since the election.

"Elizabeth, why are you slumped down in the seat like that? If I've told you once I've told you a hundred times, you're going to get curvature of the spine. Now please, dear. Sit up."

Since my father became governor, a few subtle changes had taken place in our Bel Air home; there were guards all around the house and iron gates at the foot of the driveway. To go anywhere with my father meant being accompanied by a small but heavily armed battalion. And then, of course, there was the limousine. Apparently governors are required, or expected, to travel by the most conspicuous mode of transportation available. The self-confidence that was a natural part of my demeanor at Devon vanished the instant I set foot in the elevated world my parents now occupied. My spine shriveled, turning my body into a question mark.

"I am sitting up," I said from the depths of the gray leather seat. There were moments, particularly at red lights, when I caught eyes peering at me from other cars. I had to restrain myself from diving over the partition into the front seat so they would think I was the chauffeur's daughter.

For some reason, the same moments that distressed me delighted Brian. As soon as he caught someone staring, he'd press

66

his face against the glass so his nose flattened and he looked like a mutant bulldog. Unsure of how to react, curious people would lose their curiosity quickly and stare straight ahead.

We did have another car, a station wagon that had been around for as long as I could remember. It was by this time a dingy blue and the wood paneling had long since lost its varnish. Discussions about buying a new car had always ended with my father saying, ''No, it's a waste of money. That car's got a lot of good miles left in it.'' It seemed a measure of his prudence that he would hang onto that car until no mechanic in the world could revive it. He would buy my mother sapphire earrings for Christmas, a matching necklace for their anniversary, and a Fabergé egg just because it was Sunday, but never a new car. Ironically this was probably the thing my mother needed the most since she'd been the one left with the station wagon when my father drove off to work in the luxury model given to him by National Motors.

When we reached the driveway, the heavy iron gate was opened by a policeman who was posted on the other side. He leaned in the window and said, ''Morning, ma'am. We have some men up there checking the alarm system. It won't take too long.'' Something about him reminded me of Greg; it might have been his eyes or his smile, or seeing so much youth in so much uniform.

Brian's room was my favorite place in the house. Despite the fact that the wallpaper, with its Wild West motif, seemed calculated to make one remember the Alamo, the comic books and albums scattered around in comfortable disarray had a soothing effect on me and made me want to curl up there for hours. My room was decorated with bold floral wallpaper and matching drapes and bedspread and made me feel that I was looking up from the depths of a flower pot. I often wondered if there was a back issue of *House Beautiful* that suggested, as the appropriate decor for children's rooms, guns for boys and flowers for girls.

I spent the first three days of my vacation updating my musical awareness. Brian had the latest from Jimi Hendrix and Led Zeppelin, which he played at ear-splitting volume so as not to miss one note of any instrument.

Neither of us knew many people in L.A. I'd been away at Devon for three years and he went to school in Sacramento. There were the Addisons down the street, whom our parents held in questionable esteem, making them irresistible to us. Kelly Addison was my age, her brother was three years younger, and their parents were never around, which was clearly the most attractive aspect of paying them a visit.

On Saturday morning, with a thin veil of fog hovering over the houses, we walked down the street and knocked at the Addisons' door. Neil answered and guided us through the rubble that was a normal state of affairs in their household. Beds were never made, newspapers were discarded only after they had yellowed, and dishes were washed when there was nothing left to use. The TV in the living room, which also served as a handy surface for glasses and ashtrays, was never turned off, and the sofa and chairs faced the set. The first time I was there, I thought how odd it was for people to have a TV in the living room. What was in their TV room?

Kelly was sitting cross-legged on her bed in a sea of makeup. Judging from the amount on her face, I figured she'd been at it for about half an hour. Brian disappeared with Neil.

"Hey, Bethie, how's it goin'?" With a brush in one hand and black liquid eyeliner in the other, she stopped long enough to stretch upward and give me a hug.

"I'm almost done fixing my face here. I got pretty stoned last night and my eyes look like shit. Siddown here and catch me up. How are things at the mansion on the hill? Oh, be careful—don't sit on that hash pipe."

Jim Morrison was telling his baby to light his fire. From three rooms down the hall Mr. Addison was yelling, "Turn down the goddamn music! Some people like to sleep on Saturdays!" A water pipe, a bag of grass, and an ashtray full of roaches were sitting in the middle of the floor. Things were a lot different from the mansion on the hill.

I bet you and Neil had fun growing up here," I told her, watching her paint Cleopatra lines around her eyes.

"Oh, yeah, a real blast."

"I would have. I think it's nice to be . . . well, relaxed."

She gave me a look. "Are you schiz or something? This place is a shithole. You live in a castle."

I looked around me. "It looks lived in, that's all. People enjoy themselves here."

Kelly shook her head and went back to painting. "I'll pass the compliment on to my mother. Coming from the Governor's daughter, I'm sure she'll be impressed. So what's the dirt at Devon? Get laid yet?''

I scrutinized the hash pipe I'd picked up off the floor. ''Sure, hundreds of times.'' I put it on her desk, next to a glass with a half-inch of soda in the bottom. There was no coaster underneath, and I contemplated the bottom of the glass eating its way through the wood finish, leaving a ring to join the patterns of others—ghosts of sodas past. If my mother were here to see this, I'd have to revive her with the ammonia inhaler.

''It's a new pipe. Want a hit? Gets you stoned real fast.''

''No thanks.''

She put down the eyeliner and picked up a box of green eyeshadow. ''Go ahead, take a hit.'' She threw me a pack of matches. ''I won't tell your folks.''

''I don't care about that,'' I told her. ''I just don't feel like it right now.''

''Sure,'' she told me. ''I can just hear your parents feeding you a bunch of crap about how it leads to the hard stuff. That's just crap. I mean, look at me.''

''Yeah,'' I told her. ''So what are you doing today?''

Kelly was spending the day with her boyfriend, one of the many she was juggling at the time. Neil, Brian, and I walked down to the grocery store, bought Christmas cards and ice cream cones, and then trespassed through a neighbor's estate to find a path that Neil said had been his secret before the house was built. We finally found it, overgrown but still visible. It led down a hill and brought us to a rustic-looking street with horse corrals and fragrant eucalyptus trees. We sat by one of the corrals, and grabbed clumps of grass up from the ground to feed the horses.

''How's school, Brian?'' asked Neil.

''Okay, I guess. I'd probably like it better down here in L.A. Most of the kids' fathers are in politics and—well, I don't know. It's just kind of rough.''

''In what way?'' I asked.

''Aw, nothing. It's no big deal. How's your school, Neil?''

''It sucks. Most of the kids have parents in show business. I'd probably like it better in Sacramento.''

When the sun crossed the sky and brought a chill to the canyon, we started back. We said goodbye to Neil outside the iron gate that separated our world from his. There was a pepper tree just outside the gate, and I motioned Brian over. Sitting with our backs against the trunk, we looked at the house, filling our view, splendid and secure.

"Brian, what did you mean about your school being rough?"

He looked down at the ground, and then up at the sky that was changing fast to evening colors.

"Aw, nothing. Some guys beat me up one day when I was walking home from school."

"What?" The thought of my brother pinned down by flailing fists sent a wave of nausea through me. "Did you tell Mom and Dad?"

He shook his head. "I had to say something—they gave me a pretty good shiner. So I said I got knocked down playing soccer." I thought of asking why they had picked on him, but I already knew the answer.

As we approached the gate, the same policeman who had been there the day before let us inside.

"Hi. You're Beth, aren't you? I'm Mark."

"Hi."

"It's nice to finally meet you. I've heard a lot about you."

That struck me as a pretty indiscreet remark coming from a security guard. I looked at Brian to see if he was the culprit who'd been gossiping about me, but I saw no sign of guilt.

"Oh? Like what?"

"Oh, just that you're the rebellious type and all. Hey, it's nothing to be ashamed of, you know. My wife's the rebellious type, too."

As we walked away I felt his eyes sear holes in my back. "I bet she is," said Brian.

Inside, Brian went up to his room. I found my mother in the study answering letters. She asked what we'd been up to all afternoon.

"Just over to the Addisons' for a while," I told her.

"Oh, the Addisons. Brian went with you?"

"Uh-huh. They have a TV in their living room," I said, looking over the books on her shelf.

"It doesn't surprise me."

My mother was a short, fleshy woman, blond and fair. The Swedish half of her heritage got the blame for a multitude of faults, from her easily burned skin to the extra ten pounds she could never shed—even though she refused whipped cream on her desserts and wouldn't dream of buttering her croissants. She always looked perfectly put together, and managed to achieve that perfection in record time. One morning I clocked her from pillow to front door—in a navy blue Chanel suit, matching shoes, and pearl earrings—at twenty-nine minutes and thirty-six seconds. During the power failure at school, I imagined her in my predicament, spending five minutes before a mirror by candlelight with a comb and some melted snow and emerging as though she'd just stepped out of *Town and Country*. When she picked me up at the airport in my bedraggled state, I pictured the next day's newspaper running a story about the governor's wife taking pity on a bag lady at LAX.

"You've always been fascinated with those Addison children," she said. "I've never understood it. And I would appreciate it if you didn't take Brian over there with you. He's at a very impressionable age."

"What do you have against them?"

"Those children grew up without supervision," she said, punctuating the air with her pen. "They practically raised themselves. Who knows what goes on in that household?"

"You're right, Mom. It's too terrible to ponder. Pizza crusts fermenting on the living room floor, moldy washcloths malingering in the bathtub. And the sofa cushions—they're everywhere but where they belong! You know, I don't think I'll ever go there again." My mother looked at me as though I were speaking in tongues. I waved goodbye and made my exit.

In our house, the term "living room" was a misnomer; the elegant furniture was scrupulously arranged to eliminate any possibility of conversation below a roar, much less an intimate exchange. "Living" was more likely to be carried on in the den, which had a TV and a bar and was evidently designated for fun. To test its potential after leaving the Addisons', where fun might occur in any room at any time without warning, I went to the mahogany bar and made myself a drink. I filled a crystal tumbler with ice and poured ginger ale over it. It didn't seem very exciting, so I added some gin. Then I turned on the TV and sank into the leather sofa. I switched channels, stopping when I saw Elizabeth Taylor pacing the floor in a white slip—a scene from *Cat on a Hot Tin Roof*. After several minutes I noticed that everyone on the screen seemed to be enjoying their cocktails much more than I was mine. Ginger ale and gin is a revolting drink.

The next morning the sun blazed through the eyelet curtains

into my bedroom and woke me early. As far back as I could remember, the sun always seemed to shine on Sundays. I couldn't remember ever going to church in the rain.

After my father was elected governor, our simple Sunday ritual of attending church took on new dimensions. We rode there in the limousine, and when we arrived a battery of photographers and reporters awaited us. On this day we pushed our way through shouts of "What are you going to do about Berkeley, Governor?" and "What about the abortion bill?" My father smiled, but never answered them. There was a time and a place for such questions, and it wasn't church.

Throughout the service I brooded about this new intrusion into our lives, and I decided that if this was what church was going to be from now on, I would rather pass.

"Dad, can I talk to you for a minute?" It was midafternoon, when most people were watching football or otherwise relaxing. My father was writing in his study.

"Sure, Beth. I was just working on a speech I've got to give next week." He put down his pen. "What's on your mind?"

There was a leather chair right in front of his desk but I decided to stand. "I'm not going to church anymore."

"Oh?" He pushed his notepad to one side. "And why is that?"

I couldn't bring myself to tell him that I hated riding in the limousine and fighting the throng of reporters. As an excuse for not going to church, it would never make it.

"I'm an agnostic," I told him.

"I see." There was a long pause. He picked up his pen, turned it in his hand, and put it down again. "Beth, this saddens me. Your mother and I have tried to raise you with a respect for God and for His teachings. Now God says in the Bible that we should gather together and worship Him."

"God didn't write the Bible, Dad. Men did."

He looked at me patiently. "No, Beth, that's not true. They may have put it down on paper, but they were delivering God's message. Are you trying to tell me you don't believe in God? Is that what this is all about?"

I realized I should have just told the truth about the damn limousine. "I didn't say that, Dad. Agnostic doesn't mean you don't believe in God. It just means you're not sure."

"Well, I can only say that I hope you give this some more thought. Your mother will be very disappointed."

I stood there in front of his desk staring down at the glass. A brass elephant paperweight gave me a mocking look.

"This is ridiculous, Dad. I haven't told you the truth at all. The real reason I don't like going to church is"—I looked up at him—"the limo and the reporters, Dad. It's just not my idea of church, that's all."

He looked at me with understanding. "Beth, just because you're ashamed to disgrace your family by being a nonbeliever that's no reason to make up some woolly tale about reporters."

"Dad, it's the truth. The whole thing makes me feel like I'm —in a goldfish bowl. You're used to being the center of attention all the time, but I feel conspicuous and awkward. It's as if we have no private lives anymore. Don't you see?"

"Well now, I'm not sure, Beth. I thought young ladies liked being the focus of attention."

I sighed, and turned to go.

"Beth, promise me one thing, will you? Don't mention any of this agnostic business to Grandpa Samuel. It would just break his heart."

That night I dreamed I was standing in the middle of an intersection near my parents' home. I'd heard that God was going to come by there, but I didn't know which road He would choose. I stood in the middle so that no matter what path He took, I wouldn't miss Him. I was still standing there, waiting, when I woke up.

I wanted to tell my father about my dream. I thought he could unravel it for me; he might also see that I wasn't the heathen he thought me to be. The next morning I found him in the kitchen trying to fix one of the cabinets. He was down on the tile floor on one knee with a screwdriver in one hand and a door in the other.

"Hi, Beth. I can't seem to get this damn door on straight. Here, why don't you hold the bottom while I try to get this hinge on."

"When you finish this," I said, trying to hold the door steady, "do you want to take a walk? Maybe we can find a good kite-flying hill like the one behind our old house."

"I'd like to, Beth, but I have my work to do. There are bills to read, and I still have my speech to polish up."

I sat there on the floor wondering whether I should bring up the business about church again. I decided to let it drop. I never did tell him about my dream. Years later he would still refer to the day I stopped believing in God.

My mother had taken Brian to get a haircut, so I walked around Bel Air by myself, coming back in the late afternoon, apparently just in time for Mark's shift. He opened the gate for me and, despite my intention to say "Hi" and keep walking, I gave in to his intention, which was conversation. For some reason I didn't understand, small talk about Christmas led to more intimate revelations about his marraige and how he and his wife always fought during the holidays. When he started to express some real discontent about the "foreverness" of his marital status, it was time to end the conversation.

"I gotta go, Mark. See you later." As I walked away he was shaking his head saying, "Forever is a long time."

When I went back to my room, I lay down on my bed and stared at Greg's picture. What was it about Mark that reminded me so much of Greg? Maybe nothing. Maybe I just missed Greg so much that I looked for him everywhere—even on the nightly news. At the dinner table the conversation turned to Vietnam with predictable frequency. Brian usually stayed well out of the line of fire by simply keeping his mouth shut. It was a strategy I soon adopted after blurting out my opinions several times and finding myself drowning in a lecture from my father about the domino theory, our obligation to help any country threatened by communism, and Communist agitators who were secretly behind the antiwar movement.

At some point I realized that I didn't care that much about the political motivations of this or any war. I just wanted the killing to stop. I wanted Greg to come home. I wanted to wake up from the nightmare of the seven o'clock news.

Three days before Christmas, I paid another visit to the Addisons. My mother was right to wonder about my attraction to them; even I couldn't figure it out. I couldn't have been more fascinated if they were aliens from another galaxy. When I got there I noticed a new addition to the living room: a hammock, which was at that moment sagging with Mr. Addison's weight. I could hear Mrs. Addison, who was almost never home, talking on the phone in the kitchen. Her Rosalind Russell voice carried through the rooms, and as Neil let me in the front door and I walked upstairs, I could hear her saying, "I'll be goddamned if

I'm going to chair that goddamn committee again. I've been the goddamn chair for eight years running, and I'll be goddamned ..."

I found Kelly in her room. The curtains were drawn, as usual and, as usual, she was stoned. She was lying on her bed staring into the portable TV on her nightstand, with an empty bag of Fritos and a can of Vernors at her side. She didn't seem to notice me when I came into the dark room, and I hesitated to speak up for fear that stirring her from her present state would cause a spontaneous acid flashback.

"Hey, Bethie," she whispered suddenly. *"Qué pasa?"*

I sat down on the edge of the bed. As usual, she offered to get me high. For the first time, I accepted. If I were busted I would tell the police that aliens from another galaxy plied me with an indigenous substance which they promised me was no stronger than Mateus rosé. I felt the smoke hit my lungs and Kelly ordered me to hold my breath. When I was sure I had turned blue, she said, "Okay, let it out now." No sense asphyxiating a neighbor just before Christmas.

"I don't feel anything."

"Take another hit."

The second time around I began feeling light-headed and a little giddy. We passed the pipe back and forth a few times, and pretended that we were Alice in Wonderland and the Mad Hatter sharing a hookah.

"Hey, wait!" said Kelly, jumping around and running to the closet. "You can't be the Mad Hatter without hats! Here—" She tossed a bunch of hats at me. We started laughing and I said, "I'm not the Mad Hatter—you are!"

"I am? Shit, I don't remember. Want to see my imitation of Jimi Hendrix?" Kelly straddled an imaginary guitar and got two lines into "Purple Haze" before she fell on the floor giggling.

I walked home grinning at the trees. When Mark opened the gate for me, I looked at him as if he were the Easter Bunny. "Hey, I never noticed your hat before! Can we borrow it next time we play Mad Hatter?"

"Beth ... are you okay? You haven't been drinking, have you?"

"Drinking? Drinking ... me?" I put my hand on his sleeve and leaned in closer. "Mark, since you've been so nice to me, I'll tell you a secret. I don't drink! No, wait—that's not the secret. The secret is''—I leaned in further and whispered—''I'm stoned! Now,'' I said, standing back, ''I'm going to put on a straight face—oops, pardon the pun—and walk right up there to the governor's house. If it's all right with you, of course.''

I wandered into the living room, and plopped myself down on the brocade sofa. A few feet away was a burgundy velvet chair. I walked over and took off the bottom cushion, brought it back to the sofa, and set it on end for a headrest. My eyes wandered from wall to wall, dancing around the patterns in the wallpaper, then back to the sofa where my finger traced a winding thread of jade green through the brocade. I had no idea how much time had passed when I realized Brian was standing there watching me.

''Hi. I didn't hear you come in.''

''Yeah, you do look a little out of it. Pretty good stuff, huh, Beth?''

''Pretty good stuff? What do you mean? I mean, what are you talking about?''

''What am I talking about? What are *you* talking about?''

''Wait a minute. What am *I* talking about? Wait! Shh ...'' I could hear my mother's high heels in the hallway.

She walked in, wearing a long evening dress and carrying a mink coat. After giving us and the sofa an odd look, she said, ''Your father and I will be leaving for dinner in a few minutes.''

''Okay,'' I said, trying to sound normal. She continued her scrutiny from where she stood, then finally she walked over to where I was sitting, removed the velvet cushion, put it back on the chair, and smoothed it out.

''Maria has some broiled chicken for you two. We won't be too late.''

''Good. Beth is probably real hungry,'' said Brian.

By nine o'clock I was so tired my eyes were crossing. I went to bed and slept until ten the next morning. I spent the day by myself, riding my bike around Bel Air, looking at all the elaborate Christmas decorations. Mark was aloof when I got back, but I didn't give it a lot of thought. I assumed he'd had another fight with his wife.

As I walked upstairs, my mother called from the bedroom, ''Elizabeth, would you come in here for a moment, please?''

My parents were sitting in the chairs usually used for interrogations and other weighty matters.

"Sit down, Elizabeth," she said, pointing to a chair near the fireplace. I sat down, and promptly started heating up like a marshmallow in a campfire.

My father cleared his throat. "We've just been given some very disturbing news. The young guard outside, Nick—no, what was his name, honey?" My father's sharp memory retained everything but names.

"Mark, dear."

"Yes, Mark—whom I guess you've been spending some time talking to—told us you've been experimenting with drugs. Now the young man said he had to search his soul to come to us, but he said he'd feel awful if something happened and he hadn't spoken up."

Something? Like what? Would I stroll into the Bel Air Shop Easy stark naked? Sell the Lalique crystal to buy my next fix? "I'm not experimenting. I just tried grass one time, that's all."

"Now, Elizabeth," my mother said—this was no time to correct her about my name—"your friend told us—"

"He's not my friend!"

"All right, whatever. But he seemed to think it was more serious than just trying it one time. And where did you get this—uh —marijuana? She dispatched the word with obvious disgust for the substance and the whole subject in general.

"I got it from someone at school. I don't remember who. I've had it for a while. I was laying around and I just decided to try it the other day. I don't have any more." Did I cover everything?

"Oh, Elizabeth," my mother said, waving her hand to dismiss my explanation, "I don't believe for a minute that this was the first and only time. I've heard that music you kids listen to. Don't think I don't know what 'Light My Fire' means. I wasn't born yesterday."

"You think 'Light My Fire' is a drug song?"

"Don't insult my intelligence. They're obviously singing about lighting each other's ... joints, or whatever you call them. Songs like that have a great deal to do with encouraging all this experimentation and tripping out."

"Beth, do you promise you have no more?" my father asked. I nodded. The remainder of the lecture was a blur of words and *Reader's Digest* prophecies: Grass leads to heroin, teenagers are headed for Sodom and Gomorrah, and by the year 2000, 99 percent of high school students will be junkies. Every year my parents received a leather-bound collection of *Reader's Digest*. They now took up two bookshelves and, as I glanced up at them, I wondered how they had come to replace Dr. Spock as the definitive treatise on child-rearing.

I was grounded for a week, and forbidden to use the phone as insurance that I would feel the full deprivation of my removal from society. I tried to blame Mark, or my parents, but I knew I was to blame, particularly for whispering in a cop's ear that I'd been indulging in illegal activities.

Unable to go out for last-minute Christmas shopping, I spent the next two days making a collage for my parents. I used glass beads and shells and whatever else I could find. I had no idea what it was supposed to be, nor would my parents, but I knew they would keep it anyway, just as they had the other strange art pieces I'd made for them over the years. Paper ornaments I'd pasted together in kindergarten were still brought out every Christmas and hung on the tree.

The entire Christmas season had great sentimental importance in our house. It was probably the worst time of year to get caught ingesting illegal substances. There were practices and patterns that had become as comfortable as old shoes. There were friends and distant relatives who surfaced only at Christmas, but they appeared every year without fail. There were dishes that were only used once a year for turkey and dressing, and a huge bowl that was brought out of some secret hiding place and filled with Grandpa Samuel's ancient recipe for eggnog. Such is the stuff traditions are made of, and my parents were not about to let their daughter's descent into delinquency tarnish what Christmas was supposed to be.

On Christmas Eve night we each got to open one present. Brian gave me a Led Zeppelin album and I gave him an arrowhead from Arizona. My father reminisced about Christmases in years past when we used to leave milk and cookies for Santa and he read ''The Night Before Christmas'' to us in front of the fire. Some traditions are born only to die.

On Christmas morning, the rest of the presents were exchanged. My parents thanked me for my collage, discreetly turning it this way and that, trying to make some sense of it.

My presents included a flannel nightgown from an aunt I'd never met, who had apparently lost track of time somewhere around my ninth birthday, and a pair of bedroom slippers that might have resembled moccasins but for the band of pink fur glued to them—again, from someone I didn't know. Presents like these were usually left out to admire for the day and then retired to a closet where no one ever saw them again. I received from my parents two sweaters, a book on horses, a transistor radio, and in an attempt to spark in me some sense of fashion, a dress for "special occasions." It was made of crinkly fabric with silver and gold stripes, the kind of thing my mother could have carried off with aplomb. I looked like a stalk of celery wrapped in tinfoil.

There was a steady stream of relatives and guests throughout the day. Extra help had been brought in; quiet people in stiff uniforms who stood at a respectable distance until a dirty glass or full ashtray caught their eye, when they'd swoop down on the offending object and carry it off on a silver tray.

Miraculously, everyone vanished at precisely five o'clock except for the ten dinner guests. Visitors started dropping by again at eight, coming and going for the remainder of the evening.

The days after Christmas had always seemed sad to me; trees and decorations ended up in trash cans, hauled off as in some ritual dismemberment. My somber mood was intensified this particular year because I was still grounded. When my sentence finally ended and I emerged from the house, I discovered that Mark was gone, transferred "downtown," one of the other guards said, for reasons unknown. I spent the remainder of the holiday alone, contemplating the hazards of trusting anyone, particularly anyone in uniform. I made an exception for Greg, though, and composed a letter outlining the trauma my vacation had become. On the plane back to Phoenix I copied it over neatly, but I never mailed it.

The letter that was waiting for me when I arrived at Devon was reason enough to change my mind about sending Greg my chorus of small grievances.

★　★　★

Dear Betsy,

To us over here Christmas meant a chance to blow it all out, and that's what we did. Some of the guys had been sent fifths for Christmas presents, and we started by passing them around. Then instead of our usual C-rations (commonly called C-rats 'cause that's what they taste like) we cooked steaks, hamburgers, and hot dogs on a grill. There was enough beer for about two hundred guys to get pretty shitfaced. By the time we finished all that, about a dozen parties had already begun, so Trent and I started traveling between them. Thank God for old Trent—that crazy s.o.b. keeps my spirits up. Without him this place would be even more of a hell than it is.

By the time ten rolled around there wasn't a sober man in the squadron. A few of us began stumbling around the various living areas, caroling. We weren't too good on most of the songs, but we were great on ''Silent Night.'' Everywhere we went—even the officers' area—they either gave us beer or passed around a bottle. We just kept wandering to different hootches drinking and caroling. We were pretty fucked up so our singing was worse-than-awful, but we kept doing better on ''Silent Night.''

I couldn't help thinking about a buddy of mine, and how he would have gotten off on our Christmas celebration. He died three days ago. He was standing right next to me when I heard the shots—I hit the ground and reached over to pull him down, but he was already down—with blood pouring out of him and his legs fifty feet from the rest of him. The thing that really gets me is that he only had twenty-seven days left in country. I held him while the rest of the life just ran out of him. I thought about him every time we sang ''Silent Night.''

''I'm due to leave Vietland on the 21st of May, which gives me 146 days left. I hope to spend the rest of my enlistment at a Naval Air Station on the West Coast going to college. The important thing is to think positively about the future, to have a goal and keep focused on it. I've heard of guys who leave this place thinking the worst is behind them, then go straight to hell when they hit the States. That's not going to happen to me.

Merry Christmas—I love you,

Greg

★   ★   ★

⋆ 9 ⋆

A FEW NIGHTS OF TORRENTIAL RAIN LEFT DEVON THICK and slushy with mud. My horse came back underweight but healthy; my roommates came back overweight but ecstatic about their lavish Christmas presents, and I was thinking about college. I would be graduating from Devon in June, and from time to time I entertained fantasies of attending Berkeley, where I'd be surrounded by people who felt as I did about the war, but I knew there was no point in pursuing it. My parents would sooner have paid for a trip to Moscow.

Once during my nightly vigil in front of the evening news, I saw a young black woman debating the vice president on the issue of the Vietnam war. In her eloquent and charming way she made him look like he'd been lobotomized. The woman's name was Alicia Washington, and she was president of the student body at a small college in Illinois called Mountclaire. I sent for an application and a brochure. The school appeared to be a conservative, ivy-covered cloister populated by the somber and the morally upstanding. Reading the copy and looking at the color photos of happy and exclusively white students strolling across the quad, chatting by the fire in the lounge, shooting baskets in the gym, I assumed I'd gotten the school's name wrong. Only if the entire student body had been drugged and the board of directors bound and gagged could Alicia Washington get elected president in this

81

place. I called the news program to make sure I had my facts straight, and the research desk assured me Alicia was from Mountclaire. Evidently the school had undergone a few changes since the brochure was printed. I sent off my application, and waited.

As winter faded, I spent more time on my poetry, and dreamed of someday making it my primary occupation. Up to this point Greg was the only person to read my poems. I flirted with the idea of sending one to our school paper, but it took me weeks to get up the nerve. One morning I impulsively stuck the poem I'd been working on all week in an envelope, ran over to the paper's office and shoved it through the mail slot—all without giving myself a chance to back out.

A MARRIAGE
by Beth Canfield

> *before the altar*
> *the old-enough-to-know youth and his gun*
> *trembled in holy wedlock,*
> *and sealed their union with salute.*
> *but beyond the altar*
> *death's blood blurted out the half-mast truth.*
>
> *he was just one of many*
> *to offer his hand.*
> *camouflaging fear*
> *he'd hold tight his partner*
> *and do-si-do, round we go*
> *sidestep here, duck and dive,*
> *you never know, you might get out alive.*
>
> *but it only takes a flash*
> *to end the dance.*
> *the music fades, the band packs it in,*
> *and the already drunk soil*
> *slurps up the rest of him.*

he was just one of the many scars
on this bloody earth
but there are always more,
so many more who will offer their hands
and join the dance.

and the sun grips its sides
in aching laughter.

"Beth? It's Dad."

"Oh, hi. I was going to call you later today. It's kind of early, isn't it? You must have just gotten up."

I babbled on about the weather while I wondered why he was calling. My father only called or wrote on occasions that were deemed serious. On hearing his voice unexpectedly on the other end of the line I felt the blood draining from my face, and my heart beginning to pound. Something was wrong at home. Or was it something I had done? I couldn't think of anything I had done recently to provoke a phone call. Oh, no—that must be it—the night watchman. In a fit of moral responsibility he had called my parents and told them about finding Greg and me in the hay barn. That had to be it. I'd hold my ground, defend my rights. After all, in two months I would be eighteen.

"Yes, we'll be leaving for church in a little while. Beth, yesterday we received a copy of your school paper with your poem in it."

"Oh? I didn't know you subscribed to our paper."

"We don't. I'm sure someone there thought we might be interested in seeing your poem, which of course we were. Now, Beth, I'm afraid you're letting yourself be indoctrinated by people who are bent on tearing down this country. I don't know who you've been talking to or what kind of propaganda you've been reading, but we're trying to help another country that's in trouble. The protests here are being stirred up by Communist agitators who would like to see the wrong side win."

"Dad, I don't recall any mention of Vietnam in my poem. It's a poem about war, and yeah, against war—all wars."

"Now, Beth, don't get smart. Since you're too young to recall any other war, I think it's obvious you were talking about Vietnam."

"You know, I don't think we're going to accomplish anything arguing about this. We happen to disagree. Let's just leave it at that, okay?"

"No, it's not okay. You know, Beth, I have access to a lot of information about Vietnam that could help you understand why we're there, but you never ask. You just form your own opinions without the facts. Your generation is so quick to call us narrow-minded, but you're the one who's being narrow-minded now."

I suspected I was already familiar with the information to which he referred. I had heard it before. The essence of it was that America was always right; that her soldiers only go where they need to go in the name of freedom, democracy, and God. "Tell that to the Indians," I once said to my father in response to his unqualified patriotism, "or to the Japanese-Americans who were thrown into internment camps by our good-will government."

"Do you consider anyone who disagrees with you to be narrow-minded?"

"Well, more often than not, that's the case," he laughed. "Beth, I wish you would do one thing for me. Think about what I said about how you form your opinions. Don't assume that just because people your own age tell you something that it's right, and don't be so quick to take sides against your country. Do some thinking of your own."

"You can count on it, Dad."

"Good. I'll tell your mother hello for you."

I was so excited when I received my acceptance letter from Mountclaire that the first thing I did was pick up a pen to write to Greg. But once I began, I found myself avoiding my real reasons for choosing that school. For all of Greg's stories and remarks about the war, I still couldn't tell what his political sentiments were. I was afraid of hurting him; afraid that he might take my views on the war as some kind of rejection of him. He wrote back:

★ ★ ★

Dear Betsy,

Congratulations on being accepted at Mountclaire. It's exciting to plan your future, isn't it? It's something I think about all the time. Some people's idea of war may be constant combat, but the truth is when we're not getting our asses shot at we're sitting around for long periods of time just thinking out loud. We think about what life will be like when we get back to the World. For me, I know I probably won't do a whole lot of talking. I might even seem cold and unable to get excited about anything. Over here life-and-death matters become routine—aside from a flashing realization of one's own mortality, you just don't get thrown when you get shot at or when mortars start impacting around the area. It's afterward that you're scared shitless. It might sound inhuman, but after a while, killing doesn't even faze you. It's like they're not people—they're just targets. It don't mean nuthin'.

Over a can of brew a couple of buddies and I talked about the changes our Stateside friends will find in us when we return to the World. We all agreed that for the first week or so we may seem morose and reserved. But when we're up for a blow-out we'll be a hell of a lot wilder than we used to be. We'll anger faster, work harder, shuck conventionalism, and be far more uninhibited than we were before Nam. We'll tend to be loners, and resent being told to do something, or how to do it. Maybe we'll gross 'em out in Fat City and maybe Mr. Straight won't be able to hack it when we say screw the world, but we'll never infringe on the rights of others. Personally, I just want to live life my own way, setting my own standards. I know this is a hell of a turnabout for me, the law-abiding high school football hero, but I find that for my friends here the story is the same.

I don't know if I expect you to scope out this bag, but anybody who has been here will be coming home a realist. It may sound harsh, but it's the only way I know to prepare you for the relative stranger you'll meet when I make my Freedom Bird.

Take Care,

Greg

★　★　★

Despite his warnings, I fought the fact the Greg was becoming someone I didn't know and, in some ways, didn't want to know. My letters to him were taking more time to write; I chose my words carefully, edited my thoughts, felt nervous about how he would react.

I spent that spring talking more to Harmony than to members of the human race. More of my poems were published in the school paper, but my parents never mentioned it again. Occasionally I would overhear boys in my class discussing what they would do if they were drafted. Canada was one option, failing the physical was another, going to Vietnam was generally at the bottom of the list. Most of them felt confident, though, that they wouldn't have to confront this dilemma. Student deferments were still a reality, and their families could easily provide them with college educations. I wondered what would happen to the boys all across America for whom college was as out of reach as a Mediterranean cruise. Was this war fought only by those too poor to avoid it?

★ ★ ★

Dear Betsy,

I've been meaning to write to you for a while, but after a certain amount of time in the Nam, you slip into a rut and the only thing that occupies your mind is making a hat back to the World. That may sound like I'm mentally going to pot, but it'll probably pass after a few weeks back in the States.

After giving it a lot of thought, I've decided that there's no reason for this war. At least no one that I've asked can come up with a reason—probably not even the bigwigs in Washington could think of a good one, so it kind of makes you wonder why we're over here waiting to die.

I'm presently assigned to an infantry company and for the month of April I'll be a regular "mud marine," going on patrols and standing bunker duty with the best of them. I got a ride back to the squadron today to pick up my mail and get out of the clothes I've been wearing for the last ten days in the bush.

Through my experiences here I've become aware of

man's physical, emotional, mental, and spiritual frailty. I
think that once two people have attained true love and developed a mental and emotional rapport, then marriage can
provide a sense of security that is vital to the happiness
and emotional well-being of most of us delicate individuals.
But over here, the guys who have something heavy going at
home are the most homesick and the loneliest. You've got
to realize that loneliness is a horrible, horrible thing. A lot
of the guys take trips to the villa near here to shack up
with one of the nasty old Vietnamese peasants. Other guys
appear bloodthirsty, but even this is only a release from
the terrible pressure of being away from loved ones for as
long as thirteen months. I never realized how long a year
was until I came over here.

I'm going to jump into the river with a bar of soap before my chopper leaves in forty-five minutes. Please take
care, and write whenever you get the chance.

Love always,

Greg

★ ★ ★

When I wrote back, I wanted to tell him that I was afraid I
didn't know him anymore, that I missed him terribly . . . but I
couldn't. I sealed the envelope and walked to the mailbox. My
father once told me that if we found out tomorrow that the world
was going to end, all the roads and phone lines would be jammed
with people trying desperately to get to someone to say "I love
you." Standing next to the mailbox I tore open the envelope and
wrote a P.S. "I guess I want you home so badly because I love
you."

The weeks prior to graduation were hectic and emotional. Belongings were packed up and shipped home, yearbooks signed,
addresses exchanged. Chris and Marin were both going to the
University of Arizona. "No one's throwing bricks through windows there," said Chris pointedly. Doug was going to Columbia,
undaunted, apparently, by the recent demonstrations.

The prospect of leaving high school was both exciting and
frightening. Boys who hadn't had to think too seriously about

such things as war now walked a thin line: with college and parental pressure to succeed on one side, and the reality of a faraway war on the other. There would be no "just getting by" anymore—failure or expulsion from college could cost them their lives. Boys who had been somewhat apathetic before became vehemently antiwar, transformed from ambling, carefree youths to tightly coiled springs; determined to take a stand against the war, dead-set against going, scared as hell they'd have to. In this feverish atmosphere, a plan was hatched to wear red armbands to the graduation ceremony, signifying opposition to the war. Being one of the first at Devon to express strong antiwar sentiments, I was expected to participate, and I never doubted that I would, but one detail put me in a precarious position. The graduation speaker was my father. I regarded it as a test of my convictions. The night before graduation we sat in the rec room cutting strips of red cloth.

The next morning I took out the white dress I'd bought for the occasion, and laid it out on my bed. Suddenly I felt the way I used to feel when I dressed up in my mother's clothes. I'd wait until she was gone for the afternoon, and lock myself in her dressing room—spending hours in front of the mirror, posing in her silk blouses, pearl-embroidered sweaters, and fur-trimmed jackets. Looking at my dress lying there, it seemed almost as foreign to me as her clothes had. But it was fresh and festive and feminine, all the things I wanted to be for Greg to help him forget the mud and the stench of death that surrounded him for so many months. White, fresh and pure, untainted. A clean slate on which to compose our future, any way we wanted it. In a few short weeks he would be free, and safe. Welcome home.

I slipped the dress carefully over my head, and stepped into white leather pumps. I brushed my hair and, for this special occasion, applied lipstick, blush-on, and a little of the mascara I hadn't worn since Delia helped me revamp my scandalous image. I sprayed some cologne. A glimpse of myself in the mirror as I sat on the bed brushing my hair left me with an image of a bride and brought a smile to my lips. Greg had mentioned marriage in his letter; not with reference to us, I knew, but it wasn't the furthest thing from my mind. Though time and distance separated us I now felt closer to him with every passing week; what little bond we nurtured months before seemed to have grown in his absence. Sometimes the fact that I loved him came as a surprise to me.

My parents were due to arrive at eleven o'clock. When I heard the knock at the door I looked at my watch; it was ten of. I opened the door and said, "Hi, Mo—"

"Happy graduation, baby." Greg stood there with a cigarette in one hand and a glorious bouquet of white roses in the other. I stood there stunned. He was tanned and smiling and radiant in his crisp uniform.

"Well, aren't you gonna invite me in?" he asked, opening his arms wide, and I entered them. I put my arms around his waist and cherished the life in his body. Once again, he had survived. He felt more real to me than ever—stronger, sturdier, and yet I was aware of how vulnerable he was out there, only flesh after all. I held him tight.

"Hey, does this mean you're glad to see me?" I lifted my face from where it rested on his shoulder, and looked at him before we kissed. His eyes were older.

"Yeah, that's what it means." We went into my room, and I closed the door. He handed me the bouquet, and I let the pungent smell fill my senses.

"These are . . . I love them, Greg. Thank you."

"Beautiful flowers for a beautiful lady," he said, following it with a little laugh. "Hey, this whole thing is like something out of a greeting card, huh?"

"I don't mind if you don't."

He shook his head. "I guess I can take it," he said, looking around him, then walking over to the window to put out his cigarette on the sill. He sat down on the edge of my bed; he extended his hand to me, and I went to him. He patted the bed at his side.

"Sit here for a minute," he said. "I wanna take you in."

He stared at me for a long moment. I fiddled with my hair, smoothed out my dress. I looked back at him. He was still staring.

He brought his fingers up to my cheek, and let them graze down my face, my neck. "This is the hardest part," he said quietly. "This is what I miss most."

I looked at him with a question.

"Just . . . being gentle. I never realized what a luxury it is. I'm so fucking sick of vigilance. Sometimes I hardly recognize myself anymore. I forget there's another way to be. I miss you, Betsy." He nibbled my ear, and kissed my cheek. Then he picked me up and sat me down on his lap, and with his arm around me, rested his head on my chest.

"Every day out there, I think about making love to you. I keep it in my mind all the time. The guys and me, sometimes we talk about the different things we do to keep ourselves from going fuckin' nuts out there. Trent says he thinks about going to see the Cardinals play on a beautiful spring day. Boynton—Boing Boing we call him—thinks about how when he was a kid his mother used to take him to the zoo to feed peanuts to the elephants. She took him on the subway from Harlem to the Bronx and all the way there he'd be thinking about how he couldn't wait to get there and give those elephants their lunch. He said there were two adults and a baby, and he had names for all of them. They ask me what I think about, but I tell 'em it's a secret. I have my own secret antidote, I tell them."

His kiss made it clear how much he wanted me, and I responded to let him know I felt the same. For a few moments I forgot graduation and my parents and our class protest and was aware only of an overwhelming closeness, so intense, so strong that nothing could harm us. I believed that my love for Greg could protect him from all the terrible blows the war was ready to inflict . . . even death.

Through my reverie, I heard, as if from miles away, my name over the PA system out in the corridor. No . . . Can't we have just a few more minutes, a little more time to pretend that the world begins and ends right here?

"My parents are here," I whispered.

Greg looked around. "You mean, under the bed?"

"Of course." I attempted to get up, but he held me fast in his lap.

"Say it," he said.

"Say what?"

"What you said in the letter."

"I said a lot of things in the letter." I knew damn well what he meant. He was waiting.

"I love you," I said, and though I hadn't spoken those words to anyone since I was a little girl, and then only to my parents, they flowed as if I had said them a thousand times.

Graduation took place on the shaded lawn outside the administration building. Chairs and an all-white podium were set up. When the graduating class filed in wearing white dresses and dark suits, our armbands were angry red slashes in an otherwise perfect picture. To avoid any last-minute disciplinary action, we had waited until just before the ceremony to put them on. Parents and school officials gave us intense looks as we walked, our heads high, up the center aisle and to our seats in the front as "Pomp and Circumstance" was played by the school band. At the time I thought we shocked the administration with our bold gesture of defiance on such an important day, but I later realized they must have known all along what we were planning. They placated us, knowing that an attempt to stop us would only inflame us and create adverse publicity for the school. As a peaceful demonstration, it harmed no one.

I introduced Greg to my parents and Brian before the ceremony, and they sat together in the audience.

My father's speech was a glowing eulogy to an America that granted young people the opportunity for education, a career, and the glory of serving their country. I thought of the speech he made at my grade school so many years before, and how proud I had been. At one point he scanned the audience as if to single out the bearers of the red armbands, and said, "And to those of you who feel compelled to demonstrate against our great nation, I can only hope that you will someday realize how fortunate you are to live in a land that allows you this freedom of expression. The hope of our country is that the rest of the world will someday be free of oppression and the tyranny of communism"

Everyone applauded. Greg seemed to be applauding the loudest, and from where I stood he almost looked as though he had tears in his eyes. As I approached them after the ceremony, my parents were all smiles and rapt attention as they listened to what I assumed were Greg's stories of the war. Brian stood back, taking it all in, showing nothing. Often I thought that Brian was much older than the body he inhabited. When I got there, my father told me he thought Greg was a fine boy. "We've invited Greg to come home and stay with us for a while, Beth, but he says it's up to you. What do you think?"

The governor's mansion was a sprawling, white-pillared house that looked as though it had been plucked off a Southern estate. It was located on a quiet street, unpretentious except for the army of security personnel, the electric eyes dotting the front lawn, and the helicopters periodically cruising overhead. The building was two stories with five bedrooms, plus a basement with a recreation room and a laundry room where the maid and the housekeeper hung out and smoked cigarettes. There was also a pool man, a gardener and son, and a cook named Irma, who had been born in Austria and specialized in sauerbraten, a sumptuous dish which took two days to prepare and four to digest. She had an extensive repertoire of German and Hungarian recipes, one more delicious than the next, each of which seemed to have a considerable half-life in the system.

In the parlor, paintings graced the walls and Lalique figurines adorned the end tables. The draperies, couches, and rugs were various shades of white. My mother invited Greg to make himself at home, and I wondered how she would respond if he took her literally, since his home for the past year had been the jungle. Although I was used to the way the mansion looked, I was aware that it could intimidate some people. I once took Delia there for a weekend and she told me it made her nervous. She had the strange feeling that everywhere she went she was being watched. I told her that was probably because she *was* being watched. I suggested to her that she avoid doing anything funny in her bed at night because there were cameras and microphones planted in her room.

Brian found a way to remain unaffected by the formality around him. He'd run in from the pool trailing puddles of water across the polished floors, and defuse any disciplinary repercussions with the flash of a smile and a "Sorry—forgot my towel." He would slide down the banister when dinner was announced, in stockinged feet and a T-shirt large enough to make one question if he was wearing anything underneath. Sideways looks from starched-shirt butlers and patient reprimands from our mother rolled right over him. He'd shrug his shoulders, go back upstairs, and slide back down in shoes and a smaller shirt.

You'd have thought Greg had spent his whole life in a pristine palace with security guards and servants who called him "sir." "Can I bring you an aperitif, sir?" the butler asked. "Sure, I'll have a brew," said Greg. "Would you like your brew with a head on it, sir?" At dinner he used the right forks, sipped vintage California Cabernet from a Waterford goblet, and answered in detail all of my parents' inquiries about what was going on "over there."

"Well, the problem is, sir, that the VC can be anywhere and anyone—little kids, old ladies. A kid you stop to talk to can toss a grenade between your legs. Or they'll come around selling Cokes to us and then tell the VC where we are, how many we are. ... You just have to assume that they're all gooks—oh, excuse me''—my mother smiled forgivingly—''that they're all VC. And the biggest dangers are the mines and booby traps they set. They're so well hidden, you feel it's just a matter of time till one gets you.''

I excused myself from the table for a moment, not wanting to hear any more about mines and VC. When I returned, I heard my father telling Greg he thought he would be a ''good influence on Beth.''

''I'm sure, Greg,'' he said, his words coinciding with my entrance, ''that you were quite embarrassed and put off by that little display of antiwar sentiment at graduation. I mean, having seen things firsthand, and having participated in defending your country—''

''Well, sir, I—'' Either my father didn't hear him, or he didn't want to give him the chance to disagree.

''I just hope that some of your common sense will rub off on Beth,'' he went on. ''Maybe she'll listen to you and we'll all be spared the discomfort of another incident like that.''

''Looks like they might want to adopt you, Greg,'' Brian said, leaning around the floral centerpiece to wink at me.

Greg had been given the guest bedroom at the end of the hall rather than the one next to my room. I couldn't help but notice that my parents' suite was conveniently located between Greg's room and mine. After we had all gone to bed, I peeked out of my door periodically, waiting to see the light in my parents' room go out. The maid brought them a tray with two glasses of milk every night at eleven, and they were usually asleep within ten minutes, but for some reason on this night they seemed to be staying up forever. I figured they were in there talking about Greg, and how he was going to straighten me right out. I peeked out the door again and saw Brian walking down the hall.

''What are you doing?'' I whispered.

''I'm hungry—going down to the kitchen. What are you doing?'' He looked over to the slit of light that signified parents-on-alert and said, ''Waiting for their light to go out?''

''Brian, if you tell anyone ...''

''Hey, no sweat. Just don't make too much noise in there. I need my beauty sleep, okay?''

I picked up a book and read until finally their room was dark, then I walked quietly down the hall. I tapped lightly on Greg's door and heard him say, ''Come on in.'' When I opened the door I found him sitting up in the dark with his hands behind his head. ''What kept you?'' he said.

''What do you mean? What made you think I was coming in here?''

He smiled. ''How could you resist?''

''Easily. My parents are asleep twenty feet from here, or hadn't you noticed?''

''What makes you think they're sleeping?'' he said, grinning.

''Don't be silly.'' Like all children, I assumed that my parents only had sex for purposes of conception, which meant twice in the course of their marriage.

''You mean you're not allowed to do it in the governor's mansion?'' he asked, pulling me down to the bed. ''Does a siren go off?''

Before I knew what was happening, I was lying on top of him looking down into his eyes.

''I've been dreaming about you for seven months,'' he whispered. He ran his hands through my hair. ''It seems like every picture I have in my head, you're at the center of it. Anywhere I see myself, you're there, too. How'd you do this to me, anyway?''

''We had a Haitian housekeeper once. She taught me voodoo.''

He gave me a slow smile, and his eyes gleamed in the darkness as we kissed. I tried to tell myself this wasn't what I'd come in for; that I hadn't had any time alone with him since morning and I just wanted to talk. It wasn't a lie, but it certainly wasn't the truth. I even went to the trouble of propping some pillows up under the covers on my bed in case my mother went in to check on me.

Greg rolled us over so that my back was to the mattress, and he was on his side facing me. I had on a light cotton nightgown, which he slowly slid up my body, until it was gathered just under my arms. Then I felt the fingers I remembered so well begin to explore me. As his hand moved to places never touched before, I felt myself tense up. ''Relax, Betsy,'' he whispered, placing kisses on my stomach. ''I'm gonna show you something.'' It didn't seem possible that Greg could know more about my body than I did, but in a few minutes he brought to life something inside me that would have scared me to death if I'd had the time to think about it. A violence roared up from within and screamed from every corner of my body, a thousand high notes shattering a thousand panes of glass. To keep from crying out, and to keep from flailing away at Greg's shoulder, I bit at my wrist. Gradually I came down, feeling like my blood had been drained and I couldn't do anything but lie there. . . .

When I remembered the English language, I turned to Greg and said, "What did you do to me?"

"You tell me," he said, then smiled.

"How did you . . . learn that?"

"Killing isn't all we learn over there," he said, rolling over toward the nightstand. I was sure there was a story behind that remark. I was also sure I didn't need to hear it. He lit a cigarette.

"You're not really going to smoke now," I teased.

"Really I am," he said, blowing smoke rings to the ceiling.

"Something else you learned over there?"

He put his arm around my shoulders and pulled me close. I pushed myself into his body, luxuriating in the smell, the warmth of him. "I better get back to my room," I whispered. "I shouldn't press my luck." I put my arm around his chest. "Just think, Greg. In four more weeks, you'll be coming home for good. You know, I was wondering . . . why would they give you a leave so close to the end of your time?"

He stared at his cigarette, then turned to the nightstand to put it out.

"Greg?"

He turned back to look at me. "Betsy, I've got something to tell you."

"What do you mean you've got . . . oh, no. You mean they're making you stay?"

"No, Betsy—"

"Then—"

"I've signed on for another six months."

"Greg!" I cried. Then, aware of the loudness of my voice, I whispered, "What do you mean you signed on? I don't understand!"

"I'm going back, Betsy. It's what I want."

"What you—you want to get killed, is that what you're trying to tell me?"

"I just can't come home yet. It's hard to explain, but . . . I'm just not ready. It's like . . . I don't know, unfinished business. Can you understand?"

"I understand that you may be finished if you go back there!

Didn't you think about that?'' Of course he thought about that. He must have. That's what hurt the most—that he was going back anyway. ''What about me? What about *us?*''

''I can't help it, Betsy. This is what I have to do. Don't worry about me. I'll survive. I'm just not the type that gets killed.''

''This is some . . . ideological thing with you, is that it? You're gung ho on this war and you want to go back and kill some more gooks. It looks like that bloodlust you were telling me about in your letters has hit you, too, Greg. You told me I might not recognize you—that I'd find you a stranger when you came home. This morning when I first saw you I didn't know what you were talking about, but now I see. You're right, I don't know you. Maybe you believe all that propaganda they shoved down your throat in boot camp. Maybe you're—''

''You don't know what you're talking about, Betsy. That's not the way it is. If you would just—''

''You're right. I don't know you, I don't.'' I was crying. I started shaking my head, saying, ''You bastard, you bastard. You made love to me. You knew you were going back all the time, and you made love to me just as if everything were wonderful . . .''

''Betsy, please—''

I ran out of his room and down the hall. He followed. I shut my door and locked it. He kept tapping on it and begging me to let him in; I buried my head under my pillow and shut him out —shut everything out. Shut everything out with my sobs, until sleep took me.

⋆ *10* ⋆

*A*T BREAKFAST, I SIPPED MY COFFEE AND NIBBLED AT A croissant and tried to appear as though nothing at all unusual had occurred the night before. I was sure the looks my parents exchanged had something to do with my cries and Greg's knocking at my door, but they refrained from questions. There was the pressure of tears behind my eyes and a quivering around my mouth that I was sure was visible to everyone. I tried to avoid their eyes and just sit in silence, knowing that if I spoke my voice would tremble and break.

When we finished eating Greg thanked my parents for their hospitality, and said that he was going to San Francisco to stay with some friends.

"We hope to see you again, Greg," my father said, shaking his hand. "You're a fine young man."

"Yes," my mother chimed in, "feel free to come see us anytime."

When I drove him to the airport, he told me he wished I would at least try to understand why he had to go back. I told him I was trying, but that wasn't the truth. I felt betrayed and violated. I didn't walk him to the gate; I dropped him off at the terminal, without affection, holding back my tears. He leaned over and kissed my cheek, and then he was gone. As I drove away, I thought of something my father once told me; of a time he'd felt compelled to embrace his own father after years of simply shaking hands. This first embrace was their last; he never again saw his father alive.

Sacramento was a city I neither knew nor liked, not that I'd given it much of a chance. Though it was my parents' home much of the time, it never really had been mine. I regarded it as a place for state business, and never thought of it as a town where families went about their daily lives. I remember driving by the supermarket and the dry cleaner's, almost surprised to see them there. Although I knew better, it seemed as if governments weren't run by actual people; something in me clung to an image of government as dusty old buildings in a sea of papers, fleshless and impersonal. This is the picture I nurtured as a child, and even after seeing my father on countless afternoons laboring at his desk in his shirtsleeves, scratching his head, making government happen, I retained my old bias. I had time now to discover the capital, and my father urged me to do so, but I spent it reading, lolling by the pool, and watching television. In the summer months, the temperature in Sacramento rarely dips below one hundred. The heat clamps down like a vise. There is no wind to stir the air, and night brings little relief.

One afternoon, bored and restless, I borrowed a state car, equipped with air conditioning and telephone and antenna, and drove out of the city for over an hour until I saw the gray buildings of Folsom Prison crouching in the distance. I hung around the gift shop studying the artwork by the inmates, trying to decipher, from their paintings and sculpture—some ordinary, some bizarre and elusive—what crimes they had committed. The trip became a frequent excursion for me. Eventually Brian's curiosity was aroused and he started going with me. We'd pack soft drinks and oranges and drive out of the city with the radio on full blast.

The land around Sacramento is flat and monotonous; your eyes can see so far in every direction that the heat turns the land into undulating waves at the edge of your vision. One afternoon as we drove past miles of dry fields, I turned to my brother and said, "You know, Brian, you never told me what you thought of Greg."

"Well"—he paused—"I find it hard to believe the guy enjoys what he's doing as much as he acts like he does."

My eyes focused on the endless road ahead. "He's changed

since he's been in Vietnam. In some ways I don't know him anymore. In some ways I don't even like him anymore.''

"Maybe you'd change, too, if you'd been where he's been. I mean, it seems like he's got a better chance of making it if he believes he's right and the other guys are wrong." He looked out the window. "You know what I don't like about land like this? You can always see what's up ahead. There are never any surprises.''

We walked around the gift shop, looking at the paintings and the other art pieces. There was a miniature stagecoach, carved from wood, on which everything moved as it should—the reins, the lanterns, even the rifle.

The trustees who ran the shop stood in front of a glass partition, where they could be easily observed. One man in particular, with thinning hair and wire-rimmed glasses adorning his quiet, kindly face, reminded me of a math teacher I had in junior high. We asked him some questions about the art. I asked if he'd met Eldridge Cleaver. Brian asked if Johnny Cash really performed there. I hesitated for a moment, then said, ''Excuse me, but do you mind my asking, well, what you're in for?''

"I killed my wife," he said, and blew some dust off a model car.

That night at dinner, Brian and I talked about our day at the prison. ''This man looked so sweet,'' I said, ''and then he told us he murdered his wife.''

"Well, you know, Beth, that's a common crime," said my father, balancing some rice on his fork. ''Men whom you'd never suspect—who've never committed a crime before. You see, it's a crime of passion and—''

''Can we please change the subject?'' my mother interrupted, looking as though she were having a bout of indigestion.

Brian struggled to keep from laughing. ''But, Mom, don't you want to know how he did it?''

★ ★ ★

Dear Betsy,

Nothing that's happened to me in this war has made me feel as shitty as I felt leaving you at the airport that way. I'm so sorry—those words sound and look so empty to me on this piece of paper—but please believe me, I didn't want to hurt you. I know that's the reason I didn't tell you right away about extending my tour, though still I had no idea it would hit you so hard. I guess that means I'm denser than I thought, and I hope you'll forgive me. I know you will, because I know you still love me as I love you, in spite of what has happened. I learned a sad lesson that day you drove me to the airport. I sat there watching you, knowing for the first time how bad it feels to hurt someone you love. It's something I hope I won't experience again too soon and I'm going to try like hell to avoid it.

Maybe someday you'll understand why I had to come back here. There's more than one reason, but I can tell you right now that my PCS orders had me assigned to Camp Pendleton once I leave here. I've been stationed there before, and I hated every minute of it. They had this mock Vietnamese village complete with trip wires and punji sticks and officers hovering over the trainees screaming "Kill those gooks! Kill those gooks!" For thirteen months now I've been using an M-16 and an M-60 machine gun to do exactly that. So what in hell difference can it make to me whether or not some boot second lieutenant straight out of officers' school can find a speck of dirt on my rifle with his white gloves? I'd rather stay here and do what I know how to do. The way I see it, it's my job. I've stopped feeling sorry for myself—if I've hacked thirteen months in this place I can stick it out for another six.

All my love,

Greg

★ ★ ★

Mountclaire was about an hour outside of Chicago in a small, quaint town close to Lake Michigan. The campus was shaded with enormous old trees, and thick with ivy that crawled up the brick buildings in a determined effort to reach the rooftops. I was given my dorm assignment and, when I reached my room, weighted down with luggage and a winter coat that resisted all my efforts to squeeze it into a suitcase, I saw that my roommate had already arrived.

Her name was Belinda. She had an ample figure that belonged in a Rubens painting, an unruly mane of dark curls, and granny glasses. She had already decorated her half of the room with macramé wall hangings which, I quickly learned, she made both in her spare time and for grades. She was a second year art major.

"Now, Beth," she told me, "since we're going to be living together I think it's important that we communicate. I need to know what kind of music you like. I mean I'm not really into Iron Butterfly and that kind of thing, but if you are, we can work out hours and stuff. I'm into July Collins and Dylan. Also, is it going to hang you up if I burn incense? It relaxes my mind and stimulates creativity."

"No, incense is fine with me. I don't mind about the music either, whatever you like. I didn't bring any albums. I was sort of wondering, though. Where did you buy your clothes?"

Belinda wore an Indian print cotton skirt and crocheted top, and her arms were adorned with bangles and bracelets that looked as though an entire family of gypsies had struck a deal with her. I felt conspicuously out of fashion in my loafers and straight skirt, and was tempted to dispose of my suitcases without even unpacking them.

"Oh, I make my clothes. It's easy—I'll show you how. You just have to get some bedspreads at the head shop in town."

In a couple of weeks I was using Belinda's sewing machine to make skirts out of bedspreads. I discarded my penny loafers for a pair of leather boots I'd found at a secondhand store. They were already scuffed and worn when I bought them, giving the impression that I'd been dressing this way for years.

English was my intended major, and I registered for classes in contemporary lit, creative writing, and modern poetry. The poetry class was soon my favorite. When the instructor, Wilder Hayes, was enthusiastic about something—which was almost all the time—he gesticulated frantically, as if his arms could draw pictures in the air. He'd tug at his frizzy brown hair as if to pull from his brain the words that temporarily eluded him. After each class he was deluged by students who wanted to ask him questions, dispute his interpretation of a poem, or pursue into infinity some point he'd made in passing. His brow would furrow and his eyes widen with intensity when he pointed to the student and announced, "I'm glad you asked that," before delivering his feverish rejoinder. Or he'd scratch his head, fold his arms, and say, "Let's explore that for a moment—it's something I've always wondered about myself."

Throughout this he would gradually gather his papers and close his briefcase until he was finally ready to leave the room, at which time his entourage would accompany him out into the corridor, through the building, and across campus to his office, the group getting smaller as students were satisfied and went about their business. I imagined that by the time he got to his office there would be that one last student waiting it out for his or her chance. Whenever I saw Wilder Hayes around campus, in the dining hall, on the quad, or walking to his class, he was surrounded—a tall, slim figure with a bushy head protruding from a band of eager followers, not unlike the gaggle of reporters and photographers that trailed my father everywhere from the steps of the Capitol to the restaurants where he dined to the lawn outside our church. I sometimes wondered if one day while my father was in the shower, soaping his back with the tortoiseshell long-handled scrubber my mother had bought him and singing, "It's a Long Way to Tipperary" slightly off-key, the window would pop open and some enterprising journalist on top of a ladder would appear and say, "Excuse me, Governor, but about that new garbage collection bill—"

The one person I'd been hoping to meet from my first day on campus remained a mystery. Asking around I learned that Alicia Washington was a junior, a political science major, and the organizing force behind all campus demonstrations. But I hadn't found anyone who had met her, or who knew anything about her personally. One night Belinda came in and said, "Guess who I saw down at the union? The lady you've been wanting to see. I think they were holding a meeting or something."

I began taking my books down to the student union each night, ostensibly to study, but after too many evenings and far too many cups of watery coffee, I still hadn't met Alicia.

One night, as I sat at a table staring into my textbooks, I overheard some students in the next booth.

"All I can say is we're lucky we're not on a campus in California."

"Yeah," another chimed in, "Canfield would probably have us shot for protesting. That's what it's coming to, man. He's just gonna call out the National Guard and have everyone blown away."

I slid down in the booth, and felt a throbbing in my head. Once, on a plane to Sacramento, my mother heard the passengers behind her lambasting my father. She turned around, kneeling on her seat to face them, and "really gave them a piece of my mind," she told me. "I won't let anyone talk that way about your father."

Laughter came from the next booth. I felt hurt to hear my father maligned, but, at the same time, was I able to defend him? I continued staring at my books.

Finally one evening I spotted Alicia, huddled in a booth with a few others, their heads together in quiet conversation. A girl from the group got up and began handing out leaflets. I walked over to get one, and saw that it was an announcement for an antiwar rally the following afternoon. One of the speakers scheduled was a member of SDS who, during the march on the Pentagon in 1967, had been beaten and tear-gassed by police and had later written a book about his ordeal. Another speaker was Alicia.

Belinda didn't want to go to the rally. She said large groups weren't her thing. There was no one else I knew well enough to ask, so I went alone. A couple of hundred people had gathered out on the quad in front of the administration building; only a small percentage of the school's population, but a crowd nevertheless. Some held signs reading STOP THE BOMBING and HELL NO, WE WON'T GO. Someone had taken the slogan from the recruiting poster—MARINES MAKE MEN—and added the word DEAD in dripping red paint.

By the time Alicia's turn came to speak, dusk had chilled the air and the wind gathered to shake leaves from the trees; they blew past our faces and stuck to our sweaters. I remembered an autumn visit to Illinois, where my mother grew up; I rolled around in piles of leaves the gardener had raked up. My mother knelt down beside me and picked them off my sweater and out of my hair.

Alicia Washington was tall and strong and erect. I immediately recognized the manner—impassioned, forceful, and seductive—with which she had quietly decimated the vice president on television the first time I had seen her. She spoke in carefully constructed sentences about genocide overseas, about an immoral war, which had not even been declared a war.

"Do you know that napalm sticks to whatever it is thrown onto, that it literally melts the flesh?" The audience was dead silent. "Have you seen the pictures of little children with flesh running down their faces onto their chests? Do you know that eight-hundred-pound containers of napalm are being dropped into Vietcong trenches and tunnels where it sucks out the oxygen, so that whoever is inside suffocates if they don't burn to death first? If you know that this is the kind of war we are waging, then you must not tolerate it. This is not a war that can be won, and it must be stopped!''

When she finished her speech, I made my way over and waited for some of the people to drift away. As the number of people between us dwindled I got an unexpected case of stage fright and found myself retreating into the crowd. I felt like a fan at a rock concert hanging around the stage door; maybe this wasn't a good time to approach her after all. Before turning to go I looked her way one last time, and found her looking directly at me. Someone I didn't recognize was whispering in her ear as she caught my eye, and in seconds she was headed in my direction.

''I heard you want to meet me,'' she said, extending her hand.

''Well . . . yes, that's right.'' I shook her hand. ''My name is Beth. Beth Canfield.''

''I heard that, too,'' she said. ''You're not what I would have expected.'' She was looking over my clothes.

I smiled. ''I'm probably not what my parents expected, either.''

She laughed, a radiant gesture that changed her face and made her somber speech of moments ago evaporate in the night air.

''Listen,'' she said, ''we should talk sometime. I'll give you my home number. I live in an apartment just off campus. What dorm are you in?''

When I got back to my room, I copied her phone number down in three separate places, and all that night felt overwhelmed by a feeling of being on the brink of something I had anticipated for weeks, months, years. I didn't sleep.

I reread the letter I had received from Greg just before leaving for Mountclaire. I knew that it was I who should have asked *his* forgiveness. I realized how selfishly I had acted at the airport and how, by lashing out at him, I'd wasted the few hours we had together. As time passed, the hurt I felt when he told me he'd extended his tour was hard to understand, harder to justify, leaving me with an overwhelming sense of regret and sadness. Now it would be six more months before I could see his face again, and hear his voice and his laughter, and tell him how much

I loved him. It would be six months before I could look into his eyes, the one part of him that had told me, perhaps against his will, of his anguish. I wrote him that the only thing in the world I cared about was seeing him come home.

Alicia was usually surrounded by a small group of students who functioned as advisers and coworkers. Jake was a sophomore majoring in law. No one knew exactly how much money had been left to him by his stepfather, a millionaire industrialist, but Jake used his trust fund to travel to other campuses and bring back information on the latest strategies. Dissension between him and Alicia erupted periodically when Jake advocated violent demonstrations to "up the ante," only to be overruled by Alicia's insistence that peaceful demonstrations alone would be effective. Jake smoked Shermans, bit his nails, and was never without his spiral notebook of facts and observations.

Trina grew up in Brooklyn and spoke with a thick New York accent. She had chosen as her uniform a pair of faded overalls and an assortment of tattered sweaters and men's Pendleton's. Somewhere along the line she had abandoned her bra, casting her voluminous breasts adrift beneath her bulky clothing. The males in the group seemed oblivious to this, as if only revolution consumed them. Trina saw herself as Alicia's aide-de-camp, always on the alert to perform whatever function was required of her.

Dennis had studied revolutions; he could reel off facts and details of any movement in the country for the last two centuries. With silky blond hair that fell to his shoulders and eyes the color of the sea, he looked as though he would be more at home on a beach in California looking for the perfect wave. Perhaps that's where he would have been had he not chosen to shun his upper-middle-class background in Orange County and join the movement.

I had seen Jamal in Wilder Hayes's poetry class; his deep voice parted the room with his inquiry as to whether or not we would be studying LeRoi Jones. The answer was "of course." On another campus Jamal would have been a member of the Black Panthers, but there was no chapter at Mountclaire. He frequently drew parallels between the war and the treatment of blacks in the U.S. A large number of blacks ended up in Vietnam, with no chance for student deferments, and Jamal pointed to this as another example of the way blacks were made to do the white man's dirty work. "Hey, it's like the man said, no Vietcong ever called us nigger.'' I never figured out exactly who the man was who said that, but the expression found its way often onto placards and in arguments.

When Alicia first brought me to a meeting, the others eyed me suspiciously, as if trying to sniff out any signs that the enemy had infiltrated them. Jamal looked at me with hard eyes and asked, ''How many blacks your folks got slavin' for em?''

''None,'' I said, wondering if Ramona, our laundress, and DeLese, our housekeeper, and Harry, our handyman, all civil servants on the state payroll, ever regarded themselves as slave labor.

Trina seemed the most willing to accept me, probably because Alicia brought me. Eager to prove myself and to gain their confidence, I went to the printer's to have leaflets and fliers made up, spent hours passing them out, made phone calls, and ran errands. I got a book of LeRoi Jones's poetry and discussed it with Jamal, hoping he would forgive me for being white, as well as for other aspects of my heritage. Gradually I put in enough hours and showed enough dedication to abate their suspicions, which gave way to amusement at the addition of a governor's daughter to their group. Jamal, however, remained distant.

Alicia watched this initiation process with her usual, calm, detached air. She had a way of remaining grounded and analytical, letting everything buzz around her but never losing control. It was for this reason that the final objective word was always hers, and for this reason that everyone, including me, was drawn to her.

She put her arm around me and said, ''Well, kid, I guess you're in. They're a tough bunch, but I always knew you'd make it.'' My convictions about the war had been growing on their own, but now I felt they could grow as part of a movement that had a chance to change the country.

On several occasions I walked through the lounge area of the dorm and saw students talking, laughing, smoking, paying no attention to the television in the corner that was bringing images of anguished faces and wounded bodies right into their midst. Flames billowed through the jungle half a world away, leaving human wreckage behind. Flashed across the screen were faces contorted with pain or masked with wide grins that did little to conceal the fear underneath—haunted faces that had lived lifetimes in a few short months. But in this dorm lounge it was just background, no more distracting than Muzak would have been.

I wondered if the scene was similar in homes across the country. Did people fix dinner, make love, diaper their children, oblivious to the grisly events being played out in their living rooms?

Trina and I talked about it one day, as I watched her embroider a peace symbol on her sweatshirt. "I guess I'm kinda jaded about the fact that other people are jaded, you know? And I can tell you exactly when that started happening, too. November 1965. I came home from school and on the evening news they were saying that that afternoon a Quaker—to protest the war—had stood near the Pentagon, doused himself with kerosene, and set himself on fire. He was in full view of McNamara's office and all these office workers saw it, but it was too late for anyone to save him. My mother came in and said, 'Turn off the TV, Trina, it's time for dinner.' I tried to tell her what had happened—that this was more important than dinner. but she just walked over and turned off the set and said, 'We don't watch TV during dinner.' I couldn't believe it, man. This guy was so opposed to the war that he had turned himself into a human torch and all she could think about was her fucking pot roast."

On phone calls home, I said little about who my friends were or what I was up to, but as usual that didn't prevent them from "hearing" things. One Sunday afternoon, with the sun shining through the prisms Belinda had hung in our windows, I listened to my mother as she said, "Elizabeth, it appears you've managed to align yourself with quite a radical element there."

I watched rainbows dance across the walls and make little puddles of color on the phone that was transporting this long-distance confrontation.

"What are you talking about, Mom? I don't remember mentioning that I had aligned myself with anyone."

I felt her pause patiently. "Surely you must realize that because of who your father is, you're a highly visible person. If you attend these demonstrations and such, you can be certain it won't go unnoticed."

"Is that how I'm supposed to spend my four years at college? Going unnoticed?"

"All I'm asking is that you keep your father in mind when you choose your friends and your activities. Think of how it reflects on him. Is that too much to ask?"

"I don't know yet, Mom."

On Mondays I had no morning classes, so if I could endure Belinda's drawer slamming and the clanking of her jewelry, I was rewarded with a couple of extra hours of sleep. On this particular day I woke up around nine, and made my way sleepily down the hall to the showers. When I came back I found Dennis sprawled on my unmade bed reading a newspaper.

"Hi, Dennis, make yourself at home." I unwound the towel from my head and shook my wet hair, spraying him with water.

"Hey, watch it! I figured you were somewhere nearby since the door was open."

Men were not allowed upstairs in the women's dorms. It was one of those rules that were written somewhere—no one was quite sure where—and looked great on paper, but probably hadn't been enforced for the last ten years.

"What's on your mind, Dennis?"

"Have you read the paper this morning?"

"No, I just got up." I sat opposite him on Belinda's bed, rubbing my hair with the towel. He handed me the newspaper.

"You better read this." He grabbed a rubber band off my dresser and started pulling his hair into a ponytail. The story he handed me was on the front page.

In the wake of student demonstrations and sit-ins that threaten to close down many of California's campuses, Governor Robert Canfield stated today that schools will stay open "at gunpoint if necessary." In a press conference . . .

I handed the paper back to him, and went back to my closet for something to wear.

"Is that it?" he wanted to know. "Aren't you going to finish reading?"

"I got the gist of it."

"Alicia asked me to show it to you. She thinks you'll probably get calls about it from some of the papers. She was already called this morning. They know you're friends with her."

I guess I had finally gotten used to the fact that my life was an open book, because this last remark didn't faze me.

"She didn't make a statement, but she thought we should tell you about it."

"Well, I don't plan to make a statement, either."

He stood up. "Can't play ostrich forever, kid. Well, I got a class."

Before I finished getting dressed the phone rang.

"Beth Canfield?"

"Yes?"

It was a reporter from the same Chicago paper that Dennis had shown me, and he just wanted to ask me "a few questions."

"I have no comment," I told him.

"Your politics are quite the opposite of your father's," he went on. "We know you've been active here in—"

"I said I have no comment."

"Have you discussed this with your father?"

I hung up. I knew Dennis was right, but it was all happening too fast.

I finally reached Alicia in the late afternoon, after being unable to find her all day. We sat in her apartment, amid the clutter of pamphlets and yellow notepads, drinking instant coffee.

"If the rest of us demonstrate—that's one thing, Beth. We're nobodies. But they're going to focus on you because you're more newsworthy. You better get used to it, and you better figure out how to handle it. You won't always be able to say 'no comment' and hang up, especially if your father has the aspirations most of us think he has."

I gave her a puzzled look.

"Don't tell me it hasn't occurred to you that he might run for president?"

I had the unnerving feeling that it had occurred to me a long time ago, when I began falling off my chair at the dinner table.

It was November 10, 1969. We had scheduled a huge demonstration for Saturday, the fifteenth, to coincide with the final day of the March Against Death in Washington, D.C. More than fifty thousand people were expected to protest in front of the White House, each carrying a sign bearing the name of an American serviceman killed in Vietnam or a village that had been destroyed. Jake, the only one among us with ready cash, was flying to Washington on Wednesday to join the march. The rest of us organized the demonstration at Mountclaire.

Anyone who was at all prominent in the antiwar movement was going to be in Washington, so we scheduled local speakers and musicians. Our fires were fueled by a story that broke in the newspapers on Thursday. A Vietnam vet had written to government officials with a horrific story of the massacre of Vietnamese civilians in a hamlet called My Lai, in March 1968. Each day more on the story appeared, and as it spread through campus so did support for the demonstration and a renewed commitment to our cause.

My days were swamped with preparations and details, my nights tormented by thoughts not only of the victims of the massacre, but of Greg. For so long my one hope was that he would come back alive, but if he were to become part of a tragedy such as this one, what would his life be worth? Breathing or not, did any soldier get out alive?

Jake called us on Friday night from Washington.

"There were a few arrests, but for the most part everything's going smoothly. Looks like they're prepared for something, though. I see a lot of cops around—and a lot of Secret Service. Maybe they think we're going to storm the White House."

At noon on Saturday people started gathering at the administration building. There were more than we'd expected, and not only students. The massacre at My Lai had enraged housewives, grandmothers, and an entire conservative-looking contingent from town. One neatly dressed middle-aged woman held a placard that read TYRANNY HAS ALWAYS DEPENDED ON A SILENT MAJORITY.

These weren't the only new faces that day. A few men lingered on the outskirts of the crowd, conspicuous because of their dark suits and because they never applauded the speakers along with the rest of the crowd. They just observed from behind their dark glasses. As the last speaker got up, I saw one of the men take out a camera and start photographing the crowd. Trina came over to me and said, "Smile—you just got your picture in the FBI files." I looked around. "Over there," she said, pointing blatantly, "Mr. White Socks."

She wasn't joking about the socks, and I didn't care about the picture. The crowd began to chant, ONE, TWO, THREE, FOUR, WE DON'T WANT THIS BLOODY WAR! My voice rose to become part of the hundreds of voices until it became hoarse and tears filled my eyes. I thrust my fist into the air with the hundreds of other fists, felt my heart pound with the stomping of feet on the ground beneath me, and gave myself willingly to something inside me that for too long had only been a dream.

⋆ *11* ⋆

T HE END OF THE YEAR WOULD BRING AN END TO GREG'S extended tour in Vietnam; my prayers for him became urgent and frightened. As time wound down, the weeks dragged infuriatingly, as if stalling for one last opportunity to seal his fate. Some days it seemed that time had stopped altogether, to freeze him in an eternity on the other side of the world. When I stared at the calendar above my desk it felt like a contest of wills; if I had to glare at its pages incessantly to make sure the year came to a close, I was determined to do it.

The nippy November days passed with no letters from him. He had warned me that he would be writing less frequently; he said he sometimes felt that his days were repeating themselves, that he was running out of things to say, or that when he did write something down, he couldn't tell if it was what he really meant to say. I kept writing throughout this dry spell, filling my letters with hope and praying he wouldn't notice how frightened I was that in his last days, moments, seconds, the worst would happen. You're almost home, I reminded him; soon it will be over for good. But I wondered if it would. Maybe wars never end for those who fight them.

Jake, the youngest of Alicia's disciples, found himself watching the calendar, too. December 1 marked the beginning of the draft lottery. We began meeting for coffee to console and reas-

sure each other that everything would be all right, though neither of us had any reason to assume it would be. We'd sit in the
union making jokes and talking strong, in control of our lives,
pretending not to notice that we had absolutely no control over
what happened to us. Strings would be pulled, and we would be
on the ends of those strings, and all the commiserating in the
world wasn't going to change it. Nevertheless, we sat, and from
time to time managed to make each other smile.

There was a bar off campus called Stairway to Heaven. One
night Jake and I got high and decided, at ten-thirty, to walk the
three miles there. We finished ourselves off with a pitcher of beer
at a little round table in the corner, amid sawdust on the floor
and the Strawberry Alarm Clock on the jukebox. We hitchhiked
back in the snow trying to sing "Mrs. Robinson" from *The Graduate,* which we'd seen in town the week before, and since we
couldn't remember most of the words we kept going back to
"And here's to you, Mrs. Robinson ..."

Alicia invited me to go with her for the weekend to visit her
parents. Grateful for a chance to forget the tension that the
upcoming lottery had created on campus, I said yes.

The Washingtons lived on the outskirts of Chicago in a neighborhood where the local grocery store was a converted garage.
The only evidence that their house had once been white was the
chips of paint that clung stubbornly to otherwise naked wood.

Mrs. Washington appeared from behind a clothesline where
sheets billowed in the afternoon breeze. She came toward the car
with outstretched arms.

"Lisha, it's so good to see you. How are you, baby?"

"Fine, Mama, this is—"

"I know, I know, this is Beth. Welcome. It's not much, but
we're real glad you're here. Well, come on in. Alicia, your father's inside."

We carried some groceries in that we'd bought and set them
on the kitchen table.

"Oh, you shouldn't have done this. My Lord, look at all this
food! Well, we sure eat better when Alicia comes home. Poppa,
Poppa, where are you? The girls are here!"

Mr. Washington was a tall, wiry man. He used all of his
concentration to move his feet, but when he sat down he came
alive.

"We're so proud of our Lisha," he said, easing himself down in his favorite chair after a dinner of meat loaf and baked beans. "I knew when she was just a little thing, somehow she'd go to college. I just knew it. You know, I was a janitor for goin' on thirty years—the only thing I could do without good schooling —but Lisha, I knew she'd amount to good. She was the smartest thing I ever saw. I remember one day this little white girl knocked her down and pulled all the ribbons outa her hair. Alicia came home with her hair stickin' out every which way and her dress all torn and she sat down and wrote the girl a letter saying how she shouldn't treat folks like that just 'cause they're different."

"Come on, Poppa," Alicia said. She put her hand on his shoulder. "You're making me sound like an angel." I'd never seen Alicia's face look so soft. It was clear how much she loved being there.

"Poppa, do you remember that vegetable garden we used to have?"

"Oh, I remember," Mrs. Washington cut in. "Lisha decided she'd help us put food on the table so she got some seeds and started herself a garden. I don't think she realized how much work it would be, though. She kind of lost interest after a while."

"There was one day," Alicia said, "Mama, you'd asked me a lot of times to go out and pull the weeds. It was my responsibility, but I was playing or something and I didn't do it. I looked out the window and there was Poppa in his good suit squatting down in the garden pulling up the weeds that I was supposed to have taken care of. Do you remember that, Poppa?"

"Nope, don't think so."

"It hurt me so much that I'd been so irresponsible." She looked out the window for a long moment.

Alicia insisted that I sleep in her bed. She spread out a sleeping bag on the floor for herself. The next day we walked around the neighborhood where she'd grown up. She told me how she used to look at the people there, barely making it and working so hard to get by, and she made up her mind that someday she'd be able to help them.

"Poppa used to say 'Alicia, you're the smart one, you go to college and be a lawyer or something important.' And now I'm trying to do just that."

"Do they ever disagree with your politics, Alicia?"

"I don't know. If they do, they don't say anything. I think they're just so proud that I stand up for what I think is right that it doesn't matter if they agree or not."

We drove back to Mountclaire Sunday night. The warmth of the Washingtons' home had seeped through my skin and curled up inside me, but there was a sadness there, too. The pride they showed in their daughter was the one thing I had always wanted and had never known; it was a hunger that couldn't be satisfied. I was about to tell her how lucky she was, but I was sure she already knew.

A container filled with 365 white balls, each marked with a date of the year, was the vehicle designed to assign lottery numbers to every draft-age man in America. This struck me as a perversely game-showlike approach to a subject that was deadly serious. Did they plan to lighten things up with a television host as master of ceremonies, bathing beauties in bouffant hairdos to withdraw the numbers, banks of flashing lights to erupt like a Vegas marquee every time a new one was selected? On the morning of December 1, 1969, we gathered in Alicia's apartment to witness the event on a portable black-and-white television atop two crates of books. It was all happening in Washington, D.C. Each birthdate carried with it a number; those with low numbers could start saying their goodbyes right away. In the middle range there was a fifty-fifty chance of being called, and the boys with high numbers could breathe easily.

Trina and I had gone out earlier to buy firewood, and with Girl Scout efficiency created a blaze in Alicia's fireplace. I looked past the flames and out the window. Christmas decorations were strung from the street lamps, and a light snow was falling—an incongruous setting for such a somber vigil. Jamal sat on the floor with his back to the wall, waiting. Dennis tried to read a magazine. Alicia sat in a big old overstuffed chair nursing a cup of tea, watching the screen intently. Trina paced, sat, and paced. I sat on the rug next to Jake's chair, my arm resting on his knee. I suggested that later we could go out and buy a Christmas tree. Nobody responded. The next moment, Washington's game of roulette discharged a full chamber in Jake's direction: He was number seven.

We all turned to face him. "I'll go to Canada," he said grimly. "I fight nobody's fucking war."

Dennis bolted up from his chair. "Listen, Jake, we'll go to my old man. He pushes politicians around all the time. Maybe he can pull some strings for us."

"Goddamn!" said Jamal, "this ain't no lottery, this is fixed. This ain't no random selection. His number came up because they know what he's doin' for the movement and they want him the hell out. You wait and see, they're gonna try and do it to all of us, everyone who's tryin' to stop the war. Just wait and see if any straight little rich kids get called."

"Jake *is* a rich kid," I reminded him.

"He's different. He's a troublemaker and they want him out." Jamal's bellowing voice was nothing if not authoritative, but I knew he was wrong about this. It was nothing more than bad luck.

"I'll be in Canada so fast they'll think I never existed," Jake said.

"You won't have to," I pleaded. His angry eyes stared into space. "You won't have to leave the country, Jake. There has got to be another way out. I know we can find a way."

"Oh, yeah?" said Jamal. "I suppose you'll just get on the phone with the Governor of California and see if he could do a little favor for his daughter."

"Go to hell, Jamal!"

"My, my, my, sensitive, aren't we? I'm right, ain't I? I mean you got the privilege, so why not take advantage of it? You'd be a fool not to."

"Listen, Jamal, I'm no different from anyone else in this room. We're all fighting against this war and that makes us equal as far as I'm concerned. What my father happens to do for a living has nothing to do with it."

"Convince yourself, baby. It's not my problem."

"That's enough, you two," Alicia said. I turned away from him.

Time stretched out endlessly as we waited the remaining numbers. Both Dennis and Jamal drew high. So much for Jamal's theory.

Jake had always given the impression that he needed no one, which, if finances were the issue, would easily pass as the truth. He had money, he had a brilliant mind, and—to hear him tell it —enough information on every aspect of revolution to single-handedly start one in any country at any time. But something funny happened to him when he was dealt a bad card; he started needing people. The one who had never made phone calls—people usually had to call him if they wanted to talk to him—began reaching out, especially to me.

I told him I would find a way to help him and I meant it. From Alicia I obtained the names of two lawyers who helped boys evade the draft. I felt certain that one of them would be able to help Jake. Draft evasion had become a routine procedure and Jake's case should be no exception.

It took me days to get through to them by phone; evidently others who had been stung with low numbers had the same idea. I was so grateful finally to get the first lawyer on the line that from the excitement in my voice he probably thought I was a crank. I told him about Jake's predicament and waited for his offer to set up an appointment.

"I'd love to help your friend out, Miss Canfield, but..." I was so flustered by his refusal that it took a minute or two to hear his reason: He was swamped with draft cases and couldn't possibly handle one more. The second lawyer offered the same apologies. After assuring Jake that these lawyers could help us out, I dreaded having to tell him it was a dead end. I pleaded with the second lawyer to take just one more case; what could one more mean after so many? But he refused. "You don't understand," he said. "I get calls like yours every day." He did offer, though, to make a phone call to a psychiatrist he knew, but the doctor declined to sign his name to any false statement; apparently he had done it before and his credibility was now in jeopardy. But he did offer some off-the-record advice as to Jake's options. When I went to Jake's room to break the bad news to him about the lawyers, I quickly followed it with good news—or news I tried to make sound good—from the psychiatrist.

"Now let me get this straight," Jake said, pacing the floor. "This shrink says I should act berserk. Berserk, huh? Well, that shouldn't be too difficult because I *am* berserk—perhaps you've noticed. Maybe I'm overreacting, but hell, I can't help it. This is the way I get when I think of being blown to bits in some hellhole on the other side of the world. Hey, maybe I'm oversensitive—whaddaya think?"

"Jake—"

"No, wait. Then he says I should go berserk but not *too* berserk, because then they'll know I'm faking. Well, I guess that lets me out. They're gonna take one look at me and say, 'This guy's a lying s.o.b.—draft his ass!' "

"Jake, you're upset now. You think I don't understand that? But after you've calmed down you'll be able to—"

"Oh, and his second suggestion—my 'other option' as he put it—I like even better. Act like a faggot, make a pass at the induction officer. That's cool all right, I like that one. I can just see having that on my record for the rest of my life."

"Jake, be reasonable! Is it worse than getting killed? What was it that you were just saying a minute ago about getting blown to bits? Would you like that better?" I sighed. "I'm sorry, Jake. This whole thing is making me crazy."

"Making you crazy? Well, relax. *You* won't get drafted." It was hard not to feel guilty about that: being protected by something as accidental as gender from a war that was taking the lives of thousands of boys my age.

"Well, what about his third suggestion?" I said. "That didn't sound like such a bad idea."

"Oh, the one about the blood? I should pretend the sight of blood makes me puke? That's another brilliant idea. I can just hear the officer. 'Son, you're right, that is a terrible problem. And a year on the front lines is the perfect cure'!"

"You hate all the shrink's suggestions," I responded. "Have you got a better idea, short of running off to Canada or spending the next few years in jail?"

Jake walked to the window and looked out. In the distance the football field was deserted and frozen. He sat down at his desk and put his head in his hands.

"We're going to find a way, Jake. We'll think of something."

I tried to think positively about seeing my parents over the Christmas vacation, but I wasn't looking forward to it. Mountclaire's holiday officially began on December 15, but I didn't leave school until the twentieth. I told my mother I had some tests to make up, which was untrue. Also untrue was my explanation for taking a cab home instead of being met at the airport by the limo. I told her all the flights were booked and I was on standby, and had no idea what time I'd be getting in.

The taxi pulled up to the iron gates that surrounded our house. When the security guard came out and peered into the back seat, the driver turned around and squinted at me. "You gotta be kiddin'. You live here or just visiting?"

"Just visiting," I told him. "My mother does the cleaning here." He looked at my long, stringy hair and the wool hat I'd bought at the Salvation Army.

"Thought so," he said.

I rang the doorbell and heard my mother's high heels clipping along the black slate hallway.

"Well, there you are, Elizabeth." She kissed my cheek and promptly wiped off the lipstick she'd left behind. "We were just finishing lunch. Would you like me to have a plate fixed for you?"

"No, I ate on the plane. I think I'll go unpack. Is Brian here?"

"He's at a friend's house."

I took my time putting away my clothes, hoping the afternoon would pass quickly, but looking at the clock every ten minutes didn't help. A few more things were missing from my room since my last visit—specifically, the clothes that my mother had long ago deemed "ready for the rag bin," just as I was breaking them in.

I took out a copy of Eldridge Cleaver's *Soul on Ice* that I'd begun on the plane, contemplated hiding it, but instead tossed it on the bed where it would be in full view of whoever happened to walk in—most likely my mother, who had a habit of patrolling the house at regular intervals.

"Elizabeth, why don't you come down and visit with us a bit. We'd like to know about your new school." She glanced at the book, but didn't break her smile.

"Mom, you know what I'd like for Christmas?"

"What, dear?"

"I'd like you to start calling me by my name, which is Beth."

"Of course, Elizabeth, if that's what you want."

I gave them what I thought was a sufficiently unprovocative account of my life at Mountclaire. My classes were interesting, my friends were nice, the dorm was pleasant, the weather was fine . . .

"And your friend Greg?" asked my father. "Is he back yet?"

"I don't know. He's supposed to be back in the States anytime now, but I haven't heard from him yet."

I hoped that I would be hearing from Greg soon. It was now seven weeks since I'd had a letter, but I was concentrating on the fact that soon I would be seeing him, that all the waiting would finally be over. At any second the phone could ring and I would hear his voice.

That night after dinner, my father had a visitor. "Beth," he said, "you remember Jeb Henley." He was my father's campaign manager. "We have some business to discuss, so if you don't mind leaving us alone in the den here ..."

Brian was watching "Hogan's Heroes" in his room. I sat down on the floor beside him, but after about ten minutes the temptation to eavesdrop was more than I could resist. "Brian, don't you want to know what they're talking about in there?" We walked quietly out of the room and across the hall to the den. Our mother was downstairs in her study. We stood by the closed door and listened to their muffled voices.

"Governor, we've been keeping track of your daughter's political activities." I heard the click of a briefcase, and the rustling of papers. "Here's a photo we obtained from the FBI, taken at a recent antiwar demonstration." Trina was right—old Mr. White Socks got his picture. I could just imagine it: one of those fuzzy blowups with a little round blur circled in red, ostensibly my head. "Here we have a file," he went on, "on a gal named Alicia Washington, a Negro gal who organizes all of Mountclaire college's antiwar activities. She claims to advocate peaceful demonstrations, but she's been seen associating with known members of the Black Panthers. Your daughter's been spending all her time with this Washington girl."

Brian giggled and said, "You don't take showers together, do you?"

"Shh."

"You understand, if her involvement in this revolutionary crap continues, it could prove a real liability to you politically. As far as I can see at the moment, it would be your biggest stumbling block, image-wise, if you wanted to go for the presidency." The word "presidency" vibrated through me like a chill. "It won't do for people to think you can't control your own daughter."

"I think it's just a phase, Jeb," my father told him. "You know how teenagers are the minute they get away from home. What puzzles me, though, is that school she's going to. She showed her mother and me the brochure. It looked like such a clean-cut kind of place."

"Well, that's changed, Governor. Even your good schools have these troublemakers nowadays. Goddamn slugs are cropping up everywhere."

"Well, if you feel it's serious, Jeb, I'll discuss it with her."

This was the first more or less official mention I'd heard of my father's possible candidacy for president, and it wasn't even meant for my ears. I went back to the bedroom and turned up the volume on the television.

The next day ticked away like a time bomb. I waited for my father to commence his discussion, and when that wasn't forthcoming I waited for the phone to ring. No call from Greg, no telegram, no letter. Just more waiting.

I had to get out of the house to keep from going crazy, so I took a walk down the street to the Addisons'. Mr. Addison lay napping on the couch under an ocean of newspapers, head sticking out one end and socks protruding from the other. On the television behind his head was a soap opera, in which a woman had just discovered she was pregnant by her husband's friend from high school who had recently been paroled and now worked in the local hardware store. One character explained all this to another in the time it took me to get from the bottom of the staircase to the top, where I was not surprised to smell an incriminating aroma seeping out of Kelly's room.

Status quo, I thought. But once I sat down Kelly was quick to inform me that her hash pipe was no longer merely a recreational indulgence. She explained that after numerous acid trips hash was expanding her consciousness. She offered me a joint, which I took, feeling quite comfortable with it as a recreational indulgence. Whatever consciousness I had was already giving me a headache. As I took two hits and slowly drifted into another time zone, it became more difficult to pay attention to Kelly's lengthy dissertation, which had something to do with mystics and nirvana. When I felt like it was safe to get up, I went home.

On the day before Christmas, I sat in my room reading Cleaver's book. My mother walked in wearing a red wool suit, in a cloud of Jungle Gardenia. This time she looked at the book more closely.

"Good heavens, Elizabeth, isn't that man a convicted rapist?"

"He's paid his debt to society," I told her. That didn't seem to make her feel any better. "Really, Mom, the book has a lot to offer. I'll lend it to you when I'm done."

"Well, I have to go to the dedication ceremony for a new

hospital wing. Why don't you come along with me? I'd like some company.''

Dedicating a hospital wing seemed harmless enough and it was obvious that I had no other plans, so I got dressed and followed her out to the driveway where the limousine waited to claim us.

''I think you'll be glad you came, Elizabeth,'' she said, smoothing an invisible wrinkle from her skirt. ''This hospital has been treating some of the more seriously injured boys from Vietnam and doing some wonderful things for them. This new wing was built completely from private donations.''

I didn't say anything. I was thinking of boys with smooth faces and white teeth lying in beds where their feet would have once hung over the end, only now their legs ended at the knees, or the hips. And I was thinking about Greg's strong, gentle hands, and about boys whose hands were left to rot somewhere in the jungle while the rest of them came home.

''Elizabeth, are you all right? You're not coming down with anything, are you?''

''I'm okay.''

As we pulled up to the hospital I could see a roped-off area with people crowded behind it. We were taken inside where dark-suited men and primly dressed women bustled around, frantically offering us food, drink, chairs, or ''anything at all, don't hesitate to ask.''

When we were led outside again, the crowd had grown. I could see signs reading CANFIELD OILS WAR MACHINE and GOVERNOR HAWK, and noise swelled up from the crowd as soon as we stepped into view.

The ceremony began as it was supposed to, with introductory remarks from a bald-headed man with a carnation in his lapel. But no one could hear him. The noise from the crowd was getting louder, and more signs were thrust at the sky. Suddenly objects started flying through the air. A tomato landed inches from my mother's feet, exploding red pulp on her Gucci shoes. I didn't dare look at anyone, not the crowd, and certainly not at my mother. We were whisked back inside and, amid a torrent of apologies, led out through a back exit.

In the limousine, my mother stared straight ahead. There was probably something I could have said, but I had no idea what it might be. Finally she looked over at me and said, ''How can you do this to us? Don't you have any feelings of family loyalty?''

''Do what? Mom, I wasn't out there throwing things at you.''

"Well, you may as well have been. These are the types of people with whom you've chosen to associate yourself. You have no idea how much you hurt your father when you participate in these ... demonstrations." She was clutching the handle of her purse so tightly that her knuckles were bluish-white. "I've tried to give your father a good home life, and you and Brian, too. Families should stick together," she continued, "but you just insist on ruining it. We were so happy when you were born. You were such a lovely little girl. . . . What went wrong? Why did this happen? I don't know when it happened, but you just changed. And then it was one problem after another."

"Mom, look, I don't know what to say to you. It's too bad about what happened today. But just because I stand up for my beliefs doesn't mean I'm responsible for the actions of everyone else who has those same beliefs."

"You don't have to keep repeating what you call your beliefs! By now, the entire country knows how you feel. You don't need to keep attending these rallies and ... and letting it all hang out, for heaven's sake."

"Mom, you don't change things by saying something once and then shutting your mouth. I'm quite sure you wouldn't accept that advice if it were directed at Dad. I have every right to speak out against what I think is wrong, and to keep speaking out until it's changed."

"We have never denied you your right to believe what you want. But when you start publicizing your opinions and throwing this family into turmoil, and humiliating us, I—" Her voice broke off and she reached in her purse for a handkerchief. She turned back to me after a minute and, her voice softer now, said, "Don't you understand, Elizabeth? We're all entitled to our opinions, but it doesn't mean we have the right to express them anywhere anytime. With a father in a position like your father is in, there are other things that are more important. And there are sacrifices we must make as a family because these things *are* more important. If only I could make you understand. . . ."

When we got home, I went into Brian's room and told him what had happened. I knew the same story was being related to my father behind their closed door.

A few minutes later, I heard my father's footsteps. "Beth, could you come into our room, please? We'd like to have a word with you." He filled up the doorway, the way he had when I was little and couldn't sleep. The door would open and light would spill in, and then it would be dark again, with only strips of yellow lamplight around his body, large and comforting in the open door.

I went into their room and took my usual seat next to the fire.

"Well, Beth," my father said, "what do you have to say about what happened today? Unless I'm mistaken, and I don't think I am, this is the group you've chosen to affiliate yourself with, people who use an innocent event like the opening of a hospital wing to hurl obscenities and—"

My mother looked up at him. "You should have heard some of the words they used, Robert. I never in my life . . ."

He patted her on the shoulder. "I know, dear. Beth, there is such a thing as guilt by association."

"Well, there shouldn't be. Dad, I can't control every person or every faction of the antiwar movement. I'm trying to work against something I believe is wrong."

"That's what you think, but you're being duped by outside agitators—members of the Communist Party. They're playing all of you for fools. I can't tell you how it frustrates your mother and me that you can't see that."

"Excuse me, but I am not a fool! We didn't just arbitrarily decide to be against this war! This is an immoral war and we're dedicated to proving that. If anyone is being fooled, it's the American public which is being lied to about the real motives behind the war."

"Oh, Elizabeth." My mother sniffed, a new wave of tears about to crest. "Where did you get *that?*"

I stood up to go. "Why is it that every time I express an idea you don't like I must have heard it or picked it up somewhere? I do have a mind, you know. I can think for myself!"

"Now don't use that tone of voice with me, young lady. I have been abused and heckled by some of your 'comrades' today. I will not sit here and be smart-mouthed by my own daughter!"

"Harriet, I'll handle this," my father said firmly. "Beth, sit down." I obeyed. "You and your friends are wrong. It's as simple as that. What you are doing is playing right into the hands of people who want to undermine this country. Now, I may as well tell you—if I decide at some point to seek higher office, this obsession of yours could prove quite damaging to me."

"If? *If* you seek higher office? Is this your way of telling me you might run for president?"

"Well, I'm not ruling it out."

"I'm glad you finally got around to letting me know," I said, heading for the door.

"You come right back here, young lady!" His voice stopped me. "Can't you see that you and your friends are just going off half-cocked, making fools of yourselves?"

"Dad, can you tell me why it is that everyone praises you for standing up for your beliefs, but when I do the same thing, I'm called a fool?"

"Because that's what you're acting like."

I went back to Brian's room, where I knew he'd been listening from the doorway. "Brian, why don't you ever get into these situations with them? Why is it always me?"

"I don't know. I guess I wouldn't be as much fun to fuck with."

"What's that supposed to mean?" I demanded. But all I got was a smile.

I got my jacket and purse and went back to their room to say I was taking the station wagon to have dinner at an old friend's. Actually there was no old friend, except for the old car itself, which was comforting. I drove into Westwood, walked around, and had dinner in the darkest restaurant I could find. After nursing two glasses of wine, I drove home, knowing my parents would be asleep.

Christmas morning was thick with fog. By a roaring fire, with colored lights blinking in our midst, we began the perfunctory opening of presents. Brian had asked for a black light, and my parents, having no idea what a black light was, bought it for him. In his closet were half a dozen posters just waiting for the right light to bring them to life and transform Brian's room into a Haight-Ashbury haven. I knew he'd be occupied for the rest of the morning. Wanting to escape the empty house between gifts and the arrival of guests, I took the car down to the beach. The streets were still except for the rattling of the station wagon. It was like the sound I used to get by putting playing cards in the spokes of my bicycle wheels.

I walked by the gray, churning sea, glad that mine were the only footprints. It was the kind of day I pictured when I used to dream of living in a lighthouse—days huddled in fog with only the sounds of sea gulls and waves crashing. In my mind a picture came into focus—one I'd painted long ago—of my father sitting in my lighthouse with me, warming his hands by the potbellied stove and listening to the sea. Maybe I'd painted him into too many pictures.

When I got home I went up to my room, and took out my notebook. What emerged was

> *i am afraid*
> *afraid my words,*
> *hollow as matchbooks,*
> *hobble to ashes.*
>
> *i stumble,*
> *heavy with memories*
> *of days somersaulted past—*
> *days swaddled in comfortable hands,*
> *turning to your eyes for seasons.*
> *hours lapped like ocean foam*
> *on the shore of a rooted earth,*
> *dreams were like plump sails*
> *in syrupy sunsets.*
>
> *but they sank*
> *on my breasts and belly—*
> *i bear their bruises.*
>
> *accept these words,*
> *born of a night*
> *huddled in the milkweed distance*
> *as dawn scrapes the lowest star.*

I went in and placed it on my father's desk. Soon the doorbell rang and guests were welcomed. My mother came down the hall to get Brian and me. But when she got to Brian's door I heard, "What's going on in here?" Then her high heels clipped back across the floor and she said, "Robert? Robert, would you come in here for a minute, please?"

"What is it, Harriet? We've got company out here."

"I don't know what's going on in Brian's room! It's all dark and all I can see are fluorescent patterns on the wall, and his teeth!''

My father went down the hall and stood beside her. I watched as he peered into the room.

''Oh, he's all right. He's just ... bending his mind or something. Brian, you all right?''

''Yeah, Dad.''

''Well, do that psychedelic stuff later, would you? Folks are waiting.''

The living room was filled with the sounds of clinking ice cubes and polite laughter. There were some new faces mixed in with the friends and relatives we'd grown accustomed to seeing every Christmas; men I recognized from my father's administration.

Jeb Henley smiled and waved at me, but I pretended not to see him.

Either the conversation moved to us, or we inadvertently moved to it, but Brian and I found ourselves in the midst of a discussion about uranium deposits that were on land currently owned by some Indians.

''I don't even know how they managed to buy this land,'' one senator was saying. ''Private contributions, I think. But they have this commune for wayward Indians there or some damn thing. And there's valuable uranium on that land. We gotta get 'em off so we can mine it.'' He held a cigarette gently between impeccably manicured fingers, and his hairpiece almost matched what was left of his natural hair.

Brian and I looked at each other as if to say, ''Are we going to get into this or not?'' I was hoping he would, being the more diplomatic one.

''Do you know they even have some buffalo there?'' the senator went on. ''Some rock-and-roll singer gave them some buffalo! For God's sake, this is 1969—what the hell are they gonna do with buffalo?''

Brian cleared his throat and said, in his best I'm-being-polite-but-aren't-you-being-an-asshole voice, ''Excuse me, but it seems to me we've taken enough land from the Indians.''

''Young man—I'm sorry, I didn't get your name.''

''Brian Canfield.''

''Oh, you're the governor's son. Well now, I'm sure coming from such a fine background you've been taught the importance of utilizing our natural resources.''

"Yes, sir. I also know how important people's right to private ownership is supposed to be in this country. What would you do if they found uranium under your house and wanted to kick *you* out?"

I should have waited for his answer; it probably would have been a good one. But my teeth had already bitten halfway through my tongue, and I gave in to the pressure.

"What do you need with uranium," I asked, "that justifies kicking people off their own land?"

"Little lady, how do you think these lights work, or your stereo, or your boyfriend's electric guitar? Nuclear power plants, that's how. And just how do you think they function? It all starts with the mining of uranium."

Displaying his usual knack for good timing, Brian said, "Let's get some eggnog, Beth."

We went to the bar and ladled eggnog out of the bowl that had made its annual Christmas appearance.

"People like that make me so mad," I said. "They're so sure they're right."

"Well." Brian shrugged. "I guess we should be used to *that* by now." We both laughed.

"I don't know, maybe they have to be like that," I said. "Maybe they have to see things as split down the middle—right on one side and wrong on the other, and nothing in between. That way they never have to change their minds and they never have to risk being confused. It makes their lives so simple."

"It doesn't hurt in getting elected, either," said Brian. "Who'd vote for some wishy-washy guy who goes around saying, 'Yeah I see your point, but on the other hand . . .' "

I stared into the glass of eggnog. "You're probably right. Everything black and white. It makes life easier. Sometimes I wish I could be like that."

Brian gave me a funny look and then patted me on the shoulder. "You sure you're not?" He escaped before I could respond.

I looked around the crowded room and was surprised to see my father standing by himself. He looked so vulnerable to me all of a sudden, and it was a strange picture—the most important person in the room forgotten for a minute as everyone around him laughed and smoked and slapped one another on the back. Finally I went over to him.

"Hello, Beth. Are you enjoying yourself?"

"Yeah ... Dad, I was wondering if you read that poem I left on your desk."

"Poem? Gee ... you know, there are so many things on my desk, I guess I didn't see it."

Something caught his eye; I looked over and saw Jeb Henley gesturing to him from across the room. Could he possibly have not seen the poem? I had placed it so carefully where I knew he would find it.

"Well," I said, "maybe you'll see it later."

He acknowledged Jeb with a nod and started moving away. "Sure, Beth, I'll look for it. Excuse me for a minute, would you, dear? I'd better see what this is all about."

As he walked away, I saw Jeb looking at me. He smiled and waved; I turned and left the room. I never mentioned the poem again, and neither did my father.

⋆ *12* ⋆

THE DAY I RETURNED TO SCHOOL I WAS FEELING LOW, and a message that Jake had called that morning made me feel lower still. As I dialed his number, I thought about how he could be called by the draft board any day. I pumped myself up to offer all the encouragement I could, and then—

"Beth? Hey, how's it goin'? Happy 1970 and all that crap. Did you have a nice holiday?"

"I'm not sure I'd use the word nice, but . . . listen, you sound terrific. Do you have some news?"

"News, that's what I got. What are you doing? Can you meet me at the union in fifteen minutes? I'll tell you all about it."

When I went over there and saw the look on his face, I thought for sure he'd had a call. "John R. Lascomb? Aka Jake? Hey, whaddaya say! U.S. government calling. Damnedest thing, Jake, it looks like we got your number wrong! Yeah, you're not seven, you're two hundred and seven. Hope we haven't inconvenienced you, and hey—have a nice day!" "Inconvenience, hell no! I've just slashed both my wrists, but it's cool. My roommate has a box of Band-Aids around here somewhere."

"Jake, you look ecstatic! What happened?"

"Ecstasy is the word for it. Siddown, I'll tell you. Cup o' cocoa?" He took the lid off of one of his—there were three lined up—and set it in front of me.

"I got this idea and I said to myself, Jake, it's foolproof. It's got to work. The excuses you told me about? I'm gay, the sight of blood makes me sick? It's all bullshit to them by now. These guys have seen it all. And they've gotta be hip to all the ways you can fuck up your body to fail the physical. So get this—"

"Yeah, what?"

"Reverse psychology, dig it? I was berserk all right, but berserk to kill! They called me in over the holidays and, man, I was gung ho all the way. I went in there and told them how I couldn't wait to decapitate all those VC, to make necklaces out of their entrails, save their fingers for my grandkids! I was such a psycho they wouldn't have ever let me loose over there."

The three kids at the next table thought it was a great idea, and gave us a chorus of "right on."

"Good idea, man," said one guy, "It beats ditching the country."

"Yeah," said another, "or having your hair permed."

"So this guy was sitting there looking at me like, 'Where the hell did this cracker escape from?' 'I remember in high school,' I said to him, 'hearing about this marine in the Korean War—they found him with the head of a Korean guy, peeling it like a grapefruit.' I said this to him real slowly, making these peeling gestures with my fingers, staring at my hands like in some kind of trance. Then I looked up at him and said, 'That's what I'd like to do to all those gooks—peel their fuckin' heads. Maybe I won't even kill them first!' This guy was turning green! Hey, I don't want to make you sick with the details—suffice it to say it got better from there. So that was it. They were real glad to turn me down and get me outa there."

We raised our cups of cocoa and drank a toast to his victory and his freedom. I wanted to share his happiness, and in part I did, but he seemed so out of control I was still worried about him. It seemed that the war was changing us in more than the obvious ways—and not for the better.

January and February were bitter cold months. An icy wind slashed across Lake Michigan and sent the temperatures plummeting even further. Venturing outdoors required layers of clothes and thick wool scarves to protect our faces from the knife-edged wind. On the street, pedestrians shuffled across slippery sidewalks, only their eyes visible above wool wrappings.

Still no word from Greg. As time passed, more of my energy

went to pushing thoughts from my mind that he might be dead. As long as there was no definite word, there was still hope; but every discussion about the war and every news broadcast brought the same fear crashing in on me—that he might have been blown into unidentifiable pieces in some murky corner of the jungle, or, an equally frightening thought, that he might be missing in action. I hadn't told anyone in our group about him. I wouldn't have known how to explain to them that I was in love with someone who not only fought in Vietnam but who had gone back voluntarily for more.

One bleak winter evening I sat on the floor in front of the television in the dorm's lounge, and watched as a couple in Florida were interviewed about the death of their son in Vietnam. The father, his saddened face trying to remain strong, had his arm around his wife, who cried as she spoke about her son the way he was in high school. She pointed to his graduation picture on the table next to her, and a photo of him in uniform, smiling radiantly. All soldiers smile radiantly, I thought, in the beatific pictures they send home, as if paradise awaited. This mother hoped it did. He deserves it, she said. His name was Russell; he was killed nine days after he got there.

I went back to my room and forced myself to write to Doug Purcell, Greg's friend from Devon, asking if he had heard anything from, or about, Greg. The two weeks that I had to wait for his reply felt familiar. I was pulled between fear that bad news would come and hope that no news was good news. A break in this emotional limbo came when I got Doug's letter. Greg had come home, he said, but he wasn't sure where he was now. He'd gotten only one letter from him, with no return address. He was alive! I said it again and again to myself to be sure I understood. I knew there had to be some reason he hadn't contacted me. Maybe he needed time to adjust.

Driven indoors by the weather, our group concentrated on planning rallies for the spring. Jake's draft evasion scheme wasn't the only thing that had claimed his attention during the holiday break; he'd been studying the radical activities of the Weathermen, and he liked what he saw.

"Just look at their efficiency," he told us one night. "Their network is underground. After they make a move nobody gets caught. And their violence is controlled—they always telephone a warning before the bombings so people can get out. And they only bomb buildings that have something to do with the war, like ROTC facilities. But the key is, people pay attention. When the Weathermen strike, people listen!''

We had taken up our usual positions in Alicia's living room. It was the beginning of March, and the snow was finally melting, making little tapping noises as it dripped off the eaves. Alicia came out of the kitchen with a cup of coffee.

''They don't *listen*, Jake,'' she told him, ''they just feel all the more justified in defaming the whole antiwar movement. They use it to prove their point and it hurts us all, don't you see that? This is supposed to be a peace movement. These Weathermen tactics will destroy everything we've been working for. They play right into the hands of the hawks who want the public to see us as mindless lunatics. I can't believe you don't see that, Jake. And by the way, people *have* been hurt in some of those bombings.''

Jake sucked on a wedge of lime and poured himself another shot of tequila. ''Look, how many years has this war been going on? I mean, I've lost count—''

''Yeah, no wonder,'' said Dennis. ''You've had enough tequila to make you lose count of your fingers. When did you give up beer for that shit?''

''Hey, back off, man. The point is, the movement isn't accomplishing what it's supposed to. The only thing that gets headlines is fighting fire with fire or bombs with bombs. What we need is attention, and a few strategically placed explosions would do it.''

''You're getting to sound like Jamal, you know that, Jake?'' I said. ''What's happened to you?''

''Well, maybe he's got the right idea after all! Where is he tonight, anyway? I bet he'd see things my way.'' We all looked at one another. ''Yeah, well, I heard a rumor he's trying to get a chapter of the Black Panthers going at Mountclaire. And he's got the right idea, because this group's not accomplishing shit!''

The door flew open and Jake was gone. I ran out after him. It was five below and I saw my breath on the air as I ran behind him, shouting his name. Finally, he stopped and turned.

''We can work this out, Jake. We've had differences of opinion before. Come back inside.''

''Later, Beth.'' He turned to go, but I grabbed his arm.

''Jake, you were always more extreme than the rest of us but at least you'd listen to reason.''

''Whose reason? Yours? Alicia's? Forget it. I've been compromising all along and I'm finished! I've got my own ideas and I'm gonna follow through.''

''Follow through with what—getting innocent people blown up?''

''It's happening over there, isn't it? It's war, baby, remember?''

I went back inside to a room full of grim faces. The long winter had left all of us restless and impatient. In the days that followed we began lining up speakers and musicians for our first event of the spring, but the unity that once existed among us was dwindling. Jake came back, but conflicting ideas about the tone of our demonstrations kept finding their way into our meetings. The days when Alicia's authority went undisputed were gone.

On March 6, an explosion destroyed a Greenwich Village townhouse where the Weathermen had been making bombs. Three Weathermen were killed, two others escaped, and when the police searched the ruins they found enough dynamite to blow up most of Fifth Avenue. Alicia's words had proved prophetic. The next day a note was slipped under her door: *They got what they deserved. Think about it, Commie.*

When I made my routine call to my parents on Sunday, my mother said, ''Just a minute, Elizabeth, your father would like a word with you.'' Not a good sign.

''Hi, Beth, how's school?''

These preliminary niceties were something that my parents regarded as good manners, but I equated them with sitting in the dentist's chair waiting for the drill.

''Beth, I assume you've heard about the bombing in New York in which some of your, uh, fellow activists died. Now, Beth, I hope this tells you something once and for all about what's behind this movement. These people were building bombs to use against innocent victims. It's just as I tried to tell you when you were home. You regard these people as saints, and they're nothing more than hoodlums.''

''Dad, we keep getting caught up on this same point. The antiwar movement is not one big group, and the Weathermen are not my fellow activists. There are splinter groups just as in political parties. Do you agree with the tactics of the John Birch Society? The Weathermen do not represent the entire antiwar movement.''

''Well, they're a major part of it,'' he said emphatically.

''They are not! There's nothing major about them! There are probably a few hundred members in the whole country.''

''Beth, you obviously refuse to listen. You've got your mind made up and, as usual, you're not going to open it to another point of view. You were stubborn the day you were born, and I'm sad to say you haven't changed a bit.''

These confrontations with my father left me frustrated and drained. I felt that nothing I said made an impression on him— that my efforts were wasted. Each time my hopes were raised that I might be able to reach him, that he might understand what was in my heart, but each time I came away deflated, feeling more distant from him than ever.

I rolled my eyes when he said I was stubborn the day I was born; I'd heard that story too many times. My mother told it this way: When she went into labor with me, the entire night and part of the following day passed, and there was still no progress. The doctors decided to do a caesarean section. What they found was that I had hooked my fingers around my mother's ribs, thwarting all her attempts to push me from her womb. I was in the eighth grade when I first saw a diagram of the female anatomy, and realized the impossibility of what she described. The unborn infant would have had to punch through the uterine wall, shove the bladder out of the way, snake through the intestines, and clutch her fingers onto the muscle-ensheathed ribs.

The day I came upon these startling facts, I came home from school with my biology book tucked under my arm, prepared to state my case. I patiently explained to my mother why the story she told couldn't possibly have happened. In refuting their fairy tale I was hoping to uncover the real story of my birth—perhaps some dark, mysterious secret they had never wanted to reveal. No such luck. My mother not only held to her story, she embellished it, telling me how I came out with abrasions on my poor little fingers. As a last resort I said, ''Could I have the phone number of the doctor who delivered me?''

''Well, you could,'' she said, ''except that he's dead.''

To avoid these disastrous phone calls with my parents, I began calling just at the time I knew they'd be leaving for church or going out to dinner. The shorter the time, the greater the chance that I'd remain safe in small-talk territory.

The antiwar movement regained some of its credibility on April 30, 1970, when the country was stunned to learn that American troops were being sent into Cambodia. It meant more lives lost and the escalation of a war that had no end in sight.

We held a frantically organized rally that night and called for a strike on campus. Other colleges and universities were also planning strikes, but Mountclaire still had a large conservative element compared to places like Berkeley and Columbia. Unanimous support for the strike, particularly near the end of the spring term with exams approaching, did not seem likely. Other campuses suffered outbreaks of violence and confrontations with police. Jake had a call from a friend of his at Stanford, who nervously recounted scenes of bloodshed and chaos. At Ohio State, and at Kent State where the ROTC building had been burned down, the National Guard was called.

They were also called out by the Governor of California, as my father fulfilled his earlier warning to keep the schools open at gunpoint, if necessary.

The invasion of Cambodia awakened a few people to the issues at hand. Even Belinda rearranged some of her macramé to make a place on the wall for a poster: WAR IS NOT HEALTHY FOR CHILDREN AND OTHER LIVING THINGS.

I was walking to the dorm on a Monday afternoon when someone I barely knew ran up to me, sobbing, and cried, ''Beth, did you hear? The National Guard's shooting people at Kent State! They've killed some students!''

As I ran back to the dorm the news was exploding everywhere. Four students were dead, and nine others wounded. The reports were sketchy and conflicting. Some said the guardsmen thought their M-1 rifles were loaded with blanks. Some said the men lost control after having rocks and bricks flung at them and, knowing their rifles were loaded, aimed directly into a crowd of students. At that point the details didn't matter. Four students were dead, and May 4 would forever have a sad significance in history.

Alicia was the first person I called. ''You better get over here,'' she said, ''we've got work to do.''

When I arrived, Jamal, an infrequent visitor by this time, was pacing the floor.

''Man, this is war—war! Don't you see that?''

''I can't believe their rifles were loaded,'' I said. ''How could they send them onto a campus with loaded guns?''

Jamal laughed. ''You are one dumb little princess. There ain't no such thing as a gun that ain't loaded.''

"Listen," bellowed Alicia, raising her hand in a "stop" gesture before I could speak, "I've been in contact with some other campuses. There's going to be a strike—a massive shutdown across the country—maybe every single college and university. I know there's going to be violence, but unless you want to see more people gunned down—maybe even some of us—we better make damn sure this campus stays peaceful."

Jake, who had been sitting in the corner chain-smoking, erupted at her suggestion.

"Shit! Are we supposed to *passively* protest this, too? Who the fuck are you, Gandhi? Four kids are dead! Jamal's right. This is war!"

"Yeah, and who do you think is gonna win?" I shouted. "They've got the guns!"

"We can always get guns, princess," Jamal said.

We stayed for the rest of the afternoon, arguing and resolving nothing. When we left the apartment to walk across campus and get something to eat, we were stunned to find hundreds of students milling around. Some seemed in a state of shock, some were in groups, talking and softly weeping; others were just standing quietly, watching and waiting. It looked like everyone had decided not to go to classes. Evening was making its shadows on the grass, and tension filled the still air.

Alicia stopped, looked around, and moved to the center of the crowd.

"Okay, I want everyone to listen to me!" she yelled. Heads turned her way, and people on the sidelines drifted in. "To protest this morning's tragedy at Kent State, this college is now officially on strike!" Cheers welled up and fists were thrust in the air. "But we will not allow this action to deteriorate into violence! Four students have died already. We can't let that happen again!"

Some continued to cheer, but others shouted back in protest. Suddenly Jamal's voice boomed over the crowd, "Fight guns with guns!" and the cheers came up again. Jake went to Jamal's side and shouted, "Blood for blood!" Dozens of kids clamored around Jake and Jamal, repeating their chants. For the first time I saw fear in Alicia's eyes. I fought my way through the throng to where Jake was standing, shoving his fist in the air and leading a chant.

"Are you out of your mind, you crazy bastard?" I screamed,

barely hearing the sound of my own voice. "Do you realize what you're doing here?"

"I told you, Beth!" he shouted back. "It's war!"

"Jake!" I grabbed his arm and tried to tear him away. "Jake, come with me, please! I've got to talk to you." But he only chanted louder. The noise of the crowd made my head feel like it would explode, like it was sucking the breath out of me. Slowly, I made my way back to my room.

There were two notes from Belinda on my bed: "Beth, your parents called," and "Beth, your father called." I waited until the following morning to call home. My mother answered and, after some brief pleasantries, handed the phone to my father.

"Beth," he said, "we think you should come home."

"Excuse me?"

"You heard me. There's liable to be violence on the campuses and we feel you should fly home immediately."

"I'm sorry, Dad, but I'm not coming home, no matter what happens on this campus. This is where I belong and this is where I'm staying."

"Beth, listen to me now. You don't know the half of it!"

"I know all I need to know, Dad. Four kids are dead—that's the only half that matters."

"As usual, you're just seeing your side of things. Those students provoked those guards. When you initiate violence—"

"What? You get shot? Are you telling me they deserved to get killed?"

"What I'm telling you is what I've been telling you all along, this is not child's play! These people you've chosen to take sides with are dangerous!"

"I don't think I can talk anymore right now," I said, close to tears. "I'll have to call you another time."

"Beth! Beth, we want you home! Is that cl—"

I slowly lowered the receiver, all too aware that I had never before hung up on him. I had a desperate, empty feeling inside, wondering how things could have gotten this way between us, yet knowing there were forces at work that made it inevitable. I was doing what I felt was right. So was he. And between those two realities was only distance.

Over the next few days there was news of fires and bombings and arrests on many other campuses. As far as we could tell, the strike was nationwide, even extending to some high schools. Jake reported that the National Guard was being called out in several more states to prevent ''violence'' on college campuses. By now no one thought the guns weren't loaded.

About fifty students had organized a sit-in at the office of Clark Ingram, Mountclaire's president. They climbed through a window and set up camp, making it impossible for him to enter. All over campus, students and professors were splitting off into groups, plotting their own methods of strategy. I was crossing the quad in front of the student union when suddenly someone grabbed me by the arm. It was Wilder Hayes, my poetry professor.

''Listen, do you know how to protect yourself if the pigs have tear gas?''

''Uh, no, I guess I don't.''

''You'd better wear a lot of clothes—long sleeves—anything to protect your skin. And have wet rags for your face if it starts coming down.'' He gave me a quick pat on the shoulder, then moved on to the next cluster of kids, spreading the word.

It was impossible for Alicia to maintain a cohesive strategy, and the few of us who were trying to organize things for her shared her frustration. Jamal had rounded up most of the black students on campus, inflamed their anger with his own, and convinced them that only militants could make a difference now. Jake was doing the same with whites who banded together under his leadership. It was just a matter of time before all these sparks burst into flames. We knew it, and apparently so did the administration, because police began to appear and, as the hours passed and tension built, they increased in numbers. My father's phrase about this not being child's play echoed in my ears as I watched the police, an army sent down to keep us in line, gently finger the nightsticks that hung from their belts, and pull them out from time to time when things got too noisy. Small confrontations threatened to become big ones.

''Hey, pigs!'' I heard Jake yell. ''Why don't you just go back to the barn where you belong? Whoever heard of *pigs* on a college campus?''

''Jake, back off!'' I said, tugging on his arm and trying to pull him away.

''What are they gonna do,'' he said loudly, ''arrest me for calling them names?'' He turned to them and spat. *''Pigs!''*

''You can't believe they need a reason to arrest you—or to

beat the hell out of you for that matter! Come on, let's get away from here." One of the guards was watching us intently. I couldn't see his eyes, because he wore dark sunglasses, but his expression told me enough.

"You know you've gone crazy?" I said quietly. "I think you're starting to believe that rap you gave the induction officer."

"You got a better way?" he shouted. The guard fingered his gun nervously.

The following day, May 8, a huge demonstration was scheduled in Washington, D.C. The Governor of Illinois must have figured we'd stage our own version, because on the morning of that day the National Guard descended on Mountclaire like invaders from another planet.

They formed a wall outside the administration building. Jamal and his followers paced up and down in front of them, shouting "White pigs!"

"You know why you boys are here," cried Jamal, "aimin' your guns at college students? Because blacks wouldn't do that —no, man, I don't see a black among you. I'll tell you where they are. They're in Vietnam, fightin' your motherfuckin' war. That's right, man, send the niggers over to fight the white man's war!"

Alicia pulled him away and said something to him I couldn't hear. He jerked his arm out of her hand and walked angrily back to the guard. He stood staring, then spat on the ground in front of them. It landed an inch from the shoe of a guard who looked at Jamal as if he'd like nothing better than to spray bullets into the mouth that had just offended him.

From that moment, time seemed to speed up. Jamal and his friends disappeared, but returned moments later with bulging knapsacks. Someone began running through the crowd handing out wet rags. Remembering Wilder's warning, I grabbed one, and within seconds Jamal and his army were hurling bricks and stones at the National Guardsmen. When I saw the guards cover their faces with gas masks, a feeling of terror shot through me. Alicia grabbed me and pulled me away, and we began running in the opposite direction. Tear gas canisters were jettisoned into the air. I thrust the rag to my face, but the canister that landed near me didn't explode. "Throw it back!" I heard someone yell, and I did—others did the same. I watched as the canisters exploded in front of the gas-masked guardsmen. When they began moving in on us, I was sure we would all be shot. The police moved in from the opposite side with nightsticks drawn, and attacked the crowd. One boy near me was clubbed across the back of his skull and, as his knees buckled, the cop moved on.

I started running. I bumped into a girl who kept shouting "Pigs!" and I tried to pull her away with me, but she tore herself from my grasp. When I turned around a cop was beating her with his nightstick. Her head was bleeding and she curled up her body to shield her chest from the blows.

"Stop, goddammit, you're killing her!" I cried. "Let go!" I pounded his back with my fists. There was blood running into her eyes, and she cried, "I can't see!"

He wheeled around and grabbed my wrist, and dragged me through the crowd. I could hear the girl's sobs grow faint. All around me people were yelling and crying, and I could hear more sounds of nightsticks against skulls, wood on bone. A paddy wagon pulled up and, when we got closer, I saw that Jamal and Jake were already inside, handcuffed. Others were there as well, and then I heard my name. I turned and saw Alicia being dragged over. Blood trickled from her head. "Hey, it's going to be okay," she said. "Don't worry." I looked at the nightmare surrounding us—so many kids were lying on the ground moaning. I couldn't even tell if some were dead.

Then I saw a man in a dark suit talking to one of the cops, and pointing at me. The cop walked over and said, "Let this one go." The one that dragged me over let go of my wrist and shoved me away. He moved on to the others and began herding them into the paddy wagon.

I ran over and tried to climb into the back with the others but a cop pushed me off. I landed on the ground, and before I could get back on my feet, they'd finished shoving the others inside. Their faces stared out at me as the wagon pulled away. "Hey, princess!" Jamal shouted. "What was it you were saying about bein' just like the rest of us?" I stood there stunned. Alicia looked at me sadly. I turned away from them to hide my tears and then, realizing that someone was watching me, I looked up. Wilder was standing a few feet away.

"Stop crying," he said, walking over to me. "You are who you are, and don't let anyone make you regret it." I wiped my eyes on the wet rag I'd used to protect my face from the tear gas.

"Thanks for telling me about this," I said, holding up the rag.

"Are you all right?" he asked.

I looked around and saw that paramedics had arrived and were giving medical attention to some of the students. "I'm fine."

"Come on," he said, "let's see if we can help out."

The smoke in the air began to disperse and, in the distance, I heard a siren.

· *13* ·

JAMAL AND THE OTHERS WERE RELEASED THE FOLLOWING day. The college didn't press charges, and apparently the police felt the students had learned their lesson. As I waited for them outside the police station I was unsure where I stood with the people I had called my friends. When they came out, Jamal gave me a cold look, then walked off without a word. Jake, Alicia, and the others rode back to campus with me on the bus. They told me about what had happened and, although no one mentioned the events of the day before, I knew things would never be the same again. Jamal was right. I was different from them . . . but not because I wanted to be.

Two more students were killed at Jackson State. The school year ended in uncertainty. Exams were given, though no one was sure why or what difference they would make.

Early one morning the phone rang. Belinda groaned and pulled the pillow over her head.

"I think it's for you, Beth—probably the *New York Times*."

I leaned out of bed and grabbed the phone cord, dragging the ringing phone across the floor.

"Hello?"

"Is that you, Betsy?"

There was static on the line, and his voice sounded like an echo.

"Greg!"

"How are you, baby?"

I sat up, wide awake. "Great! Where are you?"

"I'm coming through Chicago day after tomorrow—wanna meet me somewhere?" His voice kept fading beneath the crackling sound that would swell like a wave, then subside. I squeezed the receiver against my ear as if sheer force could bring him closer.

"Yeah, sure, how about the Drake Hotel? The bar there with the big fountain in it—it's called the Palm Court."

"Okay, I'll see you there at four."

"Yeah, okay. Greg, I—"

But the crackling grew louder and washed over him. Such a fragile connection, this telephone line we depend on to carry our feelings across miles, oceans, countries.

Belinda pushed the pillow off her head. "Since you were shouting at the top of your lungs, I can't help but ask who it was."

"An old friend of mine from high school. He's coming through Chicago."

For two days I thought about nothing but Greg. He sounded so relaxed, as if the silence between us existed only in my imagination, as if he called like that every week.

The afternoon of our meeting I spent over an hour getting ready for Greg's first glimpse of me in a year. I changed clothes three times, finally settling on an ankle-length skirt and a camisole top that Belinda had made for me out of antique lace. I dug my makeup pouch out of the bottom drawer, realizing I hadn't worn any since my graduation from Devon.

Standing back from the mirror to survey the whole picture, I tried to see myself through Greg's eyes. But I didn't know how he saw things, or what he thought and felt. I hoped I wasn't on my way to meet a stranger.

I'd spent so much time changing clothes and primping I had just enough time left to make it by four if I ran all the way to the station. Once on the el, I started picturing the bar at the Drake. The huge fountain was the centerpiece of a wood-paneled room that was adorned with tapestry couches, lush plants, and palm trees. I imagined the bar being not in the center of downtown Chicago, but on an island in the Caribbean. An empty bar, with the fountain sounding like rain on a lake, and trade winds blowing through the window, stirring the palm fronds. Greg would pick me up in his arms, carry me to the fountain and, as water sprayed over us, we would make love, never noticing the day slipping into evening. I found myself hoping he had reserved a room for us.

When I emerged from my fantasy, I realized we were already in Chicago and I'd missed my stop. It was a quarter to four, and I knew I'd never make it in time. I got off at the next stop and looked frantically for a taxi. When I finally got one, it was almost four. I tried to stay calm, but the traffic and the persistent ticking of time ripped apart my nerves.

At four-twenty, I raced through the doors of the Drake Hotel and across the black marble floor of the lobby. An agitated group surrounded the front desk; their outraged voices and angry gestures drew the attention of everyone in the room. Women in high heels and pearls were pointing at someone I couldn't see, and silk-suited men were nodding and trying to soothe them. Someone who looked like a manager was pushing his way through, saying, "All right, everyone calm down. I'll handle this." A man whose stomach was severely testing the strength of his shirt buttons was saying, "I think we should call the cops!" I tried to find an opening through, or around, the crowd when I heard a voice rise above the others. "I have as much right to be here as anyone else!" I stopped as if an iron gate had dropped in front of me.

Through the crush of people I could see the sleeve of an army jacket, and then I heard Greg's voice again. "Just let me go up to the goddamn bar! I'm not gonna make any trouble!"

"Oh my God!" I said, making my way through the crowd. "What happened?"

"I think he bumped into one of those women," a thin man in glasses said. "They wouldn't let him into the bar dressed like that and he refused to leave."

I was close enough to see him—his torn jeans and army jacket looked out of place among the tailored suits and designer dresses that surrounded him. His hair was long, pulled back in a ponytail, and his face looked older, more chiseled, as if a sculptor had whittled away all but the hard angular lines. His eyes focused on me and everything around me seemed, for a second, suspended. I felt no movement, heard no noise, though I knew that people were still talking. Greg's mouth formed my name, but no sound came out. Then he turned away from the crowd and raced toward

the door. He was out on the sidewalk before I could reach him.
Once outside I saw him almost a block away, walking with his
head down and his hands in his pockets. I ran after him, my
sandals making slapping noises against the pavement.

"Greg! Greg, wait! Please!" I was vaguely aware of people
on the sidewalk turning to stare at me. As I got closer it seemed
that he was slowing down; finally he stopped and turned.

"Greg," I said, trying to catch my breath, "what happened
back there? Why did you run out like that?"

He didn't say anything, just stood staring at me, not even
blinking. His eyes looked like ice.

"Look, Beth, I thought I could come here today and explain
some things to you." He was almost shouting to be heard over
the noise of traffic. "I wanted to make you understand. But I see
now that was a stupid idea."

"You're wrong—I would understand! Just let me try."

"Get off it, Beth. You can be so naive sometimes. Look around
you. Look around at all these properly dressed people, doing
everything the right way, not making any waves. And then take
a look at me—take a good look. I don't fit into this picture. I
don't belong! And the best thing I can do for you and everyone
else is to keep you the hell away from me so your life won't get
fucked up, too."

I tried to look past his words, past the hard angles of his face,
to the face I remembered: his wink, the smile that had reflected
moonlight years before, turning it into a glistening invitation. I
forced myself to remember that the man standing in front of me
was that same man.

"Greg, please, I've wanted to see you for so long. I just
want—"

"Don't!" he shouted. "Don't want anything from me, because
I can't give it!" Then he said softly, "Just let me go." He
started walking away. My feet couldn't move to follow him. I
was rooted there, on the gray sidewalk with the light fading and
people brushing past me . . . and Greg moving farther away.

Finally I turned and started moving off in the other direction
without looking up from the sidewalk. I could feel my eyes burning with tears and my stomach clench as I tried to walk. I didn't
know how or where to reach him, and I needed so desperately to
know what it was he'd wanted to explain to me. Now, all I had
was one more mystery.

By the time I got back to Mountclaire that night, I felt empty —of tears, of emotions, of the hopes that had consumed me since Greg's call. There was only a still, gray emptiness.

I considered telling Alicia about Greg. She was my closest friend, and I wanted to confide in someone. But I was hesitant to tell even her.

One night, after several of us had met to discuss the last rally of the school year, I stayed to help her clean up. It seemed like a good time to tell her what had been upsetting me, since she noticed that something had, but before I could say anything she said, "Listen, I didn't want to say anything in front of the others. I wanted to talk to you first. I need your help with something."

"Is something wrong?"

"Nothing we can't fix. I got a call from Columbia today. They want me to give a speech there on Saturday. It's a big event—a lot of heavyweights—so I don't want to say no. I'd like you to take my place at the rally here. I'll give you the speech I've prepared."

"Well, sure, I'll—are you sure you want me to do it?"

"I'll type it up tonight and get it to you tomorrow."

I was nervous about the speech, but also relieved. I'd been thinking of nothing but my aborted rendezvous with Greg.

The statement I delivered at the rally was a summation of the year's significant events: the invasion of Cambodia, the Kent State shooting, the deaths at Jackson State. I was tense at first, but the attention and silence of the crowd gave me confidence, and I felt my voice project with greater and greater conviction. I improvised my own conclusion.

"The important message here is that we can't give up! We've already made a difference, and we can still make a difference."

"No thanks to you!" I heard a voice cry out from the crowd.

"The vital thing is that we stand together, and not let petty differences weaken our resolve!"

The heckler shouted out again, but applause came up and slowly drowned out his words. I never found out who it was, but having to face the fact that I had real enemies in the movement gave me a chill.

"I heard there was a little problem at the rally," said Alicia when she returned from New York, "but that you handled it."

"Whoever told you that wasn't standing close enough to see my hands shaking."

"Never mind," she said. "You be glad it happened. You need to toughen up. It's always going to come down on you because of who your father is, and you'd better learn how to fight back."

I could always count on Alicia for the hard line, but she wasn't without her soft side, too. When I told her I was anxious about spending the summer at home with my parents, she mentioned a friend in Los Angeles who needed someone to house-sit and feed her cats. I accepted right away, and told my parents of my change in plans.

Tara Rose's house was tucked into a hillside in Laurel Canyon. It was old and in need of major repairs. The stale odor of cigarettes and cat litter clung to the rooms. She asked fifty dollars a month and my word that her cats would be fed. Tara was a playwright working day and night that summer on a waiver theater production in Hollywood. The bedroom she let me use had a bed and a record player so old that it could accommodate 78s, which had become extinct when I was about ten. The walls were painted royal blue and the windowpanes were covered with gray paint, defying daylight. Sitting in there was like being inside a bruise.

"Tara," I asked tentatively, "would it be all right if I took the paint off the windows and did the walls in a different color, like beige?"

She looked at me through a cloud of smoke and said, "Sure, do whatever you want." Tara always wore black, and could carry on an entire conversation with a cigarette dangling from her lips. I was tempted to take up smoking just to see if I could master that talent.

It took two days of solid labor, but I finally transformed my room. Sunlight streamed through the windows and reflected on cream-colored walls. It wasn't *Architectural Digest,* but at least it wouldn't give me nightmares.

My parents were staying in Sacramento for the summer and had shown no surprise when I told them I would be spending the summer in Los Angeles. They'd also agreed to let me take the station wagon, which I used to prowl alleys and collect discarded furniture in order to make my sparse room functional. Tara was hardly ever home. All of her time was taken up by her current project, a rock opera based on *Macbeth*.

Three weeks into the summer I started feeling pangs of guilt for not making an effort to see my parents. Other than redoing my room in Tara's house, I'd done nothing constructive with my time. My mind still wandered through memories of Greg. My emotions were constantly shunted between fear that he was in serious trouble and anger that he hadn't contacted me. I began to feel that this was the only way he could find to let me know it was over between us. In spite of this, all the things I still felt for him simmered close to the surface. In an attempt to escape myself, I finally flew up to see my parents.

When I arrived at the Sacramento airport on Friday afternoon, a state policeman was there to pick me up—uniform and all—a scenario for which I wasn't prepared. At least it was an unmarked car.

"Hey, you're not going to do anything like turn on the siren, are you?" I asked, feeling my old limousine phobia bubble up.

"No, ma'am." On the ride home I thought about what I could say to my parents to ease the tension, to lessen the distance. I felt myself stiffen at the thought of how awkward these reunions had become; even a cheerful holiday like Christmas couldn't redeem them. This time, Brian wouldn't be there to ease things along. He was away at camp. I prayed that the summer heat would somehow thaw the atmosphere inside the house, and as we drew closer I pushed my hopes higher.

As we neared our destination I heard shouting and chanting in the distance—the familiar sound of "No More War! No More War!" and "No More Kent States! Pigs off Campus!"

"Excuse me," I asked the policeman, "where is that chanting coming from?"

"Outside the mansion, ma'am—demonstrators. They've been there all night."

As we pulled into the driveway, I found myself covering my face so I wouldn't be recognized. Around my fingers I watched the angry crowd, some carrying signs and banners. One of them thrust a dummy soldier in the air, stained with fake blood, wearing a helmet and a sign that read CANFIELD KILLS.

"Pull around to the back entrance, would you? I'll go in through the kitchen."

I found my parents sitting quietly in the den. The room was almost dark, with the blinds drawn, and coming into the dim air conditioning from the bright, blistery June heat felt like entering another world. The cries of the demonstrators outside the windows filled the air with foreboding. I put my small suitcase on the floor and sat down.

"Hello, Elizabeth," said my mother. Her voice was flat and the corners of her mouth showed no inclination to smile.

"Hi, Beth," said my father. "I guess you saw what's going on outside."

I wondered if that was supposed to be funny. The only way I could have missed it was to arrive via underground tunnel. No, he didn't look amused. His look told me he was opening up the subject for discussion.

"Dad, I didn't fly up here to argue with you about politics. I just came for a visit, to see how you're doing and everything."

The feeling in the air was not merely that I was somehow indirectly responsible for what was going on outside, but that I had personally hired each and every one of those demonstrators to terrorize my parents in their home. This was the way they looked at me, though they said nothing. Our lackluster attempts at small talk enabled us to kill an hour, but it was clear that it was only a temporary truce. The battle lines were drawn, the troops just outside the gate. The chanting went on until nightfall, when some of the demonstrators left.

Later that night, I sat in the dark in the upstairs bedroom where Greg had slept, looking down at the small group that still stood outside the street. They were gathered around something, but I couldn't tell what. . . . Then, when they began to move, I saw it. Attached to the end of a long stick was an effigy of my father. They set it on fire. In seconds I heard someone yell "Stop or I'll shoot!" and then a gunshot rang out. The burning effigy was dropped to the ground, and everyone scattered. Security guards ran out into the street, and the sound of sirens began closing in.

When I heard the doorbell ring, I hurried to the top of the stairs.

"Governor, the electric eye picked up an intruder at the east corner of the lawn. We fired a warning shot and he ran off. But he dropped a Molotov cocktail when he ran. Apparently he was going to throw it at the house."

"Thank you," my father said.

Early the following morning I awakened to the chanting outside the gates. I went to the window and was shocked to see that the crowd had doubled since the day before. Three hideous effigies danced in the air, and a huge sign carried by several people depicted a pair of man's hands with blood on them. I dressed and went downstairs.

When I walked into the dining room my parents smiled and said good morning. Sunlight shimmered off the china and Irma poured fresh orange juice in our glasses. Every effort was being made to enjoy breakfast as usual and ignore the fact that hundreds of angry, vociferous people were parked outside our door. As I lifted a forkful of scrambled eggs to my lips, the droning from the street filled my ears as if it were in the next room. I dropped the fork to my plate; I hadn't intended to, but the clatter resounded in the room and startled my parents.

"Dad, don't you think you should go out there and talk to them?"

"No, Beth, I don't. The fact that you would even suggest that just shows me once again how naive you are about this whole situation."

"I see nothing naive about it. Do you think sitting in here pretending everything is normal is a solution?"

"Nobody's pretending. If anything, *you're* pretending, pretending that these radicals who are out to destroy our country are on some kind of ... virtuous mission." With his fork he pointed in the direction of the crowd outside. "For heaven's sake, Beth, do you still not see who these people are, what they're trying to do? That's what I mean by naive—that you think if I were to go out there and talk to those maniacs it would make a difference, as if they were capable of listening to reason."

At that moment we heard an explosion in the distance, and looked toward the front of the house. I got up and ran to the door.

"Elizabeth, where are you going?" my mother said. "Come right back here. You could get hurt out there!"

I went out the front door and ran down the path that led to the gate. Another Molotov cocktail had been thrown in the street and police swarmed out over the area. The chanting had stopped; desperate cries and shouts took its place. The crowd had become frantic and some were trying to climb the mansion gates.

"Please listen!" I cried, the sound of my voice vanishing into the din. "Please!" On the ground near the guard's booth I saw a police bullhorn and ran over to grab it.

"Listen to me, all of you!" Some turned to face me. I saw the puzzled faces of policemen who weren't sure what to do next. "This isn't the answer! You're only hurting our cause, not helping it!"

Cries came up. "Hypocrite! Phony!" The words were hurled at me like daggers. A guy leaped on top of a car and shouted, "You're the one who's hurting the cause. Go back where you belong!"

Suddenly I was surrounded by security guards, who rushed me back inside the gates. "No! What are you doing?" Behind me I heard the cries growing fainter. "Canfield—get the pigs off our campuses!" and "College is for students, not guns!"

My parents were waiting inside the front door. I looked helplessly at their faces, and walked upstairs. As I threw my clothes into the suitcase, tears soaked my face. Confusion made my head ache. No, he's not a murderer. And I'm not a hypocrite.

They were still in the living room when I went back down.

"I'm going back to Los Angeles."

"Elizabeth, don't be foolish," my mother said. "It's not safe out there."

"I can't stay here. I'm just making it worse for everybody."

Back in Los Angeles I got to know some of Tara's friends; they were actors and artists who spent long evenings talking over glasses of thick red wine. In the back of my mind I waited from day to day for some word from Greg, but part of me was losing hope. I began writing poetry again and showed the others some of my work. Ideas hatched—someone thought of doing a sculpture to illustrate one of my poems—but I didn't take any of it too seriously. Ideas poured as freely as the wine and lasted about as long.

My room in Tara's house had become my domain. I could transform it however I wanted and I had no one to answer to. I often tried to seduce whatever muse might be lingering on the night winds by creating the perfect environment for a poet—candles, melodic guitar music, and, testing Belinda's claims for the power of incense, long sticks of sandalwood.

One evening I was working on a poem when I heard Tara come

in downstairs. She was home early and, having become accustomed to being alone there, I almost resented this unexpected intrusion.

"Beth, are you up there? Come on down. There's someone I want you to meet."

I came downstairs in sweat clothes and bare feet, and immediately regretted my disheveled appearance.

"This is Anthony. He's doing the set design for my play. And when he's not doing that he does brilliant paintings and sculptures that a few galleries have been smart enough to exhibit."

"Looks like we got you away from something," he said. Anthony had huge brown eyes that made me think of deer or Keene paintings.

"We were going to open a bottle of champagne," Tara went on, "in celebration of the great rehearsal we had tonight. Why don't you join us?"

"Well, I don't know... I was working on a poem."

"Oh, you write poetry?" Anthony said, folding himself into an overstuffed chair and dangling his legs over the arm.

"Not professionally or anything. I mean, I haven't had anything published... well, I guess I can stop working for now. Sure, I'll have some champagne with you."

It was after midnight before I got to bed. It seemed our conversation covered every aspect of the art world, even architecture. Anthony's dream was someday to build his own dome-shaped house.

"It's so practical and so much cheaper than your standard house." He had a way of leaning forward whenever he was trying to get a point across, as if his body could propel his ideas. "I learned all this from reading Buckminster Fuller, you know, all about geodesic domes and everything."

It was the first time in a long while that I'd spent an evening in which politics and the war were not mentioned. In some ways it was a relief.

Anthony started dropping by often and, after turning down several invitations, I finally agreed to have dinner with him. We went to Chinatown, to a tiny restaurant with Formica tables that he said was his favorite. "How did you even find this place?" I laughed. "It's so small."

"I live over in Silverlake, so I come here a lot. I'll show you my house after dinner if you want. It used to be an old hotel.

Actually I think it used to be a bordello. It was vacant and I talked the owner into renting it to me real cheap. It's great—I have a different room for every phase of my work.''

We started seeing each other almost every day. We built sand-castles on the beach at sunset, went to Chinatown and bought paper lanterns. We visited the Planetarium in Griffith Park and watched the dark ceiling come alive with patterns of the constellations. To look at us, people would have thought we were blissful lovers . . . but they would have been wrong.

Greg was the one who slept beside me each night. Balanced on the edge of sleep, I'd feel his hands on my skin, his breath in my mouth.

''Beth,'' Anthony said, ''I always get the feeling you're holding back from me.'' It was a warm Saturday afternoon and we were sitting on the grass outside his front window. A few kids were playing catch in the street, and a little girl on a tricycle rode by on the sidewalk and waved at us. ''You're involved with someone, aren't you?''

I was looking down at the grass. ''Sort of.''

''There's no 'sort of,' Beth. Yes or no.''

''It may be all over between us, but he's still on my mind.''

''Is it somebody at Mountclaire?''

''No, he's . . .''

Anthony looked at me. ''Hey, I won't press you for details. It's none of my business anyway. C'mon, let's walk up to the deli and get a beer.''

Weeks passed and I didn't watch the news or even think very much about the war. I was bothered about this a little, as if total apathy might be just around the corner—an abyss waiting to engulf me. But every time I tried to engage Anthony in a political discussion he'd say, ''Hey, I know all that's important, but it's a beautiful day out. Let's enjoy it, okay?''

''Anthony, you've never said anything about the draft. Don't you worry about it?''

We were drinking milkshakes in an ancient ice cream parlor near the theater where Tara's play was rehearsing.

''I worry about it for other guys, sure,'' he said, twirling the straw between his fingers. ''But they don't want me. I get asthma attacks sometimes. I haven't had one in quite a while but I don't think they want to take a chance if you've got a history of it. Anyway, they let me out. I told you this hole-in-the-wall makes the best milkshakes in town. Tastes like when you were a kid, huh?''

Finally it was time for Tara's opening night. From what both she and Anthony had told me about the play, I had some trepidations about going and, as I watched Lady Macbeth romping across the stage in a leopard-print leotard, I was sure I heard poor old William grumbling in his grave.

I managed to smile, and I told everyone, including Tara, how much I enjoyed it. When Anthony brought me home after a brief opening-night celebration, he turned me around to face him and said, ''Beth, I'd like to stay with you tonight.''

''I just don't think it would be fair to either of us.''

''Let's just sleep together. I promise I won't try to change your mind about making love. I just want to sleep with you and hold you.''

We slept in each other's arms, drifting through the night, but I woke in the morning feeling sad. Greg and I never had an opportunity to spend an entire night together, and I wished it were he beside me. Anthony was vital and smart, even sexy, but he wasn't Greg. I slid out of bed and sat by the window, watching the sun burn off the early morning mist. When I heard Anthony stir, I looked back to the bed and saw his quizzical look.

''I just don't think this is going to work out,'' I said. ''You want more from me than I can give you right now. Maybe in another time, when I'm not still thinking about this other person. But it just isn't fair to you. I don't want to hurt you. I know that sounds corny, but it's true.''

He climbed out of bed, where sunlight was waiting to splash across his body.

''Hey, don't worry about me—I'm fine. It's you I'm concerned about. You know, I've got the feeling you've had more fun in the last two weeks with me than you've had in a long time. Maybe even more than you had with this guy you're hung up on.''

I thought about my times with Greg; we did have fun. But now it seemed like so long ago, and I wondered if it was even possible to have it that way again. After what he'd been through, could he be carefree as he'd once been? I tried to remember him being happy and having fun, but it became so hard to separate him from the war, the relentless conflict with my parents, and everything that seemed to be smothering me. He was part of a tangle I couldn't undo.

I turned to Anthony and said, "I know. I have a lot of things to think about."

He smiled. "I'll be here."

As I watched him drive away, I thought how right it could have been ... in another time, when Greg's voice was just a faint echo and his memory was fleeting as a spark.

I wanted so much to smooth things out with my parents, but I didn't know how. It seemed that our relationship had deteriorated to little more than a clash of political views, ideologies milling around bumping into each other. The gap that separated us had become a chasm, yet it seemed not that long ago that my father and I walked up the hill behind our house in the valley, and he listened to my dreams of living in a lighthouse. Now the pain of being strangers was so great I couldn't even spend twenty-four hours under their roof.

One morning Tara said, "You know, Anthony's got a show opening at a gallery on Melrose this Tuesday. You should go. You'll run into a lot of people you know, and I hear his new work is dynamite."

I remembered his telling me he had a show opening soon; all his recent work had already been shipped off to the gallery by the time we met.

It was Sunday, and my parents were flying into town that night to stay at the house in Bel Air. An art gallery might be good neutral ground on which to meet, but going with my father, with all the security personnel in tow, would have been a major production. I called to invite my mother.

"Hi, Mom, how are you?"

"Fine. We just got in last night."

"Yes, I know. Listen, if you're not busy Tuesday night I wonder if you'd like to go to an art gallery opening with me, just the two of us. You know, sort of girls' night out."

"Oh?" She sounded suspicious. It occurred to me that she probably hadn't spent an evening away from my father since they were married, and she might not be anxious to start now. Maybe this wasn't a good idea after all. . . .

"Where is this gallery?"

"It's down on Melrose."

"Well, I guess that would be all right. What time?"

"I'll come get you about seven-thirty."

"Fine. Elizabeth?"

"Yes?"

"Were you planning on picking me up in the station wagon?"

"Well, I suppose so. My Mercedes is in the shop."

"Would you please be sure to get it washed that day?"

Tuesday evening, as she got into the car, I could see her scrutinizing it outside and in.

"It's waxed, too, Mom."

I headed for West Hollywood. The drive down Sunset was scenic, but it was impossible to relax with my mother in the passenger seat; she had a habit of slamming her right foot down at unpredictable moments as if an unseen brake pedal could bring the car to a screeching halt.

"Elizabeth, what sort of gallery is this?" she asked, punctuating the question with a slam of her foot.

She made me nervous and I sped around the curve. "I don't know, Mom, a nice gallery. Could you please stop doing that with your foot?"

People were spilling out of the gallery and I could see a few photographers snapping pictures of the guests as they arrived. I didn't want my picture taken and, without asking my mother's opinion on the subject, I drove past the valet parking sign and found a spot around the corner.

We slipped through the crowd without being recognized, behind a couple of tall men in cowboy hats. Once inside, I looked forward to having some enjoyable, civilized conversation with my mother about the avant-garde art Tara had described as "dynamite." Suddenly I felt like Alice down in the rabbit hole, but instead of a tea party, I'd been dropped into a world of giant-sized genitalia. There was a six-foot penis painted in Day-Glo colors, and giant breasts with blinking red lights instead of nipples . . .

"Elizabeth, get me out of here *now!*"

When we were out again on the sidewalk and safely past the crowd, my mother extended her stride and put enough distance between us to allow a Mack truck through. We got in the station wagon and pulled out onto Melrose. Streetlights were blinking on in summer's late sunset. I watched the white line, wondering what to say.

"Elizabeth, how could you? What possessed you to bring me

to a place like that? Are you trying to—to gross me out, is that it? You want to humiliate me completely—and in a public place! My heavens, haven't you done enough to—"

"Mom, come on! I had no idea that was a gallery for erotic art. It never even occurred to me that it might be."

"Well, you must have had some idea what it was."

"No, I didn't, as a matter of fact. Look, you can believe me or not. I wasn't expecting to find Rembrandt, but I didn't think it would be quite *that* contemporary."

"I see. You're telling me you don't even bother to investigate things before you pursue them."

"No, not everything. Do you?"

"Of course."

"Great."

"Good heavens, Elizabeth, what if someone were to recognize me in there? How would I possibly explain it? The press would have a field day!"

"No one recognized you, Mom. Nobody even saw us, for Christ's sake, we—"

"You might watch your tongue if you don't mind."

"We weren't even there for ten seconds. Come on, Mom, don't get all worked up. You're safe. We're miles from there and you'll never have to see the place again. Pretend it never happened. Pretend it happened to someone else. Pretend it was a bad dream —something you ate."

She sighed loudly. We were almost in Beverly Hills, and after several long moments of silence, she said, "Elizabeth, can we stop for a drink?"

The only thing that would have shocked me more was if she'd asked me to turn around and go back to the gallery—"I'd just like to take one more look at that penis, dear, if you don't mind." My mother had about one drink a year, usually on New Year's Eve.

"Sure, Mom, where would you like to go?"

"Well, how about the Beverly Wilshire? They have a nice bar."

"Okay. Pardon me for asking, but how do you know about the bar at the Beverly Wilshire?"

"Your father and I used to go there sometimes for a nightcap when we were courting."

"Uh-huh."

We found an empty table in the corner, and when the waiter came over we both asked for white wine.

My mother turned to me and whispered, "Elizabeth, that ... artist wasn't a friend of yours, was he?"

"Are you kidding? Of course not."

"Thank heaven."

"I heard a rumor, though, that his studio used to be a brothel. Maybe that's what inspired him."

She let that pass. "Just make sure you don't breathe a word of this to your father." She set her purse on the table. "So, Elizabeth, are you seeing anyone these days?"

My mother had never asked about my private life before. It must have been those erotic sculptures.

"I was seeing someone recently, but it didn't work out." Yeah, I thought, when he started bringing out those giant breasts and neon sex organs, things really went on the skids.

"Well, I only hope you find the happiness that I've found with your father. I can truly say my life began again when I met him."

"Mom, what did you want to do before you got married? I mean, career-wise."

She took a long sip of her wine. "Oh, I didn't have any career ambitions. I was working in a department store when we met. It was a nice job, but it was just a job."

She took out her compact, touched up her lipstick, and checked her hair for any misplaced strands, of which there were none. There never were. Her hair was always perfectly in place, framing her face in the most flattering way possible. I couldn't remember it ever looking any different. One night I had stayed awake waiting for the tooth fairy to come and leave a quarter under my pillow in exchange for the tooth that had ended up on my dinner plate. When I heard the door open, I hid under the covers and pretended to be asleep, but when she got closer I opened one eye just enough to see the top of her head. In the morning I ran into my parents' room with the exciting news that "the tooth fairy has the same hairstyle as Mommy."

"All I ever wanted," my mother said, "was a husband and a family. And if I'd had a career, I'd have given it up without a second thought. You'll have to choose someday, Elizabeth. You can't have both a career and marriage. It just doesn't work."

The waiter came by and, after hesitating for a few seconds, she giggled and said, ''Well, I guess I'll have another glass. So will my daughter.''

''Mom, you can't make a generalization like that—that having a career and marriage is impossible. Plenty of women make it work out just fine.''

''I think if you looked closely you'd find that it's put a strain on the marriage. Look, Elizabeth, there are many things I might have liked to do, places I'd have liked to visit, or maybe even have lived in. But that all had to take a back seat to your father's work and his goals.''

''That's a pretty high price to pay, Mom.''

''You have to be unselfish in marriage. Someday you'll find that out. Do you remember during the campaign when I was so sick?''

''Yes, I think so. You had a bad flu or something, didn't you?'' I remembered calling home from Devon and hearing her pathetic rasp straining over the telephone line.

''Well, the doctor insisted that I stay home and not go on whatever campaign trip it was. I can't even remember now where we were going. He said it could turn into pneumonia. But I couldn't let your father go out there by himself. After all, there are so many things I can take care of, so why should he have to worry about them? Besides, it wouldn't have looked right. So I went.... Thank God I didn't get pneumonia.''

''Did you tell Dad what the doctor said? I'm sure he wouldn't have wanted you to go.''

''No, I didn't tell him. I couldn't give him that to worry about along with everything else he had on his mind.''

''But what about the pressure you put on yourself by hiding things from him? Wouldn't it be easier if you could just be more honest?''

She shook her head slowly. ''Elizabeth, this attitude of your generation, this 'letting it all hang out' and confronting one another with every little thing, I don't mind telling you I find it just a bit ridiculous. I was reading an article in the *Ladies' Home Journal* about these encounter groups and the things that husbands and wives say to each other—well, it's just embarrassing.'' She took a small sip of wine, then carefully replaced the glass on the table. ''I remember when my mother was so ill,'' she began. ''It wasn't until she was very close to the end that your Grandpa Samuel had any idea how serious it was. I saw how brave she was—suffering in silence like that—and I wanted to be just like her. I was in college then and—'' She paused and pulled her head back from the circle of candlelight, but not before it reflected off a tear that had escaped from her eye and traveled over her carefully applied makeup. She seemed to have withdrawn into a shadow, into a dark cave of her memory where ghosts whispered and brushed her skin.

''You were in college when she died. Did you have a boyfriend then, someone you could confide in?''

She was dabbing at her eyes and straightening her shoulders as if, by adjusting her posture, she could deflect another surge of emotion.

''No . . . no one serious, but her behavior taught me a lesson in how you should be with someone you care about, and it's a lesson I've always remembered.''

''Maybe the lesson was *not* to act like that.'' I saw my mother's face tighten. ''Maybe your mother's secrecy prevented them from sharing something really important.''

The look that came across her face was familiar. Dismissal: no more discussion, case closed, no, the dog cannot sleep in your bed tonight, yes, you have to wear shoes to school and that's that.

''Elizabeth, I'm afraid you're just too young to understand. Perhaps someday you will.'' She removed her compact from her purse and checked her makeup. No trace of tears remained. Glancing at her watch, she said, ''My heavens, look at the time. Your father will wonder what's become of us.''

When we left the bar, we walked through the lobby and stopped at a display case with an opulent collection of diamonds and rubies from Tiffany's.

''Someday, Elizabeth,'' my mother said, ''you'll be married, and your husband will buy you lovely things like this.'' I looked at her, understanding for the first time the carefully constructed image she had of marriage and family. Like building blocks placed precariously on top of one another, built on prayers that the wind would never blow. I wondered how many wishes and fantasies my mother had kept hidden—wishes left to shadows and velvet boxes where secret things are kept. How many fluttered through her mind in the empty hours between sleep and dawn, only to be caged again?

My father answered the door wearing the red terry-cloth robe that had been a Christmas present several years before. When he pulled it out of the box that morning, his face had taken on the look of a child who expected to find a toy and instead got a pair of saddle shoes. "Well, it's beautiful," he had stammered, "but I don't really need a new robe."

"Oh, honey, your old one is threadbare! There are places where Heidi chewed on it when she was a puppy. You can't hold onto things forever, you know."

The subject was dropped except for the thank-yous and kisses, but he was clearly not convinced that you couldn't hang onto things forever. After all, the station wagon still functioned, but for some rattling and sputtering, and look how long he'd hung onto that.

"Hi, dear." She leaned upward and offered her cheek for a kiss. "We had a wonderful time."

"How was the art exhibit?" he asked.

"Oh, it was just lovely, Bob. Landscapes mainly—oils, watercolors. Such a talented young artist, I think he has a wonderful future ahead. Wouldn't you say so, Elizabeth?"

I watched my mother glide through the room, chatting and smiling as she hung up her coat, confident once again that she had protected her husband from the bothersome details of an unpleasant experience.

The phone rang and my father went to answer it. There was a time when the phone never rang after ten at night. Now it rang at any hour with some sort of governmental emergency, and it would always be answered.

"Why don't you stay the night, Elizabeth?" my mother said. "It's late. You don't want to drive back to Laurel Canyon at this hour, do you?"

"No, I guess not."

"You can borrow a nightgown and robe from me. Go look in my dressing room." I walked by my father, who was sitting on the bed with his head in one hand and the phone in the other, talking about the legislature and the importance of "getting this bill through." I smiled, knowing he didn't see me, and went into my mother's dressing room.

When I emerged, wearing a pale pink silk nightgown and matching robe, I found my mother in the den drinking a cup of warm milk.

"Would you like a cup, Elizabeth?"

"No thanks. I never could figure out how you can drink that stuff."

"It's the calcium, dear. Good for the beauty sleep." She was curled up in one of the armchairs with her shoes off and her blouse untucked, looking relaxed and suddenly very young. She settled back.

"You know, I was looking forward to going to an art gallery this evening." She looked down, and laughed. "I mean, a *real* art gallery. I used to be quite a connoisseur if I say so myself."

"I remember . . . you used to go to lots of galleries and museums when we were kids."

"Oh, yes, it was my passion, all right. In fact, some people approached me about opening my own gallery; they wanted to back me. But it was just at the time your father was going to declare his candidacy for governor. I couldn't very well embark on a project like that, could I?"

"I had no idea, Mom. It sounds like it could have been a great opportunity."

"Oh, perhaps. But you can't look back and regret things, Elizabeth. You make the choices you must, and you go on from there." Her eyes took on a wistful look, a glimpse, maybe, of what life could have been like. She sipped her milk, and looked up.

"I would have been damned good though, don't you think?"

I saw my parents only once or twice the rest of the summer. Whatever reconciliation occurred that night after the fiasco in the art gallery seemed fragile as blown glass, and I didn't want to risk breaking it.

I was anxious to return to Mountclaire; it was comfortable and familiar, all the things that Los Angeles was not. Belinda and I decided to room together again. Alicia, Dennis, Trina, and Jake had all returned. Jamal had not. Jake said he thought Jamal had moved to California, and was possibly at Berkeley. I felt cheated by his leaving. There seemed to be unfinished business between us. Or maybe it was just my ego, since I knew he never quite believed I was sincere.

During the flight from Los Angeles to Chicago I tried to think beyond college to where I wanted to be ten years down the road. Somewhere over the Rockies I sipped a vodka and tonic and imagined myself giving poetry readings and holding seminars. In the hope of turning that daydream into a reality, the first class I registered for was a creative writing class with Wilder Hayes. I delved in with a new energy, spending late nights writing and rewriting. The first poem I turned in was called "After the Twain Met."

> *and what a falling off was there*
> > *there*
> > > *with*
> > > > *time*
> > > *caught in our throats*
> > > *and the snarled web of fantasy*
> > *nailed to our breast.*
> *there*
> > *with*
> > > *fallen friends*
> > > > *pressed between*
> > > > > *the pages*
> > > > > *of books we never wrote.*

> *we are the branded, brother,*
> *the scrawled omens of yellow parchment*
> *come-to-life,*
> *the desolate children of Calvary,*
> *and huge arms wave us like sprigs of laurel.*

> *another sun*
> *unglues itself from the ragged horizon*
> *and snaps us to attention.*
> *we are the stranded, brother,*
> *writing our epitaphs in rhyme,*
> *and dancing to the rhythm of no music.*

Wilder called me over after class and told me he liked the poem. He asked if he could see more of my work. That was all I needed to hear. Over the next few weeks I deluged him with poems. We began spending afternoons together at the union; cups of bitter coffee vanished along with the hours of discussing images and metaphors and analyzing other poets. He began going with me to Alicia's meetings, eager to contribute whatever political insights he could. Though we barely knew each other, our shared passions for poetry and for ending the war created a bond between us. We took long walks through autumn afternoons, crunching through brittle leaves, watching winter move in. The trees grew bare and the wind got colder; heavy jackets started to appear.

The inevitability of my father's reelection gave me time to accept it, and to decide that this time around I would call and offer my congratulations. They were taken graciously and I could hear the surprise in my mother's voice.

Two days later, on a brisk afternoon, I opened the heavy glass door of the dorm, letting a flurry of leaves in behind me, and saw a silver-haired man waiting on the other side.

"Beth Canfield?"

"Yeah?"

"I'm Ted Slauson—I'm with the FBI."

He was wearing a dark blue pinstriped suit, gold watch, and shiny black shoes.

"What color socks are you wearing?"

"Excuse me?"

"Oh, c'mon, don't put me on, okay? If you're with the FBI you've gotta be wearing white socks. If you're not in the proper uniform, how do I know you're not selling insurance or encyclopedias?"

"Miss Canfield, I really don't know what you're talking about. Here's my identification."

I studied the card as if I had the expertise to detect a forgery in a minute. "Okay, to what do I owe the honor?"

He cleared his throat and put his card away. "Is there someplace we could talk?"

This presented me with an interesting set of choices. We could get a cup of coffee somewhere, but hanging around with feds wouldn't do wonders for my credibility. We could talk in my room, but I'd never live that one down. Or we could sit in the dorm lounge, and if I sat far enough away from him, people might think he was just some stranger who had wandered in and struck up a conversation.

"Let's talk in there," I said, pointing to the lounge.

He settled on the couch and took a thick pile of papers from his briefcase. "Miss Canfield—"

"I think I'd be more relaxed if you'd call me Beth."

"No problem there. Now, I'd like to ask you about some of your associations these past couple of years. I assume you know that Miss Washington has participated in quite a number of demonstrations, and in fact has instigated some of them. Not just on this campus; there were some civil rights demonstrations in which—"

"Gee, I didn't know. I'll be sure to stop speaking to her right away. You mean she actually demonstrated for blacks having equal rights? I'm shocked."

"Miss... Beth, this is not a joking matter. I have a job to do and I'm trying to get some information here."

"Oh, yes, about your job. Who sent you anyway? My parents? My good friend Jeb Henley?"

"I'm not at liberty to say."

"Well, then, Mr. Slauson, I'm afraid I'm not at liberty to answer your questions, unless you're planning on arresting me."

"How much do you know about a certain Wilder Hayes, with whom you've been keeping company?"

"Oh—if you mean that armed robbery conviction—he didn't do it. He was framed."

"Miss Canfield, if your father becomes a candidate for president these things will be of great concern. If you don't talk to me, there'll be someone else who will come with the same questions."

"I'll take my chances. Now if you'll excuse me, I'm late for my munitions class. We're learning to make hand grenades. Wanna come? Might come in handy in your line of work."

He snapped his briefcase and showed himself to the door.

Nights, while Belinda slept, I'd light a kerosene lamp and work on my poems. Ideas were like a prairie fire burning its way through my mind. My hands could barely write fast enough to keep up with my thoughts. Wilder edited my work and urged me to submit it to college papers and magazines. I told him I didn't think I was ready. He responded by handing me a list of publications.

The first poem I had published was in the Harvard *Crimson*. The day I got the news, Wilder took me to dinner to celebrate. I watched him across the candlelit table, gulping down the house wine. With the exception of a clean shirt, Wilder was his usual disheveled self. If he'd made any attempt to comb his hair, he must have given up before the job was complete. Nevertheless, he had intense brown eyes and a dimple in his chin, and when he spoke, both his face and body participated.

I'd tried so often to define my feelings for him and always came up empty-handed. It was true that I looked forward to seeing him and talking with him, also true that there were moments

when I felt a vague attraction to him. But it was nothing like I'd
felt for Greg. Remembering those feelings, remembering how his
body felt and how he had touched me still sent shivers through
me. I doubted that Wilder could make me feel like that, but still,
there was something between us, maybe something to take its
place.

He raised his glass. "Now that we've built up your confidence
in your poetry, Beth, I'd like to encourage you to give more
speeches like the one you gave last year."

"That wasn't my speech, it was Alicia's. I just read it for
her."

"It seemed to me there was some improvising at the end. Am
I right?"

"Yeah, but I was nervous as hell."

"Well, you were good. You should write your own speeches
and give them. You could be a valuable asset to the antiwar
movement, not just as one of the sheep—as a leader."

"I don't know, Wilder, I'll think about it."

We went to his apartment after dinner. I'd never been there
before, but it was just as I'd expected—chaos.

"Can I get you some coffee or something?"

I followed him into the kitchen and, assessing the damage, said,
"Are you sure you can find it in here?"

"I have a system," he said. He walked over and put his arms
around me. "Will you stay with me tonight?"

I heard myself say yes, but I wasn't sure why. I hadn't been
ready with Anthony. I was still looking for some of the fire that
had been there with Greg, and I wasn't finding it. But I liked
Wilder, and I wanted to be with him more than I wanted to be
alone. Maybe that was enough.

His bedroom looked like it had been vandalized. There were
clothes and books everywhere. I wondered how he would even
know if it had been vandalized. It took several minutes to find
the bed under the pile of stuff that was on it, but we finally
managed.

Our lovemaking was over minutes after it began.

"What's wrong, Wilder?"

"I don't know. I guess I'm just tired. I'm sorry. Let's get some
sleep."

It was the same the next time we made love, but I told myself
it wasn't important. There was so much energy in every other

aspect of our relationship that it almost made up for it, or at least I tried to believe it did. A week before the Christmas holidays, Wilder asked me to move in with him.

"Look, you got me to clean up the place," he said. "You even put up curtains. Half your stuff is here anyway, so wouldn't it be easier?"

It had been many years since Christmas at home was any of the things I'd looked forward to as a child, any of the things that anyone looks forward to at that time of year. I dreaded adding to the usual tension by telling my parents why I had a new address. At dinner, the second night I was home, my father asked, "Tell us, Beth, what's new at school?" Brian hid his face behind his napkin. I'd already told him about my new living arrangements and his deadpan response was "That'll go over big."

"Actually there is something new I wanted to tell you about."

"Oh? I saw their eyes light up as if they expected me to announce I'd joined the Young Republicans. The food I'd just eaten churned nauseatingly in my stomach.

"I have a new address and phone number."

"Did you change dorms?" my mother asked, already suspecting that something distasteful was coming her way. She glanced over at Brian to see if he was in on whatever it was and his face quickly went blank.

"No, I've moved to an apartment—with someone else."

"What's her name?"

"Her name is—I mean, his name is Wilder. We've been seeing each other for a while. He's one of my professors."

Silence. Brian, trying to cut through the cold air that had descended on the table, said, "You know, the one who gave her an A last semester?"

"This is not a joke, Brian," my father said. "Beth, this is very disappointing. What you're telling us is that you're living in sin. Of course, since you don't believe in God, I guess I shouldn't be surprised."

"Dad, will you stop with the not-believing-in-God business? I do, but this has nothing to do with God. It has to do with . . . friendship, that's all, and there's nothing wrong with it."

"Friends of the opposite sex don't need to *live* together," my mother said.

I knew they were picturing Wilder and me in a passionate love nest—wild orgies night after night. By telling them the truth I might have been able to ease their minds, but I didn't think they wanted any details.

"The decline of morals in your generation is just horrifying," she went on. "I remember those pictures from Woodstock, all those kids having unnatural sex acts—in the mud, no less."

"It's wrong in the eyes of God," my father declared, "and it's wrong in our eyes."

"Now wait a minute, what you mean is that it's wrong in your eyes. Unless of course you've had some intimate dialogue with God that I don't know about."

Brian laughed and received a sharp look from my mother.

"Don't make a joke out of this," my father snapped. "What you're really doing here is flying"—he waved his fork in the air, searching for the words—"in the face of everything your mother and I have believed in all our lives, and taught you to believe as well. You can't blame us if we regard this as just another way of rebelling for you. That seems to be your main motivation these days."

"Excuse me," Brian cut in, "Beth, if you're not going to finish your potatoes, can I have them?" I passed my plate to him.

"Dad, that's not true. The two of you are always looking for some motive. You never give me credit for just doing something because I want to do it."

"Well, you can hardly blame us, Elizabeth," said my mother. "Look at your record."

"Record? What record? What have I done that's so ghastly? I'm moving in with a guy—I mean, that'll surely make the world come to an end."

"This isn't the first example, Elizabeth," she went on. "Just look at your behavior ever since you started at Mountclaire. Even before that: hanging around with that family down the street when I told you I didn't approve. Sometimes I think you deliberately try to bum us out."

"Okay, hanging around with the Addisons. Participating in the crime of leaving soda-can rings on the furniture—guilty as charged!"

"Don't raise your voice, and you know darn well what I'm referring to. That whole drug incident."

"I didn't exactly bring a shipment over the border."

"That's enough, Beth," my father interrupted. "I think that's about enough."

More silence.

"Beth, you're our daughter and we love you no matter what," my father stated. My mother shot him a look. He looked back at me, and went on. "You'll always be welcome here, but your friend will not."

"Fine, just fine," I told him. "Now, if you'll excuse me . . ."

I got up and passed behind Brian's chair.

"Down head trip, huh, Mom?" he said, and met my mother's glance with a smile.

14

I WAS WANDERING IN A DENSE WOOD AT NIGHT, TRYING TO get home. Moments before it had been light, but darkness fell suddenly, filling up the spaces between the trees, crowding out the stars and the moon. The fog was so thick I could hear it brushing the leaves and settling on the ground. The smell of wet pine clung everywhere.

I stood still, wondering which way to go, but with the darkness and the mist I'd lost all sense of direction. All I could do was keep walking and hope for a clearing in the woods.

Suddenly, I saw a light through the blackness. I knew it must be the light from home, so I headed that way, but it kept disappearing behind the trees, and then reemerging. It seemed to change location each time, and each time I turned in a different direction, trying to follow.

At moments I thought I heard other footsteps. I'd stop, thinking it might be someone else who was lost, or someone who had come to find me and guide me home. But it was only the echo of my own footsteps bouncing off the trees.

It was cold and still and the light kept vanishing and returning, but it never seemed to get any closer.

Then the forest ended. I turned in the direction of the last light I saw, and it took me to a clearing . . . but there was nothing there. I was alone, with only darkness and mist and the sound of my own breathing.

My head jerked up from the pillow.

"What is it, Beth?"

"I was lost in the woods. I was trying to get home, but every time I saw the light it turned me in a different direction, and then—"

Wilder yawned and sank back into the pillows. "Don't you think you should take my advice?"

"What advice?"

"You know," he said, rolling over to face the wall. "Go into therapy and get these parental hang-ups of yours worked out. For Christ's sake, that dream is right out of a textbook."

"Are you suggesting group therapy again? I've told you I don't want to talk to a group. I'd rather just talk to you."

He pulled the covers up around his head.

"Okay," came his muffled voice. "Tomorrow."

I got out of bed to get a drink of water. Getting to the kitchen meant stepping over several sleeping bags spread out in the living room—visiting revolutionaries or friends who'd been too tired or stoned to head out into the cold night. At first it seemed exciting; impassioned talk late into the night, the thrill of sharing a common goal, one that so consumed us we lost track of time. Now the apartment smelled of dirty ashtrays and stale coffee. I'd once thought this showed a remarkably generous side of Wilder's character, but now it annoyed me. When I finally spoke up, my objections to our increasingly communal quarters didn't get the response I hoped for.

"You know, Beth, you're complaining about nothing. You've got some kind of latent materialistic streak, you know that?"

"Nothing? This is nothing? I buy food and when I come in here to eat something, it's vanished—every last morsel! I mean, you'd think someone would at least save me a bite. You know? One cookie? A half a glass of milk? I'm not greedy."

"Buy more food. You've got the money. Maybe they don't."

"They? What they? Who? I don't even know who these people are!"

"Forgive me, Miss Canfield. Maybe you'd like to have them cleared by the Secret Service."

"That's not fair, Wilder, and you know it. I really don't think I'm being unreasonable here. I come home and somebody's using my typewriter. Somebody else is wearing my sweater. Half my *underwear* is missing, dammit!"

Wilder rolled his eyes, and threw his hands in the air. "Don't you see? This is exactly what I'm talking about. You just confirmed everything I've said. Your problem is that you've been more influenced by your parents than you think. You imagine you're the opposite of them and that's what causes all the conflict, but what actually causes the conflict within you is that you're exactly *like* them. And if you're ever going to change that's the first thing you've got to accept."

I stood there staring at him, squeezing an empty cookie package. He came over and put his arms around me.

"I know it's hard hearing this. Look, I know this Gestalt therapist who has a group session every week. You should go. It would really help you sort this shit out."

"No thanks."

"Suit yourself."

After the dream, though, I began to consider Wilder's suggestion seriously. I was still put off by the idea of giving a group of strangers entree into my life, but I wanted Wilder to know I was trying to "sort this shit out."

It was early February. The war was grinding along; more plastic body bags were being stuffed with the remains of young lives, more gold stars appeared in homes throughout the country, signifying the loss of a soldier's life. Our effort was in a state of limbo; we were unsure how to proceed. Alicia was consumed by her conviction that passive resistance would achieve our goal. "If we could only organize in such a way that industries were shut down, particularly war-related industries . . ." For days we delved into concepts like civil disobedience, and those aspects of the Vietnam war that made it different from all others. Together, Wilder and I made an intensive study of the use and effects of napalm, and we learned about a defoliant called Agent Orange that was raining down on the jungles of Vietnam almost daily. The magical way we pooled our efforts and our enthusiasm made our problem in bed seem trivial, but I knew it wasn't trivial.

One night, with a winter moon throwing light on the bed and Wilder snoring beside me, I lay awake trying to think of some exotic way of seducing him. I'd heard that there were Japanese women who massaged men with their whole bodies and, the more I envisioned it, the more certain I was that Wilder wouldn't be able to resist a tactic like that. I rolled over and slid on top of him, moving my body against his as if waves were passing through me.

Like lightning, Greg's image split the darkness behind my

eyes. In that second, I knew how he would react, how his body would awaken to mine. But just as quickly, I pushed his image away, forcing myself to focus on Wilder, on what I wanted to experience with him.

"Beth, what the hell are you doing?"

"What do you think I'm doing?" I whispered.

"For Christ's sake, it's the middle of the night."

I rolled off him and stared at the ceiling. "Wilder, what is it with you? Am I the only one around here who's interested in sex?"

"Jesus, Beth, it's two o'clock in the morning and I'm trying to get some sleep. Give me a break, will you?"

For the next few days, I consumed myself with our research, trying to convince myself that things were bound to get better, and that it mattered if they did, because in the darkness it wasn't Wilder I longed for.

On a night when icy winds whistled through the streets, we walked into town to get some pizza. Warming himself by the huge brick fireplace, Wilder said, "I don't know ... it's just too quiet these days. Like the lull before the storm. Something's going to happen. I just feel it."

On February 8, 1971, we heard on the news that South Vietnamese troops, backed by American bombers, had crossed the border into Laos. Within seconds after hearing the news, Wilder reached for the phone. He and Alicia set up a meeting, and a rally was scheduled for February 10. We got word that other demonstrations were also being held around the country.

Wilder grabbed me by the shoulders and said, "Okay, Beth, this is it. You're going to be one of the scheduled speakers. I've already told the college paper to list you in the program, so word should leak to the press anytime."

"Wilder, don't you think you could have discussed this with me first?"

"You'd better start working on your speech."

I glowered at him, grabbed a yellow pad, and headed for the kitchen. After a double dose of instant coffee I began composing. With all the research we'd been doing, the information just seemed to flow. Delivering the speech in front of a crowd was another story.

Wilder stuck his head through the doorway. "How's it going, champ?"

"Fine."

"See? I told you. We have an interview in an hour—a guy from the *Chicago Tribune*. It just hit the wires that you're going to be speaking."

"Wonderful." I sighed.

When the bell rang an hour later, I opened the door to a short man who looked like he'd chosen his clothes in anticipation of gaining another fifty pounds. Even his glasses were too big for him.

"Hi, I'm Nelson Evans," he said, holding out a hand that I had to reach inside his sleeve to shake.

There was someone asleep on a chair in the corner. I pushed a bunch of newspapers out of the way to make room for us to sit on the sofa, and cleared some coffee cups and ashtrays so he could set his tape recorder on the table. "Sorry about the mess," I said, shooting a quick glare in Wilder's direction.

"That's okay—makes me feel at home. Now, Beth," he said, into his microphone, "this is your first scheduled speech. What prompted it?"

"Well, I've been active in the antiwar movement for a couple of years now. I think it was just a natural progression."

"Your father is directly opposed to your stance. In fact, he's been responsible for calling out the National Guard on California campuses on several occasions. Some people think he'll be a candidate for president in the near future. How does *he* feel about your speech?"

"Look, I'm speaking out about a war I believe is wrong. I have that right, as an American citizen, to speak out. If you want my father's opinions, you'll have to ask him. I can speak only for myself."

The phone rang. Wilder went into the kitchen to answer it and called out, "It's for you, Beth." When I closed the door behind me he whispered, "It's your mother."

"Hello?"

"Elizabeth, your father's not here right now and he doesn't know I'm calling."

That was my cue she was pulling out the heavy artillery. In the next room I could hear Wilder talking about defoliants, B-52's, and American imperialism.

"I just heard that you're going to give a speech at some ... demonstration."

"That's right."

"Elizabeth, this time you've gone too far. It's bad enough that you hold these views and insist upon consorting with revolutionaries. But to go out of your way to speak in public—and at a time like this in your father's career? Have you no sense of loyalty? No sense of respect?"

"Mom, I don't think this has anything to do with loyalty. And has it ever occurred to you that I may deserve some respect, too, for standing up for what I believe in? You know, some parents would take pride in that."

"Some parents would yank their child out of that hotbed and send her off to a finishing school in Switzerland. Your father thinks that might be the only way to get you to straighten up and fly right."

"Fine. There are protests in Europe, too. I could either join one or start my own."

"Well, Elizabeth, it's easy to see where your priorities are. You come first, and your family comes later, isn't that it? You know, someday you'll regret this, I promise you. Your father won't be around forever."

"I won't be around forever, either, Mom. And I'm just trying to make the time that I am around count for something. Have you and Dad ever thought of that? Look, is this the only reason you called?"

"I felt it reason enough, young lady, but apparently it's all been a waste of time. Obviously family loyalty means nothing to you. Goodbye, Elizabeth."

Time and again she mentioned my lack of loyalty to my father. Had I betrayed him so terribly? I had to wonder if it was all my fault. She kept him so close I sometimes doubted that there was room for me.

When I went back into the living room, Wilder was wrapping up the interview. Nelson Evans said his goodbyes and, after I heard his steps fade down the staircase, I said to Wilder, "I think I'm ready for that group therapy."

"Good girl," he said. "And just to show you I'm not a complete tyrant, we'll go together. By the way, you did great with that reporter." He hugged me and planted a kiss on my forehead.

The day of the rally was still and cold. The gray skies let neither snow nor wind through, locking us into a deathly quiet corner of winter. Pressed together for warmth, students and townspeople gathered, drawn by a chilly awareness that the war had crossed yet another boundary. As I looked out over the crowd and noticed how many people from town had come out, I wondered how many had lost their sons.

I noticed a boy standing in the front; he was wearing jeans, an army jacket, and a knit ski cap. Not unusual, really, but there was something different about him that I couldn't define. When he reached up to adjust his cap I realized what it was. His hair was so short I could barely tell what color it was. He looked around self-consciously and pulled the cap down lower over his ears.

Wilder had noticed him, too. We were sitting by the side of the makeshift platform we had set up that morning. I was scheduled to speak before Alicia, and just after the folk-singing duo who were at that moment tuning their guitars. They began to sing, "Where have all the flowers gone, long time passing..."

As usual, a few of the students who made a practice of trailing after Wilder had found us and were sitting behind him, like dogs held by an invisible leash.

Wilder leaned back and said over his shoulder, "Do you see that guy over there? I'll bet he's in the military. Probably just back from Vietnam. If he's here to cause trouble..."

There were a few cops standing around; the idea of trouble wasn't far from anyone's mind.

"He's not doing anything," I said.

But he couldn't take his eyes off the boy. "Maybe not. But someone ought to find out who he is and why he's here. Why don't you go down and make some inquiries, Steve?"

Steve, a skinny, acne-faced freshman who was known for his imitation of Wilder's clothes and mannerisms, jumped at the chance to please his leader. He got off the platform and stood inches from the kid, head tilted back so he was looking down his nose.

"So what if I was in Vietnam?" I heard the boy say. "I have a right to protest the war, too, maybe more of a right."

Steve turned around and, timing his words perfectly to coincide with the end of the song, shouted, "Hey, we don't want some fuckin' baby killer here, do we?"

Voices welled up as if they'd been waiting for a cue. "No! No!" I looked over at Wilder. He was sitting back, arms crossed, with the look of someone who just had a good meal. "Wilder, do something! This isn't fair."

"That's where you're wrong, Beth. It's absolutely fair. How many women and children do you think he's killed? Don't tell me about fair."

"Get outa here, man!" Steve screamed. "We don't want your kind here!"

There were shouts of "baby killer" and "murderer" from the crowd. They wanted to flog him to death with their words. I started to get up, but Wilder pulled me back. My eyes searched the crowd frantically for Alicia. She was nowhere around.

"Fucking hypocrites!" the boy shouted back, as they drove him off.

Wilder was still smiling. "You bastard," I said, and walked to the other side of the platform.

I gave my prepared speech. I spoke about the slaughter of innocent civilians, and the bombing our government was keeping secret from us. I called it a war of economic advantage with a price tag of human lives. When I finished what I'd written, I looked around at the faces in the crowd.

"I'd just like to say one more thing. Anyone has a right to protest this war, even someone who's been there—especially someone who's been there and who's seen what's really going on. This is supposed to be a peace movement. Maybe some of us have forgotten that."

I knew that it wasn't enough, that I should have spoken out in the boy's behalf before, when it would have meant something. I stepped down to less than thundering applause, but that hardly mattered now. Alicia squeezed my hands and said, "Good for you, kid." Wilder came striding after me and wheeled me around.

"Whose side are you on, anyway?"

"That's funny coming from you! Do you think that defenseless kid is what we're fighting? You think he's the enemy?" He was just an ex-soldier. He could have been Greg.

"You're out of your mind!" he cried. "If it weren't for poor defenseless kids like that there would be no war! What the hell do you think a war is?"

"You know nothing about that boy! It's not your business to drive people away. He's here for the same reason we are."

"You fucked up a good speech with that stupid remark at the end," he said. "You don't win a crowd's support by putting them down. Obviously you never learned a thing from your father about public speaking. Or maybe you just threw that stuff in to placate your parents after all.''

His words hung on the wind that blew between us as I walked away.

I wanted to renege on our group therapy appointment but at the last minute it seemed more important to face the things that were plaguing me than to spite Wilder. We walked into a room dimly lit by a fireplace full of blazing logs and a dozen or more candles. There were pieces of African art on the floor and the walls, and no furniture to sit on—only huge pillows. Several people were already there. Dr. Freeman stood up and walked over with outstretched arms. When he and Wilder embraced, his long, gray beard caught in one of Wilder's shirt buttons.

After a few others arrived, bringing the group to seven, Dr. Freeman said, ''We have a new member tonight, Beth Canfield. I'd like to tell you the rules briefly. We advocate complete honesty here. Whatever you feel, you say. That goes for everyone.''

I listened to one girl who was carrying around about eighty extra pounds recount her attempts to lose weight, and sob over her failures. Others, whom I could barely see in the shadows left by the smoldering fire, spoke up one by one.

''You think you're shit, so you let yourself look like shit,'' one said.

''Yeah, you're afraid of interaction,'' another chimed in, ''so you stuff your face and hide behind your weight.'' This poor obese girl was bound to leave the session and shed more tears into the biggest hot fudge sundae she could find.

Eventually it was my turn. ''And why are you here, Beth?'' Dr. Freeman asked, candlelight bouncing off his glasses where his eyes should have shown through.

Had I chosen to follow their rules, I'd have said, ''Because Wilder wanted me to, but now I think the idea really stinks.'' But I figured the first flaw in their rule was that they wouldn't know if I was following it or not. I said, ''Well, I just have some problems with my parents that need to be resolved. We have political differences that get in the way of our getting along.''

''That's bullshit, Beth,'' Wilder said, his voice filling up the dim room. ''Your problem is you—you think you're different from them but you're not. You're hung up with the same conservative, materialistic values that they are.''

''Could you elaborate on that, Wilder?'' Dr. Freeman asked. I was looking at Wilder in utter shock. I wondered if I was going to be charged for this abuse, or if Wilder was planning on picking up the bill.

"Yeah, your idea of a home and relationship is identical to your parents'. You want a nice little place with lace curtains, and complete fidelity in a relationship."

"Are you telling me that fidelity is the issue here?" I said, suspecting that he'd been sitting on this one for months.

"I think we should have an *open* relationship, but I've been reluctant to bring it up to you because of your conservative hang-ups."

Candle wax dripped down onto one of the African figurines leaving red droplets on her cone-shaped breasts.

"Why don't you answer him, Beth?" someone said from the shadows of the farthest corner.

I didn't feel entirely comfortable saying what I was thinking, which was that I doubted an open relationship would make him any less impotent.

"Fine," I said, "just let me know when you want to bring someone into the bedroom. I'll go sleep in the living room with the sixty-seven transients who usually occupy it."

For the next few weeks we tolerated each other. There was no affection, no attempt at intimacy, and no mention of Wilder's desire to start a harem, which didn't surprise me.

On March 29, Lt. William Calley was found guilty of the deliberate, premeditated murder of twenty-two Vietnamese civilians at My Lai. He was sentenced to life imprisonment, but public sentiment turned in his favor. Editorials appeared in the papers protesting his conviction, calling it a way to enable the government to have a scapegoat. He was receiving hundreds of telegrams a day, all expressing support and sympathy. Letters poured into the White House.

"I don't believe this!" Wilder yelled. "Why don't they just shoot the motherfucker? That would be justice." We talked more about this than we had about anything else in weeks.

"You know what it is?" he said, pacing the living room and kicking sleeping bags out of his way. "It's denial. This is America—Americans don't do that kind of thing. Americans aren't war criminals. We're the good guys—the ones who put on the Nuremberg trials. What a lot of crap."

Wilder wrote articles for the college paper about the absurdity of America rallying behind a murderer; he lectured his poetry classes about genocide and the perils of overlooking atrocities. He was consumed. He hardly ate, and never came to bed, which eliminated one source of tension between us.

I was as appalled as he about the brutal murder at My Lai, but something else haunted me, too. I couldn't help wondering if Greg had ever killed indiscriminately like that—in a moment of panic or fury. Were contorted faces and torn bodies etched on his conscience, on his soul?

One afternoon I was returning from the printer's, loaded down with fliers I'd picked up for Wilder. "Excuse me, young lady" came a voice behind me. I turned around and saw a young black man carrying a briefcase.

"Now what's a pretty lady like you doing carrying *all* those papers *all* by yourself?"

"Oh, please, spare me the come-on. I don't have time right now, okay?" I started to walk away.

"No, wait. I have something to discuss with you. I saw you with that heap of papers and I said to myself, 'Now she could use a briefcase like this one I got here—fine leather, locks so you can protect your valuables . . .' "

"And I'll bet you'll sell that to me for a real good price, right?"

"Well, no, not this one. This one's mine. But, you see, my brother has this leather shop—fine stuff—he'd make you a good deal if I was to bring you in there."

"And I suppose your cousin has a jewelry shop with some nice watches for sale, too, or maybe you've got a few on your arm that I could see?" I said, trying not to laugh.

He smiled and shook his head. There was something about him I liked. Probably the unapologetic way he was trying to make a sale.

"Now, listen, I'm just trying to turn you on to some nice stuff. He's got leather hot pants, too—real short, cut real nice. Legs like yours should be shown off. They'd look great on you."

"Okay, look, this is real entertaining, but I gotta go." I was about to ask his name when a campus security guard walked up.

"He bothering you, miss?"

"No, everything's fine."

I'd seen the guard before. He dated a girl from the dorm I used to live in, and tales of his racist behavior were legion.

He came nose to nose with Mr. Leather Goods for Sale. "You're not a student here, are you, boy?"

"No, I was just walking through campus—it's a public place."

"That's where you're wrong, boy. This is a private college and we can kick anyone off we want. And that's what I'm doing to you right now. So get the hell outa here, boy."

"Don't call me boy."

"I'll call you any fuckin' thing I want, nigger."

Fists flew, but before anyone got hit, a pair of black hands were in handcuffs and a pair of white hands were coming down hard on a nice leather jacket.

"Move, nigger." The guard turned to me and said, "You better come along, too, young lady."

"You know, I really don't understand what this is all about, he was just—"

"Just come along, now. You can tell us all about it at the security office."

"But I have to take these papers—"

"That can wait. This way, please."

The leather man cracked a few jokes in the back seat of the car, but I found less humor in the situation than he did. I kept trying to explain to the security guard that it was all a misunderstanding, but he didn't seem interested. At the security office they questioned me, supposedly writing down my exact words.

"You said your name was Beth Canfield?"

"That's right." I saw him cast a suspicious look at my stack of fliers."

"You the daughter of the governor?"

"Yes." The two men exchanged looks, and one went over to another desk and dialed the phone.

"Now, Miss Canfield, did you initiate a conversation with the, uh, Negro man we now have in custody?"

"No, he called to me and I stopped."

"And did you imply that he was trying to sell you a watch? Possibly a stolen watch—or several stolen watches?"

"Who told you this?"

"Mr. Garrick overheard the conversation. There's no reason to protect this man, Miss Canfield."

"But I was just joking! I—"

"Fine. Did he then try to sell you some . . . some hot pants, and in doing so make some salacious remarks about your body?"

"Well, he did, but—I mean, no, not really. His brother has a store and he was just—"

"Fine. That's all we need, Miss Canfield. This man has some dangerous friends. For your own protection we're going to have you remain in a female security officer's apartment. She's waiting outside to escort you."

"This is ridiculous! Am I under arrest?"

"No, miss. We're placing you in protective custody. Because of who your father is, you could be a target for some of this man's associates."

"For Christ's sake! He was just trying to sell me a briefcase. I didn't—"

"We have your statement, Miss Canfield, it's all we need. Now if you'll just come this way ..."

"Wait a minute. I can make a phone call. I know that much."

I called Wilder at the apartment.

"No, I don't know when he'll be back," said an unfamiliar voice. "Who's this?"

"This is Beth. I live there."

"Oh, okay. I'll tell him you called."

A burly woman was waiting for me. I climbed into the back of her car and was too frantic over what was going on to heed her attempts at conversation. As we walked up the steps to her apartment, she made me go ahead of her, as if she expected me to bolt and run.

She pointed me to the living room, said, "Your bedroom's over there," and then, backing out, locked the door from the outside. When I heard the bolt slide into place the realization of what was happening hit me like a slap. I ran to the door and began calling after her, but her steps vanished down the staircase. The afternoon was such a blur I couldn't begin to grasp how I had ended up there. I called Wilder again. This time there was no answer. In a matter of moments the feeling of being trapped was almost suffocating. I went to the window for air and to look for a way out. I was three floors up, and there was no fire escape. The sun spilled the last of its orange light onto the streets and the lights blinked on in the windows across the way.

⋆ *15* ⋆

*I*CALLED THE APARTMENT AGAIN AND LEFT THE NUMBER
with someone—I didn't even bother to ask who it was. It was
an emergency, I told them, please get a message to Wilder. Two
hours passed with no return call.

The security woman said her name was Maude, and that she
was sorry about this but "it's for your own good."

I opened some of her drawers, thinking she might have left a
gun around and I could shoot the door open. But at the third
drawer I stopped. There had to be some kind of karmic repercussions for invading someone's privacy, not to mention the legal
repercussions of blowing her door off.

It was almost seven o'clock. I called Wilder again. The same
voice told me the same thing. He wasn't there. "I gave him your
message, though."

"Well, did he say when he'd be back? Did he leave any message for me?"

"No to both questions. Sorry."

I tried Alicia's apartment but there was no answer. I couldn't
think of anyone else to call, or anything else to do, so I turned on
the local news.

"Mountclaire College released a statement this evening that
Beth Canfield, Robert Canfield's daughter, is under protective
custody at her own request following an incident in which a black

man allegedly harassed her. She called security guards and the man was arrested. There are no further details at this time.''

At my own request? *I* called security guards? It was starting to make sense to me.

I heard footsteps on the stairs and then a key in the lock. Maude threw her jacket on the couch and said, ''You're supposed to call your parents, Beth. They're worried about you. They called the security office.''

''Who gave that statement that I requested to be put in protective custody?''

''I don't know.''

''Of course you don't.''

My mother's voice sounded anxious but firm. She said they'd been terribly worried, that the security office had said I'd been accosted. This was getting more and more bizarre.

''I was *not* accosted! They're making this up! I was just talking to the guy and they arrested him and now they're releasing all these lies in the press. And they've locked me up in—''

''Dear, you're upset and you're not thinking clearly. These people know what's best. They're just trying to protect you.''

''I don't believe this. You're telling me I should stay locked up here like a prisoner for my own good?''

''Elizabeth, calm down. There's no cause for hysteria. Your father and I have discussed this with the authorities and we're confident this is best.''

I hung up the phone wondering if I was the crazy one. I was the only person, it seemed, who wasn't ''confident'' that everything was fine. Even strangers were more in control over my life than I was. It was a bad dream from which I was supposed to awaken, but somehow the nightmare had crossed over into reality. It was a warm spring night, but suddenly I was cold. There was a wall heater in the bedroom and I turned it on and sat close to it, hugging my knees to my chest and looking out at the clear night sky.

There had been a heater like that in our house in Woodland Hills. I would sit by it on rainy days, setting up camp there with my books and crayons and dolls. One gray, wet afternoon I sat there holding the red balloon I'd been carrying around for days, when suddenly the heat made the balloon burst. The noise scared me so badly I don't think I ever picked up a balloon again.

I went back out to the living room where Maude was sitting on the burlap-colored couch reading a copy of *Field and Stream.* Perfect. First me, then Bambi. It was the ugliest room I'd ever seen: Formica tables, a green shag rug that resembled some virulent strain of fungus, and paintings that must have come from a Holiday Inn rummage sale. I stood in front of her.

"What did you tell my parents?"

"I didn't talk to them. Look, you're just making this harder on both of us."

"Oh, I don't think it's so hard on you. You can walk out the door anytime you want. And by the way, did you have the outside lock installed just for my benefit?"

"It was left over from a previous incident."

I went back to the bedroom, slamming the door behind me. Fighting back tears, I tried Wilder once more. Again I was told he'd gotten the message, but wasn't there.

Suddenly the full impact of being imprisoned in a stranger's apartment hit me. I felt anger flood my brain and shoot through every muscle in my body. I paced the floor, faster and faster, trying to make the feeling subside, but it only got stronger. Then, as if my arm had a will of its own, it swung around, grabbed a clock off the table, and sent it crashing through the window. Glass shattered on the floor and the street below. Maude came barreling through the door.

"What the hell are you doing?"

I felt better. My blood had stopped seething and my muscles relaxed. After a minute, during which she glared at me with clenched teeth, I said, "You shouldn't lock people up—it makes them crazy. I'll pay for your damn window."

"You bet your sweet ass you will!" she said, and slammed the door behind her.

I fell back onto the bed and, trying to push away my feelings of anger and helplessness, I let exhaustion carry me to a distant place where none of this was real. My eyes drifted across the baby-blue walls, walls I remembered from my childhood, and soon I was four years old again and back in my old bedroom. I'd been put down for a nap by my English nanny, Cleo, and having no intention of going to sleep, I wandered around the room and into the bathroom. On the counter I found a lipstick that belonged to Cleo. I removed the cap and unwound it, and the bright, shiny red seemed to sing out to me from inside the tube. Lipstick in hand, I went back to my baby-blue walls to run wherever my imagination would take me and as high and wide as my arms would reach. I was in ecstasy, and positive that when my parents saw my masterpiece they would share my joy. Instead, my nanny screamed that I'd ruined her favorite lipstick, my parents screamed that I'd ruined their walls, and I screamed that I was an artist. Couldn't they tell? The upshot of the whole thing was that the lipstick drawings remained on the walls for a good three months as a punishment for me, though I still admired my work.

Maude was quiet in the next room; I turned out the light and felt the darkness wash over me.

Sleep was a deep well, dropping me into dreams of caves with no exit and rooms where the walls were roped together with cobwebs.

The next morning I tried Alicia. She answered in a sleepy voice.

"Alicia, it's me."

"Beth, where are you? You're all over the news! What happened?"

"I'm in a security guard's apartment. Alicia, everything you've heard is a lie. I didn't have that guy arrested. I was just talking to him. And I didn't ask to be locked up in here! I've got to get out. Wilder won't return my phone calls and I don't know what to do."

"Okay, calm down," she said, the last traces of sleep leaving her voice. "First of all, I know the guy they arrested. His brother is running for alderman of one of the districts, a predominantly black district, I might add. I'm sure Mountclaire's bigwigs would love to see him lose, radical that he is. There's a lot going on here, kiddo. Anyway, the guy you were talking to—his name's Roland —has been released. They charged him with trespassing, although they probably would have liked to charge him with more than that. Anyway, there'll be a trial, so it's not over yet."

"Alicia, I've got to get out of here."

"Let me work on it. I don't think they can hold you against your will. Give me the number there."

I heard Maude in the kitchen rattling dishes, opening the refrigerator. I hadn't eaten in almost twenty-four hours, but I wasn't going out there until she left. Finally I heard the door close and the outside lock slide into place.

The contents of her refrigerator revealed that Maude had a definite fondness for Sara Lee. The only thing bordering on nutritious food was a package of Cheddar cheese but, judging by the fissures in it, I estimated it had been bought sometime last summer. I cut off the only good corner and combined it with a piece of pound cake.

An hour and a half went by before Alicia called me back.

"Okay, Beth, we're coming to get you out. A lawyer friend of mine pointed out to the security office that they had no right to hold you like this. He also got a copy of your statement; we'll bring it along. I think you'll find it interesting."

Maude was the first one through the door. She looked at me with glacial eyes and I gave her back a mirror image. Alicia and a young bearded man were behind her.

I got my purse and the pile of fliers from the bedroom, walked up to Maude, and handed her some fliers. "Here you go, Maude, you can pass them out to your friends." As we walked down the stairs she yelled, "I'm sending you a bill for the window!"

Out on the street there was a light breeze and spring flowers spilling from window boxes. I let the smells and the warm air fill my lungs. We walked around the town talking about what had happened. The lawyer's name was Martin and he showed me the statement I'd supposedly made.

"... the suspect shouted at me to stop, then proceeded to try and sell me various items such as watches and leather goods. He then made sexual comments about my legs and what I should wear ..."

"This is incredible," I said, but somehow I wasn't really surprised. Nothing surprised me anymore.

Over lunch we discussed the alternatives available to me. I could take legal action against Mountclaire, which was way beyond my financial means, or I could try giving interviews to tell the real story. I decided on the latter, and the first person I called was Nelson Evans, the reporter who had interviewed me in Wilder's apartment.

"Okay, I'll do an interview with you, Beth," he said when I called him from Alicia's apartment, "but I don't know how much coverage it will get. It's sort of after the fact, you know."

"When can we do it?"

"I'm going to be in your neck of the woods tomorrow. I have

to talk to a vet who's going to be in the march in Washington—
what are they calling it? Oh, yeah, Dewey Canyon III. Interesting, huh? Dewey Canyon I and II were military operations in
Laos so they called this one Dewey Canyon III. Anyway, I'm
sure you already know all this. I'll see you after I talk to him.''

I was too embarrassed to tell him I didn't know all about it.
The idea of vets demonstrating against the war in which they'd
fought was fascinating to me, but I wasn't sure whom to ask for
information about it. After his treatment of that vet at the rally,
I wasn't about to ask Wilder.

When I got back to the apartment, he was getting his things
together for class. As usual, there were a few sleeping bags on
the floor filled with motionless bodies—motionless except for one
who'd had the poor sense to camp out next to the door and was
introduced to morning by a slamming blow to the legs as I came
through, still weighed down with Wilder's fliers.

''Beth . . . they let you go?''

I looked at him and realized that everything I'd once found
attractive about him was now distasteful to me: his uncombed
hair, the holes in his sweater, his glasses, which I was sure he
didn't need and were pure affectation—everything about him
made me want to look the other way. Instead, I glared at him.

''No thanks to you.''

''Hey, give me a break! What was I supposed to do, ride in on
a white horse and rescue you?''

''Wilder, don't insult my intelligence by thinking I'd expect
gallantry from *you*. At least you could have returned my calls.
Alicia didn't have any trouble figuring out what to do. But I
guess you were just too busy.''

''Get off my back, will you? I have a class to teach. Maybe you
should learn to take care of yourself instead of relying on me.''
I looked down at the pile of fliers I'd been lugging around for
him and threw them at him. White pages fluttered on the air and
drifted down onto sleeping bags where hands suddenly emerged
to fend off the attackers. On my way out the door I gave him a
suggestion as to what he could do with the fliers after he picked
them up.

Nelson Evans rushed into the coffee shop twenty minutes late.
''Sorry,'' he said, trying to catch his breath, ''that took longer
than I thought it would. He's leaving for Washington tomorrow
and I want to get the story out before the march begins on Monday.''

"I know I sound ignorant," I told him, "but I haven't heard about a march on Monday."

I expected him to be surprised, but he was on a roll. "Well, the Vietnam Veterans Against the War wanted to time it for right before the big April twenty-fourth march. They've planned some pretty dramatic stuff."

"Who was this guy you interviewed?"

"Name's Jan Elliot. Nice kid—lives here in town. Just got back from Vietnam. Now, about your story."

I filled him in on the facts of my situation, the lies, the motives, the school's attempt to discredit me with the antiwar movement, but it suddenly seemed small and unimportant against a backdrop of veterans descending on Washington to protest a war they knew intimately. I realized that there was an aspect to the war I'd been overlooking—those who returned after fighting it. I remembered the vet's face, a boy's face, when Wilder had yelled at him and called him a murderer.

"Well, I think I have enough here," Nelson said. "By the way, are you going to Washington on the twenty-fourth?"

In the midst of everything else, I'd forgotten about the march on Washington. It was going to be one of the biggest demonstrations in the last few years. I hadn't considered going before, but in less than a minute I decided I would. I left Nelson and bought a round-trip ticket for Washington.

My interview was in the Sunday paper, under the heading: "Canfield's daughter to attend April 24th rally in Washington." There were two sentences at the end of the article about "the incident." Nelson was right. It was after the fact; trying to change the story seemed futile. On the same page was the story about Jan Elliot. I looked at the accompanying picture and saw the face that had haunted me for months. His hair was longer, his eyes harder than they had looked that day. Something in me had known it was he when Nelson first mentioned the interview.

The news coverage of the veterans' march showed thousands of vets, many with stumps where arms and legs should have been, in wheelchairs or on crutches, their eyes angry or tearful, making their way into Arlington National Cemetery.

I watched the television, almost hypnotized, as a young vet named Lt. John F. Kerry addressed the Senate Foreign Relations Committee:

"In our opinion, and from our experience, there is nothing in South Vietnam which could happen that realistically threatens the United States of America. Any attempt to justify the loss of one American life in Vietnam, Cambodia, or Laos by linking such loss to the preservation of freedom ... is the height of hypocrisy. . . .

"We are asking America to think about that because how do you ask a man to be the last man to die in Vietnam? How do you ask a man to be the last man to die for a mistake? . . .

"We wish that a merciful God could wipe away our own memories of that service as easily as this administration has wiped away their memories of us. But all that they have done and all that they can do by this denial is to make more clear than ever our own determination to undertake one last mission—to search out and destroy the last vestiges of this barbaric war, to pacify our own hearts, to conquer the hate and the fear that have driven this country these last ten years and more, so when thirty years from now our brothers go down the street without a leg, without an arm, or a face, and small boys ask why, we will be able to say 'Vietnam' and not mean a desert, not a filthy, obscene memory, but mean instead the place where America finally turned and where soldiers like us helped in the turning."

Wilder had come in during the speech. I could feel him standing behind me. I made a point of not noticing, not saying anything. If there was anything left between us, I couldn't find it.

On Friday the twenty-third, a thousand veterans threw their medals over a recently constructed fence onto the steps of the Capitol. Some dedicated the medals to others who had died in battle. It was the ultimate act of contempt, throwing back the medals that the government had given them for their actions in a war they had come to revile.

My plane got in around ten-thirty in the morning. Traffic into the center of Washington was backed up for miles.

"Supposed to be half a million people here today," the cabdriver said. "Traffic's backed up all the way from Maryland."

When we got to the center of town, the buildings started to look old, historic, and governmental. There was no doubt that this was where the power was, where laws were passed and wars were declared. It looked like a page out of a history book. But it felt oddly familiar to me, as if I'd been there before, or would be again. It was a strange, shadowy feeling and I pushed it aside.

The rally began at the Ellipse just behind the White House and then proceeded down Pennsylvania Avenue to the Capitol.

Not only were most of the speakers older than the college students usually associated with the antiwar movement, but many of the people in the crowd were as well. I stood by one middle-aged woman wearing a mink coat, although it was a warm day. "Are you chilly?" I finally asked.

She laughed and said, "We decided it would be a good way to show that it's not just students who are opposed to the war."

The speeches went on all day. I had never felt such a bond among so many people. There was no violence, no dissension. I knew I was taking part in one of the finest moments of the entire antiwar movement. After the rally, thousands of marchers pitched in to clean up whatever trash had been left in their wake. I didn't get back to Mountclaire until after midnight.

"Beth, I was waiting up for you." Wilder was sprawled on the couch in front of the television. "You were mentioned on the news a couple of times, about being at the rally. How was it?"

"It was great." I looked around to see how much of an audience we had, and was surprised to see no one else there. There was a time when I would have sat up until dawn sharing with Wilder what I'd experienced that day. Now, he just made me tired. I went into the bedroom.

"Listen," he called out, "tomorrow we gotta talk about how to capitalize on this. You know, do some interviews about the rally and everything. It seemed to be a big deal that you went." He came into the bedroom and stood by the door. "Next big event like that, you should be one of the speakers. We'll work on that."

"No, Wilder, we won't—I will. There's no 'we' anymore." I had thrown everything I owned on the dresser, and reached under the bed for my suitcase.

"You're kidding, right? What is this—you're moving out? After all the work we've done together you're just going to walk out of here?"

I dragged the suitcase out and threw it onto the bed. "What we've been working for is an end to the war, and that's still what I want. I'm not walking out on that, Wilder. I'm walking out on you."

"I don't believe this. You make a couple of speeches and now you're off on your own. Who encouraged you? Who supported you? When we started out your confidence was shit! You need me! We need each other!"

"Right, Wilder. I need someone who puts me down all the time and preys on my worst fears about myself. I need someone who refuses my phone calls because when it comes to trouble he's afraid to get his hands dirty.''

''That's not true.''

''You know it is.'' I slammed the suitcase shut. ''I don't need you, Wilder, and if you need me ... well, look around. Somewhere you can find yourself another partner with a newsworthy name.''

''That's not fair! We had something going!''

''Especially in bed, right?'' I grabbed the suitcase and walked past him. He followed me into the living room where I grabbed books off the shelves and tossed them into a shopping bag.

''All right, all right. Now that it's out in the open—come on, Beth. Just stick around a little longer. Next week *Time* magazine is coming out to do a story—''

''So long, Wilder.'' I slammed the door. In a second it opened and I heard him yell behind me, ''As long as we're telling the truth, you spoiled little bitch—your poetry stinks!''

I turned back to him and smiled. ''Tell it to the Harvard *Crimson.*''

I went to Alicia's for the night.

· *16* ·

ABOVE A TAKE-OUT PIZZA PARLOR I FOUND A FURNISHED single room, big enough for the few possessions I had left after my months with Wilder. His open-house policy meant that every time someone stayed there and moved on, something —usually something belonging to me—moved on, too. My new home had stark white walls, which I brought to life with posters and anything else that seemed suitable for hanging. I made book-shelves from bricks and boards, and replaced all of the light bulbs with soft amber ones.

I gave my new number to Alicia and to my parents, who were delighted that I'd finally "come to my senses." I imagined them hanging up the phone and heaving a sigh of relief that my soul might have escaped the hellfire that awaits those heathens who choose fornication over conjugal love.

Among the first things I did after moving was remove Greg's picture and letters from the locked box where I'd kept them hidden while I lived with Wilder. As I read them over again I gave myself up to the tears I knew would come. When I dried my eyes, a strange thought occurred. I wondered what would happen if I asked my father to locate him. The government could proba-bly find anyone. But on the heels of that thought came a picture of Greg opening his door to find some FBI agent like Ted Slauson: "Greg Howell? I'm with the FBI. The Governor of

California asked me to find you.'' There had to be another way.

The May Day demonstrations were scheduled in Washington and Alicia planned some rallies at Mountclaire. ''And Beth,'' she said over a lunch of pretzels and coffee, ''you're one of the speakers.''

I laughed. ''Anything else you've scheduled me for that I should know about?''

''Listen, girl, it's now or never. You've been tiptoeing around this long enough. You've been playing around the edges without getting as involved as you could. It's time you took the plunge.''

She was right. I was ready to make a total commitment and anxious to show Wilder I didn't need him.

''Alicia, there's someone I'd like to introduce at the rally, and let him say a few words. His name's Jan Elliot. He's a vet. As a matter of fact, he's the same vet the crowd harassed that day, remember?''

She smiled. ''I remember.''

The day of the rally was warm and clear, a day for kites and picnics. But several hundred of us had gathered under a robin's-egg sky for a more somber purpose. A lazy wind pushed along puffed white clouds, like balloons that had escaped into the blue.

I looked out at the sea of faces in front of me, some so intent I wondered what story was behind their expressions.

''The war we've protested so long continues to claim the lives of many and permanently scar the lives of others.'' I heard my amplified voice bounce back at me through the sound system. ''While we're assembled here, at this moment, someone is losing his leg, or his arms, or his life for a war this government says he should fight. And all of us are losing our innocence as we watch this country sanction the loss of lives for a worthless cause. How long is this government—our government—going to tell us that the war is winding down when in fact it's escalating? Words like 'Vietnamization' mean nothing while the dead continue to pile up, while bombs continue to fall, and defoliants still pour down like rain.''

There was a burst of applause and, looking over the crowd, I saw Wilder clapping his hands over his head and smiling smugly, as if he had created me.

''I don't know,'' Jan had said when I approached him about speaking. ''No one seemed to want me there last time, especially your boyfriend. What makes you think it'll be any different now?''

''He's not my boyfriend anymore,'' I'd said, ''and maybe they won't accept me either. We just have to take that risk.''

''I'd like to introduce someone who knows more about Vietnam than any of the rest of us—because he's been there. Jan Elliot is active in the Vietnam Veterans Against the War and has recently returned from the demonstration in Washington.''

He was greeted with applause that tapered off to a respectful silence, a still pool into which his words dropped like pebbles, making larger and larger ripples.

''Once I believed that America was always right. I believed that her causes were the right ones, and her wars were those that needed to be fought. So when my country said go to Vietnam, I went. But what I saw there was wrong. There was no glorious cause. The only glory was in this government's fantasies—the fantasy of Vietnamization, and whatever perverted ideals have made them escalate a war they never should have gotten into in the first place. Last year I came here and I was greeted with shouts. I was called a baby killer and a murderer. But that wasn't the first time that happened to me or others like me. People have spit at us, moved away from us on planes, glared at us in subways.

''What I want to say to you is that we didn't start this war. We're not the ones you should be spitting at. Aim your anger at those who are really responsible—your government. Those of us who have been to Vietnam and back have just as much right to protest as you do, and we may have a better idea of exactly what we're protesting. What I saw over there—what all of us saw— will be the nightmare we have to live with. But if we can help bring an end to the nightmare of this war that can't be won, a war that will leave only carnage in its wake, then our legacy will be one to be proud of.''

As he walked off, tentative applause began and then swelled. I listened for hecklers, but could hear none; he'd won them over. Alicia and I went up to hug Jan, and through the tangle of arms I could see Wilder staring at me from a safe distance. Finally he came close enough to speak.

''Beth, can I talk to you for a minute?''

''What is it, Wilder?''

''I have some of your mail at the apartment.''

"Oh, right, I forgot to have my mail forwarded. I'll come by and get it."

"Beth—wait a minute. Could we just have coffee or something? I'd like to talk to you."

"There's nothing to talk about. I'll get my mail later today."

Devon sent out an alumni newsletter every few months—an update on who was doing what and where they were living. It was something I never contributed to but always read, usually with the hope of finding some information on Greg. Time after time I came up empty, but once I saw an item about Delia. She was married, living in Montana, and had a daughter. In the newsletter I picked up at Wilder's apartment, I learned that she was expecting her second child. We'd written a few letters back and forth, token gestures that enabled us to tell ourselves we'd kept in touch. But now, seeing her name again, I wanted to talk to her.

I got her number from Information. Her voice sounded older to me; contented and relaxed. I wondered how she'd changed.

"Well, this sure is a surprise, Bethie—how are you?" I could hear a baby cooing in the background.

"I'm fine. I was just thinking about you. It's been a long time since I heard your voice."

"Yeah. I read about you sometimes in the papers, giving speeches and stuff. You sure have a talent for stirrin' things up, it seems."

"Should I take that as a compliment?"

"Oh, I don't know. I know you're against the war and all, but it just seems like someone's gotta fight the Communists. I mean, where would we be if everyone refused to go to war?"

I laughed. "Delia, you always were a Republican at heart."

"Yeah, well, oh, can you hang on for a minute?" I heard clattering and crying and footsteps coming back toward the phone. "Listen, Bethie, I gotta go. The little terror's crawlin' now and she's into everything. Why don't you come out here and visit us sometime, like durin' the summer? We got plenty of room."

"Maybe I will. 'Bye, Delia, take care of yourself."

In Washington, the May Days resulted in thousands of arrests and frequent outbursts of violence between police and demonstrators. More peaceful were the memorials that were held nationwide for the students at Kent State and Jackson State. At

Mountclaire we held a candlelight vigil, and as I looked around at the faces half in shadow and half flecked with light, I noticed Jan standing back from the crowd, holding no candle, hugging the darkness as if it could camouflage him.

I walked over to him slowly; it seemed like I did everything slowly around him. Something about the way his eyes darted back and forth reminded me of an animal who sensed danger in any quick movement.

"Hi, Jan."

"Hi." His hair was long now. He pushed it back from his eyes and looked at me. "You know, I think it's too bad those kids died like that," he said. "But there are so many guys who've died in Nam, and others who've lost so many parts of their bodies there are times they wish they'd died. Who's lighting candles for them?"

There was nothing I could say. I blew out the candle I was holding, letting drops of melted wax stay on my hand and harden there.

"Sorry," he said after several minutes. "I guess I'm kinda weirded out today. I went to see a buddy of mine in the vet hospital in Chicago. His leg was blown off. I think I'm the only visitor he's had. His girl left him—maybe she can't handle sleeping with a cripple. Man, life is sure fucked up sometimes."

Candles were being blown out, spirals of smoke were drifting into the sky, and people were leaving.

"Jan, when you go see your friend again . . . I'd like to go with you."

"Why? Sudden surge of sympathy?"

"Hey, look, you have a right to be angry, but please don't take it out on me. All I've done is try to get people to see that the war is wrong—the same as you're doing now. I never called any vet a baby killer. I really would like to go with you, Jan."

The Veterans Hospital was at Roosevelt Road and Fifth Avenue, not an area where I'd like to be stranded after dark. In fact, I had a few reservations about going there in daylight. I suddenly felt conspicuously white, as if middle-class WASPishness were emanating from my every pore, alerting the neighborhood that there was an alien in their midst. I felt eyes peering at me from dark doorways, and I hoped that Jan was a devout male chauvinist who would sweep me out of danger's way should the occasion arise.

We walked through the hospital doors into a caldron of noise.

It bubbled up around my ankles and swirled past my head. The corridors were full of nurses, wheelchairs, men on crutches and in bandages. Jan seemed unfazed. "We have to go to the amputee ward," he said. "It's on the second floor."

I'd never done well in hospitals. I'd visited my grandfather in the hospital once when he was recovering from, as my mother said, "an operation—nothing serious, dear, just a minor problem." I never found out what the minor problem was, but there were bottles hanging by his bed and the one with yellow liquid in it filled up as I stood there, holding onto my mother's hand. My grandfather was pale and his breath smelled bad, and I threw up in the bathroom.

I felt my stomach churn when we got into the elevator, and I tried to push down the nausea with deep breaths. In the amputee ward I heard laughter and yelling and whistling—not the sounds I'd expected. A man with no legs went by me in a wheelchair, winked, and said "Hey, baby" under his breath. Jan laughed. "He's being careful in case you're my wife or something. I wouldn't come in here alone if I were you."

All I knew about Jan's friend was that his name was Kurt, he'd just turned twenty, he was a "grunt"—a sheepish inquiry revealed that meant he was in the infantry—and he'd been "short, man—only a couple weeks to go" when a land mine blew off one leg and ravaged the other with second- and third-degree burns.

We walked into a section that was thick with beds and wheelchairs; I wondered how the nurses found room to move between them. In the first bed was a boy whose arms stopped at the elbows. Half his face was bandaged, and the shape of the bandages didn't hold much hope for what was underneath. A man in a wheelchair sat by the bed crooning, "Hey, you're lucky, man—now you're only half as ugly!" Jan was looking at me. "C'mon, Beth, he's over here." The air smelled of urine and medicine. Please God, don't let me be sick.

Kurt was staring at the ceiling when we walked up.

"Hey," Jan said, "you daydreamin' or something? I brought a friend with me. This is Beth."

Kurt turned to me with eyes that belonged in an old man's face. "Hi, you Jan's girl?"

"No, I'm just a friend." I wondered if Jan thought of me as a friend. I wondered what Kurt's eyes had seen that had aged them like that . . . but maybe I didn't want to know the answer to either question.

"Know what I was thinking about, Jan?" he said, turning back to the ceiling as if his thoughts were painted there. "I was thinking about high school when I used to set all the records for the broad jump. Remember? Man, I was really somethin'—really fuckin' somethin'." His voice trailed off and I expected to see tears in his eyes, but there were none.

Jan said, "Okay, so maybe you'll never make the Olympics, but they'll fit you with a leg. You'll look fine. All the girls'll be after you again."

"No, I don't think so. They told me today there might not be enough there to fit a leg to. So how many girls are gonna want some guy with a nub where a leg should be? Sharon sure as hell didn't, now did she?"

For the first time I let my eyes focus on the left side of his body. It stopped at the bottom of his hip.

"I just want to get outa here," Kurt said. His words had a cracking sound like Brian's when his voice was changing. "I just want to get on with my life."

Before Jan could say anything a doctor appeared at the foot of the bed and said, "Sorry to interrupt you, but I'll need a few minutes here."

"That's okay," Jan said, "we gotta get going. I'll be back tomorrow, Kurt. Hang in there, man."

Outside, the smells of diesel oil and sour garbage seemed refreshing after what had filled my head in the hospital. On the way back, Jan stared off into space, and—afraid that whatever I might say would sound trivial—I remained silent. Finally he said, "You know what? What's really fucked is that if any guys come back as heroes in this war it's the guys who come back in body bags. They're really the lucky ones. The rest of us come back scum."

"Jan—"

"No, don't say anything! There's nothing you can say to change that 'cause you know it's true. No one gives a fuck—they don't wanna know anything about us—they'd rather look the other way. And they sure as hell don't wanna look at guys like you saw in there. Kurt wants to get outa there 'cause he doesn't know what's facing him out here. If he knew he wouldn't be so goddamn anxious."

I wrote an article for the school paper about my visit to the hospital. Excerpts were picked up by a couple of larger papers, and there were a few calls requesting interviews. I felt presumptuous describing something which I knew I couldn't possibly understand. Still, I felt compelled to relate the experience of seeing boys whose lives had been irrevocably changed, who had come home only to be shunned by the country that had sent them off to fight its war. Maybe someone would read what I'd written and the next time they saw a vet walking toward them, they'd smile instead of crossing to the other side of the street.

It could have been that there was some genuine interest in what I had to say, or it could have been that the rumors about my father becoming a last-minute presidential candidate made me an object of curiosity. I didn't want to ponder it too much. But in the press, my name appeared more and more frequently. Among those paying attention to this were my parents, who called and demanded that I come to California for at least part of the summer. "It's time we had a long talk," they said. I had no plans to go to California, and their invitation was not the kind that would send me running out for a plane ticket. I politely declined, which seemed to have no effect. Their last words were that they were sending me a plane ticket and hoped I would not disappoint them.

·*17*·

ROUND-TRIP TICKET TO LOS ANGELES ARRIVED IN THE mail with a note from my father in his slightly squashed, backward-slanting handwriting. His unique penmanship had evolved, I'd once been told, because he had been born left-handed, something frowned upon at the time. His schoolteacher, in an attempt to remedy this defect of nature, tied his left hand behind his back and forced him to write with his right. From that time on, he obediently, but awkwardly, wrote with his right hand and did everything else with his left.

The note said: "We hope your school year went well. We look forward to seeing you." I took a long walk around the campus, through the town, beside Lake Michigan—all pieces of a place where I thought I belonged. Now they seemed like pieces of a puzzle that didn't fit. Lately I'd attended very few classes. I'd gotten an education; but what I'd learned had nothing to do with the curriculum, and I didn't feel right about my parents footing the bill. I didn't belong on this campus any more than I belonged in California, and California was definitely not where I wanted to go. I thought about sending the plane ticket back, I thought about scraping my savings together and going to Alaska—the northern lights seemed suddenly irresistible. I carried my father's note around with me for days, glancing at it every few hours, as if the message there might at some point transform itself into an answer to my dilemma.

Alicia was graduating, and with her gone it seemed like my last ties to Mountclaire were broken. On a warm afternoon, with no wind to stir the thick air and sun tumbling through the now curtainless windows, I helped Alicia pack her things into boxes.

"Well, are you going to pick up where I left off, Beth? I bet you'd have a good chance at being student body president if you wanted to go after it."

"That's about the last thing on my mind at the moment," I said, closing a box filled with books and lifting up a corner of it to determine if anyone other than Mr. Olympia could handle it. "I don't know what to do, Alicia. I don't want to go home and talk to my parents, I don't want to stay here ... I don't really even want to come back next year."

"Look, I can't help you decide about coming back next year. That's something you're going to have to work out. But there are obviously a lot of loose ends as far as your parents are concerned and if I were you I'd tie them up. It doesn't do any good to skip out on it and not deal with the problem. Even if you don't resolve anything, at least you'll know you went back and tried."

I knew she was right. "I'm really going to miss you, Alicia."

I carried her advice around with me the way I'd carried my father's note. But there was more than one journey I had to make, more than one set of loose ends. I'd never stopped thinking about Greg, wondering how he was doing and what had become of him. Even if it was over between us, I needed to know that he was all right.

Two days after I watched Alicia graduate, I was scheduled to leave for California. I sat in my apartment and thought of packing everything up and just leaving for good, sending my belongings ... somewhere. I lay down on the bed and felt the coolness of the pillowcase on my cheek, heard my heartbeat against the mattress. When I was very small I would lie awake on dark nights listening to my heart thump like this. I'd imagine it wasn't my heart at all, but someone else's—someone who was hiding under the bed waiting for me to drift into sleep so he could crawl out and grab me with long, wavy arms. I'd feel my stomach fill up with fear; it would float up like water and bubble into my throat. I felt like that now, far from the blackness of those nights, with afternoon light settling on the walls, and only my own heartbeat. . . . The fear was the same.

I fell asleep and my dreams were cradled in light. Memories

winged through my mind of shimmery afternoons when Brian and I took long walks, found a honeysuckle bush and sucked sweet liquid from the blossoms—Brian said that was why it had been named honeysuckle. There were long summer days when we'd dangle our legs into the swimming pool and eat red plums that dripped juice down our chins.

When I woke up it was dark. I pulled a suitcase down from the closet and started packing.

On the plane I had a window seat, and watched passengers file by, hoping no one had been assigned to the seat next to mine. Outside, the Chicago sky was a dusty blue. Summer was a good time to fly west. In Illinois, it is not a kind season; the air goes limp and torpor sets in. No leaves stir, and people move slowly, wiping their foreheads and fanning themselves.

A slender man slid his briefcase under the seat next to me. He wore a perfectly pressed suit and had perfectly combed hair, slicked with either water or Vitalis; I made a mental note to watch to see if it dried. He nodded an awkward hello, and sat down. So much for having an empty seat next to me. What caught my eye when he slid into his seat was a flash of white at his ankles; he was wearing white socks. Great—now the FBI was following me onto planes. I was sure of it. I looked at him again, trying to create a look in my eyes that said, "Okay, I know who you are." He smiled again and said, "Warm day out, isn't it? I'm Norman Zsweski. What's your name?"

"Beth," I said, instructing my face to read "as if you didn't know."

We left Chicago behind us and I looked down on other landscapes, wondering what states we were flying over. Maybe the FBI had been following me all year, bugging my apartment, monitoring my phone calls. His briefcase clicked open and I tried discreetly to angle my eyes for a glimpse of what was inside. Probably a gun and handcuffs, along with reams of "material" he'd gathered on me. As if he could read my thoughts, he shifted the case so all I could see was the black leather top.

"What do you do, Norman?"

"I, uh, work for the government," he said, averting his eyes and shuffling the papers he'd just extracted from his briefcase.

Poor planning on the FBI's part—they didn't even give him a cover. I wondered what would happen if I changed seats. He'd probably change, too. And I wondered if he was planning on following me all the way to Bel Air, making sure I didn't escape, tailing me right up to the iron gates and then congratulating himself on a job well done.

"Actually," he said, the sound of his voice cutting through my thoughts and bringing my eyes back to his still wet-looking hair, "I work for the Postal Service. I'm not a mailman, though. People always jump to that conclusion. That's why I just say I work for the government. I work in an administrative capacity. These here are financial reports. Looks like we're going to have to raise the price of stamps again."

I looked down at the papers and that was exactly what they were. Either this was an exceptionally clever ruse, or my paranoia had gotten way out of hand. I realized it was probably the latter.

Satisfied that I wasn't being tailed after all, I let my attention wander to the other passengers around us. The old man across the aisle was pressing on his teeth as if his dentures were loose. I remembered the first time I discovered that my grandfather wore dentures. I'd come in to ask him something and found him at the bathroom sink gargling. I said, "Grandpa?" and when he turned around he had no teeth. His lips folded into his mouth and disappeared. I started running down the hall screaming for my parents and, not knowing what was wrong, he ran after me, which only made matters worse.

Brian opened the door for me. He was taller than when I had last seen him. His skin was tanned to a golden brown and the sun had lightened his hair. I wanted to hug him longer than I did, as if by holding onto him I could reclaim some of the hours I'd missed spending with him.

"I think Mom and Dad are in the den waiting to talk to you," he said, with the same casualness he had about everything. I'd once joked with him that if there were a ten-minute warning for World War III he'd snap his fingers and say "Damn, just two days before the Super Bowl." But it was the attitude I needed at that moment to untangle some of the knots in my stomach.

Just as he'd said, my parents were sitting in the den, wordlessly waiting for my arrival. I imagined they'd checked the clock at least a dozen times, not really sure I'd show up. I wondered why they chose the den for this meeting, rather than the customary fireside chairs up in their bedroom. But I wasn't about to object. I was a lot more relaxed in the den, where the walls and the furniture didn't reverberate with years of anxious confrontations. The den was neutral territory; if anything, the memories it held were happy ones. On the television, Brian and I had watched countless hours of "Shindig" and "Star Trek." One night my mother came in after we had rearranged all the furniture, and caught us reenacting a scene on the bridge.

"My Lord," she gasped, scanning the disarray, "what have you children done in here?"

"Uh-oh," said Brian, escaping behind the bar. "Beam me up, Scotty!"

"Is something wrong, Elizabeth?" my mother said, shaking me from my reverie. "Why are you staring like that?"

"Oh, nothing. I guess I was just wondering . . . well, we usually have our talks in the bedroom."

"The bedroom's just been painted," said my father. "Have a seat, Beth. Did you have a good trip?"

My father sat in the brown leather recliner in the corner, and my mother was in the loveseat beside him. He directed me to a chair facing them both.

"It was okay except for the FBI man sitting next to me."

"What's that?"

"Nothing, Dad. Just a joke."

"Oh. Well then, Beth, your mother and I have been wondering . . ."

"Yes?"

"Well, just where are you going with your life?" he blurted out.

"Where am I going? I don't have some kind of master plan, if that's what you mean. Not yet, anyway."

"Well, maybe you should. The only thing you seem to have dedicated yourself to is embarrassing us with your continual outbursts about the war. Young people in college should be preparing themselves for a career. It doesn't seem to me you've had time to do anything like that with all your demonstrating and 'speaking out' as you call it."

His words were coming to me from a place far away, from another time when I'd looked at him with younger eyes and wanted so badly for him to understand me. That child was still there, but she was behind me, down a long road, blurred with the dust of discarded prayers. Older now, I could only regret that her eyes were still sad, but I had to turn away from her and come back to this room with leather-bound books, and an orange sunset reflected in the pool outside. My parents were waiting for answers.

"I don't see why you can't allow me the dignity of having my own beliefs and expressing them," I heard myself say, "even if they contradict yours. You look at everything I do in relation to *your* lives. It's like my beliefs and my feelings have no importance at all."

My mother's jaw tensed. "That's just a cop-out," she said. I remembered the night at the gallery when she'd used the phrase "gross me out" and wondered if she'd taken a crash course in language of the seventies. "We've never said your feelings aren't important. Don't change the subject."

"Beth," my father said, pausing as he usually did when he wanted to stitch together the fabric of his thoughts, "I may as well lay it on the line. There's been a lot of talk about my running for higher office, and I'm not sure that isn't what the good Lord intended for me. Now how is it going to look if you're running all over the country spouting off about the war and associating yourself with these radicals who—I'm sorry to say, Beth—are just using you?"

I felt my throat tighten. No, I wasn't going to cry. They were the little girl's tears, and I wasn't going to let her put them in my eyes. Not now. On the table beside me was a glass case, and in it a ship that my father had made when he was in college. It was done to scale, and every detail was accurate. I wished at that moment it could magically grow into a life-sized version and carry me off.

"Maybe they are using me. Maybe you're right about that. But what you're doing isn't much different. Either way I'm being treated as an appendage of you. And none of that has anything to do with me. Everyone has their ideas of what I should be and how I should be acting because of who my father is, but where do *I* fit into that? I've never asked you to approve of what I'm doing, but please, can't you just recognize that I have the right to do it?"

My father gazed out the window as if the landscape of my words were somewhere at the edge of the darkening sky. My mother's gaze never wavered from my face.

"This is exactly what your father's getting at—your selfishness," she said, in a voice compressed and hard. "You don't care about us. Apparently now you don't even care about the people with whom you've affiliated yourself. It's just poor Beth, no one understands you. What *do* you care about? I think it's just yourself, not anyone else, and not even your so-called cause.''

"If you really believe that, you don't have any idea who I am. Have you ever really listened to anything I've tried to say to you?"

"Yes, Beth, we *have* listened," my father said. "We know you're against the war. Now why do you have to keep saying it and embarrassing your mother and me?"

"Because the war is still going on! And as long as it's going on, I'm going to speak out against it."

"I don't know how you can do this to your father," my mother said under her breath, but loud enough to ensure I would hear.

I stood up and, as I walked toward the door, I faintly heard my mother call my name, as if over a long distance. "Elizabeth, come back here. We're not finished. We want some answers." So do I, Mom, so do I. So what's the difference between us?

I walked across the patio, grateful for the darkness and the cool breeze. I passed the pool and went into the garden, and found my way to a bench under the trees. I let the pungent fragrance of night-blooming jasmine fill my head, let the warm evening air wash over my thoughts. I heard a click and saw the colored lights come on around the pool and along the path that led to the garden. That was it—the sum of her words. All each of us thinks about are our own feelings, and it's left us with a chasm the size of the country between us.

The scent of jasmine was seductive, almost magical, as if it could take me in, carry me back through the years, so I could start over, so I could . . . change things? If the war disappeared, and politics vanished from our lives, if my father hadn't run for governor, would things be different? Maybe not. Maybe that wasn't it at all.

I heard footsteps on the path . . . my father's footsteps, I knew. He stopped next to the bench and reached up to the tree for a leaf.

"Beth," he began, rolling the leaf in his hand, "it's hard to know what to say anymore. It seems everything I say is the wrong thing."

I looked up at him, then away. "I know what you mean."

"It's not that your mother and I don't try to understand you . . ."

"I know, Dad," I said quietly.

A sudden breeze stirred the scent of flowers in the air. My father was looking beyond me to the city lights. I didn't know why words had always been so awkward between us. Maybe a time would come when things would be easier. But for now this was all it could be—stumbling attempts to reach out. The words not said were a churning river between us.

"Beth, the one thing I do want you to know is that I never thought my job would throw so much public attention on you and the rest of the family. It's more than I ever expected, and for that I'm truly sorry."

I stood beside him and gazed at the city. "Too light out there to find the North Star," I said.

"You remember that?"

"I remember the night you showed it to me, when I was little." We watched the sky in silence.

Later that evening I found Brian in his room reading a magazine. The black-light posters had been replaced by posters of surfers crouched in the curls of enormous waves. So many turns his life had taken that I hadn't been there to see.

"You leaving tomorrow?" he said.

I laughed. "I figured you were listening to everything."

"Of course. Where are you going?"

I lay down on his bed. "I don't know. I feel like there are things I left behind that I have to go back and sort out. I think I'll go to Montana to see Delia. She sort of invited me last time we talked."

Delia's voice was sleepy when I called. "Uh-huh, that's fine," she drawled when I said I knew it was sudden, but could I fly up there tomorrow? She lived in a town called Bozeman, and she woke up enough to tell me I had to change flights in Denver and she'd pick me up at the airport.

I slept that night in what had once been my room. The same floral wallpaper and white shag carpet that were the backdrop of so many memories sent me whirling back through the years, to a time when the bed seemed large and I could barely reach the top of the dresser. Now my toes touched the end of the mattress and the room felt like a doll's house. A half-moon hung in the trees outside, and somewhere in the distance a dog was barking.

· *18* ·

WHEN THE PLANE LANDED IN BOZEMAN, MONTANA, I thought for a moment there had been a mistake and we'd missed the airport terminal. But when I came down the steps I saw the terminal ahead—a small, low-lying building that resembled a ranch house. I took a seat inside on an old wooden bench that looked like a church pew, and waited for Delia. Twenty minutes later everyone had left but myself and two others who were having a fight over a friend of theirs named Stan who was never on time.

"That settles it, then, that does it once and for all," said the woman. "Next time I call Thelma."

"The hell you will!" said the man. "Damn fool woman drives like a rollie coaster! Ain't steppin' foot in that vehicle for love or money."

"Well, fine! You can stay here until Stan gets here or until hell freezes over, but I'm calling Thelma."

I heard a car radio blasting out front, so I went to the window. It was Delia, in a powder-blue convertible, waving both arms in the air. I waved back, grabbed my suitcase, and went out the door. When I passed the man I whispered to him, "Live dangerously. Ride with Thelma."

"Bethie! You're cute as a buck, just like always."

The passenger door flew open. "Have a seat, honey." I got into

209

the car, and when I leaned over to hug her we laughed at the distance we had to reach over her very pregnant belly.

"Great to see you," she said, pulling away from the curb with a modest screech of tires. "I'd like you to meet Millie." A grinning baby was strapped into a car seat in the back. I recognized her cooing from the phone. Millie had a cloud of white-blond curls and her mother's lake-blue eyes.

"She's adorable. She looks exactly like you."

Delia patted her tummy. "I promised Kenny the next one would look exactly like him. How was your flight, sugar?"

"Relaxing. This car is beautiful, Deel."

"You like my horse? Graduation present from Daddy."

"Oh. Didn't you tell me you dropped out of school?"

"You know Daddy. Enjoy the sights, honey," she said, waving her hand. "This is Bozeman's main drag."

I felt like I'd gone back in time to a western version of "Mayberry R.F.D." There were bars and fast-food joints instead of soda shops, and pickup trucks instead of bicycles. The brick-faced buildings and narrow streets made me think of milkmen and neighbor ladies who always had blueberry muffins "fresh from the oven."

"We're a college town," Delia said. "You picked a good time of year to visit. It's quiet as a graveyard when school's out."

We pulled up to a red house shaded by huge pine trees. A clothesline ran along the side and sheets billowed in the breeze. A swing set dominated the front yard, along with a large black dog who'd rearranged every square foot of dirt to his liking. He didn't look pleased about having a stranger on the property, and when he gave us a deafening sample of what his lungs could do, Delia hollered, "Bear! It's okay, quit that barkin'!"

Delia had let her hair assume its natural color, not quite as blond as she had been at Devon. She wore no makeup, yet her face and eyes still radiated their unique glow. I realized she had never needed makeup in the first place.

She lifted Millie out of the car seat.

"Can I carry her?" I offered.

"You betcha," she said, arching her back for a stretch and once again patting her belly. "For a while I thought it'd be twins, but the doc said no, just one big one." She broke away to yell once again at Bear, who was busy chasing a cab down the road. "Dog's bonkers—he has this thing for cars. C'mon inside, honey."

The front door opened into a small hallway which was an extension of the kitchen. I thought of all the expensive homes in Bel Air where the only ones who ever entered by the kitchen were servants and delivery people. Delia led me through the kitchen into the living room, a narrow rectangle with orange carpeting and wood-paneled walls. Baby toys were strewn across the floor and in the center stood a playpen.

"Put her down right there, Bethie." I lowered Millie into the playpen. "Heavy, isn't she?" Millie attempted to stand, waging a war with gravity that seemed to have no regard for the effort her legs were making to support the rest of her. She finally thudded down onto her diapered end and picked up the nearest toy, as if to forget the whole trying episode.

"We thought you could sleep in the baby's room—there's a bunk bed in there and we'll move her crib into our room."

"Thanks, Delia, but you know I don't want to inconvenience you..."

"Hey, don't be silly!" She laughed. "I'm real glad you're here. I hardly get to see anyone these days 'cept Millie and Kenny. He should be home early. He's real anxious to meet you. For years I've been bendin' his ear 'bout all our crazy times at Devon." She gave me her old rib poke.

Delia made some coffee and we sat at the kitchen table. Outside the window was the bluest sky I'd ever seen, scattered with clouds that looked like huge cotton balls. The nearest house wasn't near at all by city standards. There was enough room between for a wide view of the hills, dotted with trees.

"Bethie, why the sudden escape from California? You didn't rob a bank, did you?"

"No...I just needed to get away." She waited for me to say more, but my feelings hadn't settled enough for words.

"Well," she said, content to fill in the silence herself, "I'm real glad to see you. I think about y'a lot—the old times and everything." She stared down into her coffee cup for a long moment. "Ya know, Bethie, I never told Kenny I'd had an abortion—couldn't see any point in draggin' up that whole thing. After we were married and I got pregnant I was so scared—you know—that maybe somethin' would go wrong 'cause of what I did. I mean maybe that doctor didn't do it right, messed me up inside or somethin', ya know?"

I nodded, but I wasn't sure if I did know. It occurred to me that fear might be the same no matter what its origin. It lodges in the same place, sends tendrils through one's belly and chokes the breath whether it's the fear of a botched abortion, of an unseen enemy, or fear of the man under the bed and "things that go bump in the night."

"Anyway," Delia was saying, leaning back to hoist herself from the chair, "I was relieved when Millie was born and everything was fine. Listen, I gotta bring some stuff up from the root cellar—wanna help me?"

"Root cellar?"

"Oh, you city people. That's where we store all our canned stuff. I put up jams and vegetables and fruits. C'mon, I'll show ya."

We walked outside and the sky was filling up with clouds. On the hill there were shadows in the spaces where moments before pools of sunlight had been.

"It looks like it's going to rain, Delia."

"Yep. There's a sayin' in Montana. If you don't like the weather, wait an hour, it'll change."

I lifted up the heavy wooden door of the root cellar and we descended into a dungeonlike room that smelled of damp earth. A mouse scurried away. There were shelves filled with canned beets, corn, beans, and jams, and rows of jars that hadn't been filled yet.

"If you could just reach a coupla those jars for me—"

I got them down and we emerged from underground to falling rain. "Great," she said, "I won't need to water the garden today."

We came back in to find Millie crying and Bear whining. Delia walked into the living room in no apparent hurry saying, "She needs to be changed."

"How do you know that's why she's crying?"

"Funny, huh? That way she's cryin', I can just tell."

Kenny came home just as the rain was letting up. He was tall and lanky and wore faded jeans and a plaid shirt. One of his front teeth had been capped, obviously by a dentist not given to artistry. This didn't alter his good looks, though; he had confident posture and a long, slow stride.

He grinned and shook my hand and said, "Glad to have you here. Delia talks about you a lot." He bounced Millie on his knee and talked about the house he was building and the crew he had to "keep on top of all the time."

"Kenny's a contractor," Delia explained. Everything seemed so easy and informal there; I felt like I'd come in from a storm to a warm fire.

At the kitchen table, Kenny helped himself to another bowl of chili and said, "You know, Delia may not be the best cook in the state but at least she makes a lot. You never go away hungry around here."

"Thanks a heap," said Delia, getting up to get milk from the refrigerator. Kenny reached an arm around her and pulled her to him; he put his head on her stomach and kissed her. "How's the weather in there, son?"

"Keep wishing!" Delia laughed.

"Are you kidding—kicking up thunder like that? There he goes again! It's a boy all right."

Millie dribbled baby food on her chin, and Delia and I sent Kenny into a laughing fit with our imitation of the science teacher at Devon as he tried frantically to catch the frogs we'd set free in the lab.

For the next two days I let time slide by me as easily as the clouds slid across the sky. I took walks with Delia and we took turns pushing Millie in the stroller, its quiet squeak keeping rhythm with our steps. From time to time we lowered Millie to the ground between us, each holding one of her tiny hands, so she could test her skill at walking.

Their neighbors had horses that Kenny and Delia often rode. Since Delia was now in her seventh month, I went instead, following Kenny through the hills. We saw a pair of deer who calmly watched as we rode past. He told me how Delia had changed his life, how he had been "a real hell-raiser before she came along," but now his favorite time of the day was coming home to her and the baby.

One afternoon, as rain clouds moved in on a blue sky, I helped Delia pull weeds out of the garden and plant some new seeds. "Delia, it's so peaceful here. I never would have thought you'd end up with a life like this. What happened to the rodeo circuit?"

She wiped dirt off her hands and laughed. "I don't know. I met Kenny and I just started to look at things differently. I really wanted to get married and have kids."

"Everything seems so easy and simple here. Why do things get so complicated in my life? You know, I used to be so confident that I knew what was right, and that I had the strength to back up my convictions and to stand up for my beliefs. But it seems that everyone has ideas and motives that have nothing to do with me or with what I'm about. I feel like there are so many forces trying to pull me in different directions that I don't know if I have that confidence anymore. I thought maybe if I went back, looked behind me . . .''

She was looking at me with sweet, sad eyes. ''I don't know what to tell you, sweetie. You've told me a little about the trouble with your parents. Family's real important, takin' care of the people who care about you. But so is standin' up for what you believe in. I guess what you gotta try for is to have both, but it's hard. Kenny and I fight sometimes about how to raise Millie— we're two different people—but we don't let it come between us. I guess the bottom line is, you gotta be true to what's inside your heart.''

''I look at you and Kenny, though, and he's so accepting of you; he doesn't try to mold you or change you. Sometimes I feel like I'll never find that. Or maybe I have, and I was too blind to see it. I've been thinking a lot about Greg. Maybe it was my fault he stopped writing. Maybe I did something to drive him away.''

''I don't think so, sugar. Greg came to see me about a year ago.''

''He was here?''

She nodded. ''I thought he was going to look you up, too, but I guess he didn't. He said he wanted to, though. I don't know why he came by exactly, tell ya the truth. Said he just wanted to set things straight, clear up any bad feelings. He was . . . well, he's different, Bethie. I don't know that it wasn't for the best that he didn't come to see you.''

''Maybe you see it that way, Delia, but I'd like to know what went wrong. I've even been thinking about trying to find him, so we can talk. . . . In fact, I've made a definite decision to go look for him. That's what I'm going to do when I leave here. I never met his father, but I was thinking I'd look him up and see what I could find out. Or maybe I should start by calling Devon . . .''

Delia stared into the tangle of weeds she held in her hand. When she looked back up at me, her eyes were tense and strained, in a way I'd never seen before.

''Delia, what is it? What's wrong?''

She looked back down at her hands and began feverishly picking away at the weeds. I grabbed her wrist.

"It's Greg, isn't it? He's..." I shook her arm. "Delia, tell me!"

"Okay, honey, okay." She looked back up at me.

"Well?"

"I know where he is."

I closed my eyes and listened to my heart pound.

"He's all right?"

Delia stood up, and brushed the dirt from her overalls. "I have a letter. C'mon inside."

The sky had clouded over and we walked back to the house and into her bedroom. The bedroom was small, too small for the accumulation of furniture that had been forced into it. There was a double bed, two huge dressers, an armchair, and a trunk at the foot of the bed. The gingham curtains were hemmed unevenly, prompting me to ask if she'd sewn them herself.

"Yeah." She laughed. "Fortunately for Kenny my cookin's better'n my handiwork." She opened a drawer and dug under some sweaters. Looking through the pages of the letter she said, "Let's see ... he says he wanted to thank me for listenin' to him and—oh, here it is. He says, 'I'm living in Oregon. I've built a shelter out in the forest outside a town called Hood River. I've got an old pickup truck so I can bring in supplies. Everyone around here leaves me alone which is what I want.' "

Rain was falling lightly on the roof and I could hear Bear scratching at the door. Delia took my hands in hers "Beth, I think you should leave him alone. Ya might not like what you'll find."

"I don't care. At least I'll know. Right now all I have are a lot of questions."

We were silent a moment, then a grin spread over her face.

"Give me your hand, honey."

She took my hand in hers, then put it to her belly. I felt the baby roll beneath her skin.

"What's he *doing* in there?"

"Ridin' rodeo, sugar."

I made plane reservations that night to fly to Portland. Delia and Kenny drove me to the airport the next morning and, as I left them, I felt an ache inside me—the ache of goodbyes I hadn't wanted to say.

·*19*·

OREGON WAS AS SCENIC AS MONTANA HAD BEEN. THE soot and cement of Los Angeles seemed a remote memory as I looked down from the plane on green forests cut with blue rivers. When I got into Portland, I rented a car and managed to make some sense of the map they gave me. Once on Interstate 84, I found myself bordered by mountains and woods on one side and the Columbia River on the other. There was a cold edge to the wind, as if it were resisting the encroachment of summer. White clouds floated across the sun.

It took me a little more than an hour to reach the town of Hood River. Throughout the drive I tried to figure out what I would do once I got there, where I would go, whom I would question. I still hadn't reached a decision, but when I saw a gas station up ahead, I decided to start there.

"Excuse me," I called to the attendant, a white-haired man with grease smudges on his face. I walked up to him. "I wonder if you could help me—I'm looking for someone." He gave me a skeptical look. "His name's Greg Howell. He lives outside of town, in the forest I think, and he drives a pickup. Have you seen him, or heard of him?"

"Doesn't sound familiar," he said, squinting at me. I walked away, wondering about my approach. Would this man tell a stranger even if he did know something?

A visit to the post office got me little more than a chorus of shrugs and some reticent looks from the customers. Farther on I came to another gas station. While one of the attendants looked me up and down, the other gave my little car the once-over. The whole thing was beginnning to feel like *Invasion of the Body Snatchers*.

"Why don't you try the markets, honey? Man's gotta buy food sometime."

Twilight had settled over the town. I was exhausted, so I searched the unfamiliar buildings for a place I could spend the night. The Hood River Inn was a two-story wooden building next door to a small gift shop. I walked through the Spanish-style interior and paid for a room for the next few nights, had dinner in the dining room that overlooked the river, and fell asleep in a room that looked as though it belonged in a mountain cabin.

I couldn't sleep past six the next morning. I wandered around the town taking in the landscape, waiting for stores to open so I could resume my search. Once the doors began opening for the day, I focused on every market, small or large, that I could find: drugstores, luncheonettes, an auto parts shop, anyplace Greg might have reason to go. Again and again I repeated the same questions, but no one knew anything, or no one was saying. My words tasted stale. I had parked my car and walked through the streets; my feet were giving out. He wasn't here. He had moved on. I walked into a small corner grocery, bought some fruit and a container of orange juice, and while I watched the clerk ring them up, I wondered if I could make myself ask one more time. I changed my story a bit, hoping that might help. . . .

"Excuse me, sir, but I wonder if you could help me out. A cousin of mine moved up here not long ago—" I was startled by a loud *clank!* of metal outside the door, and bolted around. A kid had thrown his bicycle down on the pavement. He came into the store; a bell on the door jingled when it opened.

"Anyway, I'd like to surprise him, but I don't know where he's living, somewhere outside of town I think. I wonder if you've seen him around? He's a few inches taller than I am, blond, and he drives a pickup truck. . . ."

The clerk looked at the boy who'd just approached the counter, carrying a container of milk, a pound of butter, and a small box of sanitary napkins. The boy did not look pleased. He grabbed a candy bar from the rack nearby.

"Hiya, Randy," the clerk said, "your mom feelin' better?"

"Yes, sir, thank you," said the boy sheepishly. The man put the groceries in a sack.

"Excuse me," I began again, "but does he sound familiar?"

" 'Fraid not. That'll be $2.79." The boy picked up his bag and left.

Outside I stood in the street wondering where to go next, or whether to go anywhere. I began walking and heard someone come up beside me. It was the boy from the grocery store.

"Ma'am? I heard you back there. I know the guy you're talking about."

I looked at him as if he'd descended from the sky. "You do? You've seen him?"

"Yes, ma'am. I met him once when I was playing up in the forest. If you follow that road over there for a ways, you'll come to a pond by a fork in the road. Take the right fork, and you'll see an old white pickup parked off the road. There's a path up from there. I don't know exactly where he lives, but he's somewhere up there."

"Oh, my God. Thank you. Thank you, Randy." I began running to my car, turning back once to yell, "Thanks again!"

"Don't tell him I told you!" he shouted back.

I drove down the highway until I saw the truck. Clouds slid over the sun, turning everything shadowy, and I wondered if I should just turn back and forget the whole thing. I was so close now, but for the first time I considered the possibility that Delia could have been right about leaving him alone.

A path leading into the forest was embedded with footprints. The sun came out from behind the clouds and crawled up over my back, but it turned chilly as I walked deeper into the forest. Splinters of sunlight fell through the branches and the air smelled of pine and earth. I heard a car pass on the highway below, but then it was quiet again, with only the sound of birds and leaves stirring in the wind. I didn't know how long I'd been walking. A branch snapped, as if broken by a footstep. I stopped and held my breath to listen. Maybe a deer ...

"What do you want?" a voice said. I wheeled around to face the voice but it was as if the trees had spoken. "Greg?" I'd heard his voice in my sleep, in the sound of rain on the roof, in the noise of crowds. "Greg, it's Beth."

Footsteps ... then he came out from behind the trees. He was wearing fatigues and in his hand was a gun. He had a beard and was thinner than I remembered.

"Jesus Christ, Beth, how the hell did you find me?"

I thought of the boy's request. "It wasn't easy. I guess if you really want to find someone—" I took a few steps toward him, thinking maybe he'd reciprocate, but he stayed planted. Everything about him seemed darker. I remembered how he looked in high school—sky-blue eyes, blond hair, freckles—a face made for sunlight. Now he belonged to shadows.

"You live here in the woods?" I asked, feeling the awkwardness of conversation.

"Uh-huh." He turned his back to the wind and lit a cigarette. I waited for him to say something else, but he was blowing smoke rings toward the sky and watching them trail off on the wind. I was afraid to move any closer.

"Where?" My voice was almost a whisper.

"Right here. This is my backyard. Nice, huh?"

In the quiet that followed I wondered what I wanted from him, if I wanted him to ask me to stay, or just talk to me. I didn't know, but I didn't want to leave yet, although the air was getting colder and I knew the sun was sinking somewhere past the trees. My back was aching from standing in one place, but I thought if I moved, even just to sit down, he would leave. Moments stretched between us, long and empty.

"Greg, we used to be friends. We used to be able to talk. What happened?"

"What happened?" he said, turning to face me. "Vietnam happened. Or maybe you were so busy protesting the war you didn't notice that some of us were living it."

"Greg . . . that's not fair."

"I'll tell you what's not fair. When I got back to the States they put us on a bus in Oakland. There were crowds of demonstrators throwing bricks and bottles at the windows, holding up signs calling us murderers and baby killers. No ticker-tape parades for us, huh? That went out in World War II. Now you tell me about fair, Beth."

I didn't say anything. He frightened me, but I didn't want to just walk away from him . . . and there was no other place I wanted to go.

He stood up to leave. "You better be on your way. There are a couple of hotels in town if you need a place to stay."

"I know. I stayed in one last night. Can I come back tomorrow?" I said to his back. I knew he heard me, but he kept walking until he was gone behind the trees.

I went back to the Hood River Inn and spent a restless night with Delia's warning and Greg's face churning in my mind. The next day I walked back up to the same spot. I sat there a long time, finally decided he wasn't coming, and started walking back down the path. Then I heard footsteps. He came out of the trees, the gun dangling from his hand, and stared at me without saying a word.

"Look, this is my place, okay? You don't belong here. Why don't you go back to your own world?"

"Because I don't belong there, either."

He sat on the ground next to me, closer than he'd allowed himself to get the day before. Tentatively, I sat beside him. I realized I was measuring the distance he put between us as if it were a measure of his trust in me.

"I didn't come here to invade your life," I said. "I just want to know what happened. You stopped writing, Greg. I didn't know where you were, or what happened to you. Greg, I didn't even know if you were *alive*."

"It was better that way. If you understood, you'd wish you didn't."

We stared out through the trees for a long time, neither of us speaking or looking at the other. My mind went back to when we'd ridden horses under a clear desert sky and silence had seemed so comfortable. Now our silence felt like shards of glass.

"Greg, who else knows you live out here? Does your father?"

"Are you kidding? He knows I'm somewhere in Oregon, but he would never understand how I live or why. He's an old World War II soldier. The war he remembers meant glory and honor and coming back a hero just 'cause you went. That's what war means to him, and it's all he understands."

"Look, I don't like the idea that my protesting the war has upset you. But I never participated in any demonstrations against vets, so don't think of me as one of the people throwing bricks at the bus."

He didn't say anything for several long minutes. He picked up a twig and chewed the end of it.

"Beth, I'm not going to say I think the war is right. I wasn't there a week before I knew this government had fucked up. But what was I gonna do—get shot up or killed because the war sucked?" He looked away and laughed—one of those laughs that's not really a laugh. "You know, I remember when I was young seeing pictures of guys in World War II giving bubble gum to smiling kids. In Nam, the kids would stand in the road and spit and say 'Fuck you, G.I.' They didn't want us there, we didn't want to be there, but goddammit, we didn't start the fuckin' war and nobody has any right to treat us like shit 'cause we did what our country asked us to do. In the Marines they told us never to leave a man out there—always bring 'em in even if they're in a dozen pieces—and we always did. But this country left us over there—all of us."

He stood up and started walking away.

"Greg, wait! Don't go."

He turned and looked at me.

"Greg . . . can I stay with you just for a little while?"

"C'mon, Beth." He laughed. "Get serious. Look around. There's no running water, no bathroom, no bed. It's not really your style."

I just looked at him, hoping my eyes would convey that I was serious, that I hadn't come all this way just to turn and leave.

"Okay, come on."

He led me between trees and over ground strewn with leaves and dead branches. Finally we reached a cleared space with a plywood shelter and the remains of a campfire. A rifle was set on end by the shelter and there were canteens and cooking utensils scattered around.

"So there it is," he said. "Built myself a hooch out here. Keeps out the rain and the snow. The warm seasons I sleep outside. I hunt for food and I go into town only when I need to."

The sun was almost down. He built a fire and opened some cans. "Tonight the menu's canned beans. Hope you don't mind. I wasn't expecting company."

He gave me a blanket to wrap around me, said I could use the sleeping bag, and pointed to the other side of the campfire. "The latrine's that way—about twenty yards past that tree."

The sky blackened, and night sounds filled the woods. Greg sat by the fire, smoking, staring into the flames. It was as if he had forgotten that I was there. He retreated to a world inhabited only by him. Eventually he moved to his blankets, lay down, and pulled them over his shoulders. I watched him as one would watch an untamed animal, with fascination, with curiosity, but never without respect for the distance that his wariness enforced.

Throughout the night I heard him tossing. There were moans coming from some deep corner of his sleep. At dawn he got up and, through half-lidded eyes, I saw him take his gun and head up the mountain. I waited a little while, and then followed. His footfalls echoed far ahead of me but I couldn't see him until he was close to the top of the mountain where the trees thinned out. He was standing still, looking up at the sky.

Suddenly he screamed—a long, primal scream that hung on the wind and shot ice into my heart. He stayed there a few more minutes, as still as the earth he stood on, and when he turned to go I ran back, afraid he would see me.

When he came back I pretended to be waking up. I reached in my bag for my brush and started tugging at my hair.

"I have to go check some of my traps," Greg said, "and get some water."

"Can I go with you?"

He was getting some buckets out from behind the hooch. "I guess so. You can help haul water."

He had set traps at different spots in the forest for rabbits and squirrels. I shuddered at the thought of finding some furry victim in one of these devices, and was grateful when we found all the traps empty. He led me to a narrow river where we filled the buckets. Although he carried two and I only had one, he got back much sooner than I, apparently unencumbered by the weight he was carrying.

Later, after he let me help him cut potatoes and cook them over the fire, I said, "Greg, why did you stop writing to me?"

"Look, I don't fit anymore. My isolation is a way to protect other people, not just myself. I did you a favor by disappearing from your life."

"Can't you tell me what made you feel like that? Can't you give me a chance to understand?"

He walked away as if he wasn't going to answer, but then turned back. "We used to drop leaflets on villages in Nam telling them they had a few minutes. Then we'd fly over and blow 'em away. The thing about killing is you start to get good at it, then you start to enjoy it. Believe me, Beth, you don't want to understand."

When night fell he got quiet again, smoking and staring into the fire. After he moved to his blankets, I sat watching the coals smolder and die before I crawled into the sleeping bag. I lay there listening to his breathing: uneven, unsleeplike, just as it had been the night before.

I wished we could go back in time, to when we weren't strangers, to when life was more than a reminder of death. If we had anything in common now it was our reason for ending up here, the common bond of wanting to escape, from the past or to the past, it didn't matter. We were both running. Greg had built his own world here, in shadowy woods where patches of sunlight are smudged on the trees and the mountains hover protectively . . . where darkness is never too far away. But listening to the restlessness of his sleep, the strange, sad moaning, I wondered if there was such a thing as escape.

I looked at the sky, remembering the first time I discovered that the heavens held so many stars. I was nine, at camp for the summer, and I woke up one night to see the sky flocked with stars, so many they crowded out the darkness.

The night my father showed me the North Star, he said it's the one sailors look for to guide them when they're lost at sea. You'll never be lost, he told me, if you know how to find the North Star. I searched the sky and found it—the brightest one in the north —but I still felt lost.

From somewhere outside the rim of my thoughts, I heard a rustling in the bushes. Suddenly three gunshots ripped a hole in the night. I bolted up and saw Greg sitting up on the blankets, his gun still pointed at the bushes. My ears were ringing and my whole body felt like it was squeezed in a vice. My lungs wouldn't expand, my stomach was constricted, and I didn't feel I could move any of my limbs. Eternities seemed to be going by, and all I could do was watch them go. Greg's eyes were fixed on the bushes, mine were fixed on him, and the gun was still in his hands. I wasn't sure—if I uttered a word—that he wouldn't turn and shoot me. Gradually the ringing in my head started to subside, like the sound of a train moving farther away.

Simultaneously, as if following the rhythm of some strange dance, Greg lowered his hands, bringing the gun to the ground at the same moment the ringing in my head ceased.

I commanded my voice to say Greg, but there was no room in my throat for anything more than a hoarse whisper. He looked at me, then turned away. I moved myself out of the sleeping bag, shaking my leg, which had been frozen so long it had fallen asleep. I got up and walked to him slowly, surprised that my legs were holding me. I felt like I was under water.

"Greg," I said again, hearing my own voice as if through thick cotton, "Greg, it wasn't anything. Just an animal or something." He was shaking. "Greg, please talk to me—please tell me what's wrong." I knelt beside him and his head fell against me. Tears soaked through my shirt, warm against my skin.

"Dreams," he said, his voice muffled against my chest.

"Tell me what they are."

"Go back to sleep, Beth."

Afraid to push him, I crawled back into my sleeping bag, but sleep was impossible. I lay there wondering what was going on behind Greg's impenetrable eyes, the eyes I once thought I could read. Again the wood was quiet, alive with only the sound of the wind and small creatures. I don't know how much time had passed when I heard Greg cry out, and I bolted up and went to him.

"The nightmare again?"

He took a long breath, held it, and slowly let it out. I put my hand gently on his, and felt him tremble.

"Please, Greg, please tell me what's wrong. I don't think it's helping to keep it inside. Please . . ."

The shuddering in his body eased a little. "Trent—he was a buddy of mine in Nam. Maybe I wrote you about him. I don't know."

"Yes, I remember."

His unblinking eyes were fixed on a corner of the blanket. "We were hit one night. It was so dark—we couldn't see anything. We just had to shoot into the bushes—couldn't even see what we were shooting at. I didn't know where Trent was. After a while I didn't know where anyone was, but I knew a lot of us had been hit. It went on for a long time and when it stopped I knew I had to wait till it got light to come out and look. I didn't know if the VC were still out there, waiting for someone to move. When it finally got light, we started finding the bodies. Only three of us had made it. I couldn't find Trent."

He'd been talking so fast, as if caught in a rushing tide with nothing to hang onto, but then a sob cracked through his voice. His hands were clenched into tight fists. "There was no way I was gonna stop looking till I found him. There was this dead old tree lying across the ground. . . . I went to step over it and when I put my foot down . . . God, I almost stepped in him. He'd been blown in half. . . .'' He hesitated, caught in his memory. ''His eyes were staring up at the sky. I reached over and closed his eyelids. Something—I don't know—something about the way his body was turned or maybe 'cause he was so far from the others, I was sure the dinks had booby-trapped him so whoever came to get his body would be blown to pieces. I had to reach inside him, into the guts that were spilling out of him, and I knew if my hands shook I'd be dead, too. Man, he was my friend, and here I was with my hands sliding through his insides looking for—'' He stopped, wiped his face, and said, ''This is the first time I've cried. I thought I'd forgotten how. I just can't stop going back there. Every night, I'm back there with Trent, his body inside out on the ground . . . the sun, beating down—it must have been a hundred, and the smell making me want to puke. Every night . . .''

I wondered what I'd been doing at that exact moment, when Greg was on the other side of the world living this horror. I thought of the anger I felt the night he told me he'd extended his tour; anger that shut out all his attempts to explain the reasons. ''Unfinished business'' I remembered him saying. But I didn't let him tell me. How many other experiences like that came back to haunt him? The memory of that night came up in my throat like rancid food.

I held him for a long time, rocking him. Our tears ran together and were cooled by the night air. When it got so late that even the sounds of the forest seemed frozen in sleep, I felt his body relax and his breathing become steady. I gathered the blankets around to cover us, and we sank into sleep.

I woke up abruptly. The sky was ablaze with morning, and I thought I'd heard Greg scream, the same scream I'd heard from the mountain the day before. But when I looked, he wasn't there. . . . I sat wondering if it had been a dream or an echo. In a few minutes he walked out through the trees carrying a dead rabbit. Maybe I had heard an echo; I'd never know for sure.

''Want some breakfast?'' he said, taking out a knife and starting to peel the rabbit's fur. Blood dripped over his hand.

''No thanks,'' I said. I walked around in the woods long enough for him to finish his culinary preparations and came back as he was eating the finished product.

''Sure you don't want any?'' he said.

''I'm sure.''

He moved around without looking at me, cleaning dishes, folding blankets. I wanted to say something to him about what had happened during the night, but I didn't know what to say. I was sure he was thinking about it, too.

He went off to check some other traps and came back empty-handed. He walked over to me with a troubled look.

"Beth, you can't stay here anymore."

Something inside me sank. "Why?"

"Because I don't trust myself around people—not you or anyone. I belong out here alone, and that's how you gotta leave it. It's not just the nightmares—sometimes there are daymares. Just leave, Beth. It's better that way."

I couldn't say anything. Part of me wanted to cry, another part wanted to argue with him, but I knew neither would do any good. I left and walked down to the river where we'd gotten water, but I didn't feel like I was really leaving. I didn't feel like I could leave—not like that—not knowing he'd stay there with his dark memories and haunted dreams. Somewhere there had to be help.

I sat by the river, looking into the clear water, throwing rocks in and watching the ripples widen. Somewhere, cities rumbled with traffic and sirens and people hurried through another day. But it was a world I'd left far behind. Here, I felt suspended, dictated to only by the wind and the sun and the passing of time, my life sealed tightly against human intervention. It was easy to see why Greg had come here. Inside me, what had been stormy was now calm. But maybe the point was to take that feeling into the world, not nurture it at a safe distance from the world. I thought I heard something behind me, but I was too lost in my thoughts to turn around and look.

"Beth, what are you doing here?"

"Thinking."

"I watched you walk down this way. Unless you know these woods better than I do, there's no way back to town from here."

"Greg, I don't want to leave. Not after what you told me last night. How can I just leave you here knowing what you're going through?"

"There's nothing you can do."

"But maybe someone else can."

"Who? Some VA shrink who doesn't know what the hell vets are about? What does he know about guys getting blown apart? He's been sitting out the war behind his desk. I tried it once—I tried talking to one. They don't know shit. The guys that get too freaked out, they just fill 'em full of Thorazine.''

"What about other vets? They'd understand. Maybe other guys have nightmares, or other things they want to talk about, and they can't find anyone to talk to, either. Greg, if you'd let me, I'd help you find someone. I know a guy in Illinois who just got back from Vietnam. We could go there. I don't think staying alone with your torment is going to make it go away.''

He looked into the water for what seemed like an hour, then lay back on the ground and closed his eyes. I couldn't tell if he was sleeping. Eventually he said, ''I don't think so, Betsy. I've lived out here a long time ... alone.''

''You could come back again if you wanted, but can't we just try another way? I'll stay with you, Greg. We'll go to Illinois or wherever we have to.''

He got up and started walking back toward his camp. I followed at a distance, not sure whether or not he wanted me there. Night was moving in on the sky, turning it a deep shade of blue. I stood back and watched Greg build a fire, slowly, deliberately, as if every detail had taken on new importance.

He stood up, turned away, and slowly walked off. I didn't follow. He was gone an hour, maybe two, maybe longer. I added wood to the fire. I thought about the last two days, how much had happened in such a short time. I had learned more about Vietnam in the last forty-eight hours than in all the years before.

In those quiet moments my mind drifted from Greg to Delia's words about family. I couldn't very well insist that Greg stop running if I wasn't willing to do the same. Fate had planted such lofty and disparate ideals in the confined space of my family, where they would be certain to clash. But it was becoming apparent that no matter how far I went, threads of the family fabric still pulled at me. Maybe there were enough left for mending.

I heard the leaves rustle and saw Greg walking toward me. ''You'd better go now, Betsy.'' Shadows and firelight played on his face as he poked at the wood, sending sparks into the new darkness.

I stood up. ''I'll be back, Greg. Again and again—as many times as it takes.''

The day was just a faint wisp of light at the far edge of the horizon. In the tree above me a bird was singing, as if he didn't know the sun was gone and the North Star had taken its place.

· *Epilogue* ·

WOULD YOU LIKE TO TAKE YOUR PHONE CALL IN ONE
of the other rooms, miss?''

"Why don't you go into Lincoln's bedroom?'' my mother
asked. "That's a part of the White House you haven't seen yet.''

I picked up the phone and could barely hear his voice over the
din.

"Greg, where are you? Are you still at the airport? It sounds
like you're standing out on the landing strip.''

"No—I got in a couple of hours ago. I'm calling from a pay
phone. I've been to a meeting with some vets here. Listen, Betsy,
there's some stuff going down that I better fill you in on. You
can pass it along to your folks or not, whatever you think is best.
These guys are going to stage a sit-in tomorrow in front of the
White House. They've been getting shafted but good. Some of
them aren't getting the benefits they should be getting. A lot
of them were exposed to Agent Orange. Some of their kids
have been born deformed because of it. And the government
is just ignoring them. The thing is . . . I might be out there with
'em.''

I smiled at the confidence in his voice. So often I'd feared he
would go back to Oregon, to the mountains that had sheltered
him for so long. I thought of how many times I went to his refuge
there, only to find him still brooding and distant.

And I thought of the afternoon when gray clouds exploded into rain and we ran back from the stream into his hooch with our clothes soaked through. Sitting so close to him that our shoulders were pressed together, I could feel his breath rising and falling. It was the closest we'd been since the night he told me about his nightmares.

"You should get out of your wet clothes so you don't get chilled," he had said, reaching across me for a dry blanket. "Here, wrap this around you." I turned my back to him and pulled off my wet sweater, but before I could wrap the blanket around me his hands were on my shoulders, turning me around to face him and pulling me into him. He smelled like rain and the woods. "Sometimes in Nam, it'd be pouring down rain and I'd be soaked and muddy and miserable—and to make myself feel better I'd think about you. I'd think about holding you like this—"

I sank into him and started pushing his jacket off his shoulders, but he took my hands and held them away from him.

And the night when a warm wind stirred the pine trees and I lay under a star-strewn sky with a thin blanket over me. In my dream, Greg was pulling the blanket off. His face was against my neck and his hands were on my waist. Then the dream and reality tumbled together and I opened my eyes to see him there, leaning over me, framed by the trees and the sky. His body felt leaner and stronger than in my memories, but so familiar it was as if I'd never known anyone else.

And the day in Illinois when he disappeared for hours, and returned smiling as if he'd just navigated a trip to the moon with no assistance from NASA. "Here," he said, handing me a box, "I got on the el and went into Chicago to buy you something. Hope it fits." He'd bought me a sweater, which did fit although I'd have worn it even if it didn't. But the main reason for his happiness was that he "went all that way, through the store and everything, and I was okay!"

Now, listening to him talk about the plight of other vets, I felt he'd found his strongest reason yet for staying in the World.

"You should be out there, Greg, if that's where your heart is." I looked over at the portrait of Lincoln, half expecting a smile to creep across his stern features.

"Well"—he laughed—"your folks might not like me too much after that."

"That's not a good reason to back down from something you believe in."

"Sure isn't. I'll see you in about an hour, Betsy. I love you."

"I love you, too."

The outside of the window was ringed with frost—a white circle with no beginning and no end.